Also by Lance C Wilson

THE LAIRD OF BRAIDWOOD
Historical

TEARS OVER THE KIMBERLEYS

DARE TO LIVE THE DREAM

THE CHILDREN OF KIMBERLEY COTTAGE
BILLY OF THE NORTH
MY FIELD OF DREAMS

THE STONE PEOPLE

DARK SIDE OF THE ROCK

MEG'S STORY
FIFTY ACHES & PAINS

PAULINE'S JOURNEY

Set in the wilds of eastern Arnhem Land

Follow a desperate mother's quest to find her missing daughter

A search that will change her life forever

Printed and published by Kimberley Cottage Publishing

This is a work of Adult Fiction.

All characters and events are portrayed fictitiously.

National Library of Australia Cataloguing-in-Publication entry:

Author: Wilson, Lance C, 1945

Title: The Gulf

Editor: Rhonda Scott JP

Cover photo, design and book layout by Alan Jennison

ISBN: 9780 – 977 – 550 – 593

Dewey No. A 823.4

A CiP record for this book is available from the National Library of Australia

Many Thanks

Many thanks to Rhonda Scott my Editor for her valued work in turning my novel into a book and to Alan Jennison, not only for making the book print-ready but for preparing its superb cover.

Thanks too to our Aboriginal friends from Numbulwah for allowing me and my wife Cynthia to camp on their land in The Gulf at Cape Barrow while gathering information for the novel.

Special thanks as always to Cynthia for joining me on my adventures and for preparing her wonderful meals, even in the most remote parts of our country.

I hope you enjoy reading this story as much as I did writing it!

Foreword

Lucy Jones was born into a farming family in the Tunnack district of southern Tasmania. She was the third child of a family that would eventually grow to seven. Her father ran a small farm, one of many such farms in the district.

At that time the area was bustling and the township boasted two schools, one State and the other Catholic. There were two shops, two garages, one bank, fortnightly livestock sales, a post office and the local hotel which was the hub of community activities as well as successful football teams, both seniors and reserves.

Early on in her life, like in most of rural Australia sadly, the family farm became unviable as did the town, resulting in the family having to move nearby to Parattah where her father had gained employment on the railway. This too had a disastrous effect on them all as only a few years later the railway depot was closed and the family was again faced with unemployment, as were over thirty other men employed in the town when the community services followed suit and everywhere shut down.

Lucy was a plump and happy child and popular with her peers. At only sixteen she left school to support her ailing mother. As in most small, close-knit communities, Lucy met and fell head over heels in love with a local lad, Liam Walsh. Liam worked on his parents' property in the Oatlands area and it was common knowledge and belief that Lucy and Liam would eventually marry.

However misfortune struck again and Lucy's dreams were shattered. Her one true love, called up by the Army and deployed to Vietnam, was tragically killed in the first week of his arrival. Lucy was broken and initially sank into a deep depression until her close friends managed to persuade her to start socialising.

One night, while drinking far too much with her friends, something happened that would change her life forever. She certainly did not anticipate living her life in the wilds of eastern Arnhem Land but only a mother – on a quest to find her missing child – would endure and tolerate absolutely anything.

Chapter One

Lucy turned over in bed, awakened by her snoring husband who was also breaking wind loudly. The smell was sickening. Immediately she rolled out of the bed, grabbed her faded dressing gown and made her way to the kitchen.

Although she had been married to Rex Jacobs for twenty-five years she was still disgusted with his behaviour and last night he had again staggered home drunk from a mate's place at midnight. Over the years Lucy had often thought of leaving but had never had the faith in herself to start a new life, mainly because of her daughter, their only child, and now it was all too late. Having made herself a strong coffee she sat at the table and reminisced about her life. It had become a habit to reflect on the past, no doubt due to the hopeless situation in which she found herself.

Rex had always treated her like rubbish, deriding her for the love he knew she felt for her first and only love Liam Walsh, and his wealthy family. How often Lucy harked back to that fateful night when she had been out drinking with her girlfriends at the hotel and, unaccustomed to alcohol drank far too much. During the evening she had been aware of Rex and his mates drinking at the bar.

Feeling ill from all the alcohol, Lucy rushed outside and was violently sick. She decided to make her way home and after informing her friends, left the hotel. Lucy felt the presence of someone following her as she walked down the dark lane but before she could turn around Rex

Jacobs had grabbed her roughly and kissed her forcefully while at the same time pushing her to the ground. He ripped off her panties and raped her repeatedly over the next few hours. Arriving home at daylight Lucy hurriedly washed and went to bed, too ashamed and terrified to tell her parents. Looking back after the shocking incident she still remembered the looks Rex's friends had given her - she was now 'his' girlfriend.

Two months later Lucy discovered she was pregnant and when her parents learned of the father, a hasty wedding was arranged. After twenty-five years of a loveless marriage the only light in Lucy's life was her beloved daughter Sheridan, now twenty-four years old and who would soon be home for the weekend before heading off with a friend on a trip around Australia.

Sipping her coffee, Lucy sat staring out at the rundown houses that surrounded her and compared it to her life and the happy times they all shared on her father's farm. A tear slid down her cheek as she recalled the family life they had all enjoyed, the special times with the animals and how much happier and safer she had felt. She loved joining in the community events, especially going to watch the football on a Saturday afternoon and barracking for the local boys who were playing on their 'field of dreams'.

Lucy appreciated now that, despite her parents never having much money, they still ate well from their fresh farm produce and all the neighbours helped each other by sharing whatever bounty they had - indeed a freshly killed chook for Christmas was a huge treat. On frosty nights they made ice-cream by leaving the mixture on the tank stand to freeze and the whole family woke up early to enjoy the delicacy. All such sweet precious memories now brought a glow to her face as did the wonderful community hall dances where she watched her parents sweep each other around the dance floor to the local musicians belting out old favourites on the piano, drums and accordion.

Conversely, Lucy also reflected on the anguish of her parents and many others as they were forced to sell the family farms and move nearby to Parattah to gain employment on the railway. Even so, in the early days with the running of the famous Parattah Gift footrace and other events, life did resume some normality but only for a few short years until modernisation caught up with Parattah and the railway closed along with the hotel, shops and garages in the town.

Fast forward and Lucy finds herself unhappily married to a man who lost his job and never worked again, who was content to drink with his mates, get the odd load of wood for her fuel stove, demand meals and do everything to make her feel and look useless in front of his friends.

The death of her parents remains vivid in her memory. They passed away within weeks of each other, her father first then her mother after losing her zest for life without him. Their deaths resulted in the remaining family leaving town with the exception of Lucy. Her daughter Sheridan left home after finishing school and having excelled was goaded by Lucy to attend college, from which she graduated with Honours and now held a great job in Hobart working for a well-known firm of solicitors. Having saved for many months she was now off to follow her dreams and to see Australia with a girlfriend. Lucy smiled to herself. Sheridan until now had only left Parattah a few times to go to Hobart and had never even been north of Oatlands.

Lucy rose slowly to her feet and returned quietly to the bedroom. She dressed quickly as she knew that Rex would not surface until his usual mid-day, when he would demand some food and wander off to spend time with his mates, coming home late and possibly drunk again. Today she was driving the short distance to Oatlands to buy a few groceries. Each dole pay, Rex gave her three hundred dollars. Spending frugally and saving money Sheridan had given her for Christmas and birthdays, Lucy had managed to hoard over twenty thousand dollars! Her plan had been to leave and start a new life but she was still too insecure to take such a huge step.

Popping into the spare room Lucy applied a little make-up and somehow it made her feel like a real person again. Opening a drawer she lifted out some old papers and found a photo she had hidden for years. The photo was of Liam with her, they were smiling, so in love and so happy. Lucy could never understand why Liam had chosen her as he was a handsome boy and she was a little on the chubby side but she knew he had adored her. Today, she decided, she would visit his parents who were now living in a retirement village in Oatlands. They had always treated her like a daughter even after her marriage to Rex and sent her presents each year on her birthday and for Christmas, much to the ire of Rex who, like a spoilt child, made life miserable for her on each such occasion.

How many times had Lucy wished she had fallen pregnant to Liam instead! He had been such a gentle soul and on many occasions Lucy had been more than willing to become sexually involved and give herself to him but he had insisted on waiting until they married on his return from Vietnam. Clutching the photo to her heart she shed a tear and whispered to herself, 'If only'.

Picking up her shoulder bag, Lucy closed the door and walked towards the old ute that she and Rex owned. Like the house it was old and in poor condition but at least it was theirs. Turning the key, it at first blew smoke but eventually settled as she drove slowly into town, parking outside the supermarket. She made her selections and after chatting to a few acquaintances made her way to the retirement village.

Liam's parents, Mary and Bill Walsh, greeted her warmly. She always felt ashamed that she did not visit them more often but if Rex found out, which he easily could, it would be to her detriment. Living in such a small community did have its disadvantages.

Mary immediately put the kettle on and Bill took her by the hand and sat her down on the small settee.

"How is life treating you Lucy?" asked Bill warmly.

"No complaints Bill, heaps worse off than I am! What about yourselves?" Lucy replied.

"Well Lucy, age is catching up with us and for that reason I am glad you called because there is something we both want to discuss with you," said Bill in earnest.

Lucy felt a bit uncomfortable as Mary placed cakes and biscuits on the coffee table in front of her then pulled up a chair so that all three sat in close proximity to each other.

"My dear Lucy," Mary started slowly, "there are a few things we feel we must discuss with you while we are still capable. As Bill said, time is catching up with us and as you know Liam was our only child. We were both shattered by his death."

Lucy knew Mary was suffering and gently reached out and took her by the hand. Even as a young girl they had always made her feel welcome. She had a great affinity with the old couple.

Drawing breath Mary continued, "We've never told you but Liam could have escaped National Service. Since he was our only son and we needed him on the property he was eligible for exemption. He refused, saying it was not fair for him to shirk his duties when others had to go, but we were not surprised by his reaction. That was our Liam, a special human being."

A tear trickled down Lucy's face as she shook her head and uttered quietly "I never knew."

"That was the nature of our wonderful son Lucy. He also told us that you two would marry on his discharge. In fact, we had started to make arrangements. You were perfect for each other and we love you for the happiness you brought into his short life." Mary struggled to continue, her voice breaking up as the women squeezed each other's hands tightly.

Never before had Mary disclosed her feelings about Liam and Lucy but now needed to get whatever she had to say off her chest. Lucy sensed more revelations were about to unfold.

"As you are aware we sold the farm a few years ago since we had no family to pass it on to apart from you Lucy. We know what happened to you and under what circumstances. Bill has cancer and in a few short months his life will end so we are now obliged to make plans," Mary said, looking straight ahead, desperate to not break down.

"You see Lucy, our son loved only you! You were the sunshine of his life and we regarded you as our daughter-in-law, married or not, for it was you he chose out of all the others to spend his life with. I want you to know that on Bill's death you will inherit what would have been our son's inheritance. We are positive he would've wanted it that way," Mary added, then stopped and gave a huge sigh of relief. She slumped back in her seat, her strength having left her body.

"But," Lucy stammered, "Mary will need money to live on and I surely do not deserve this!"

"Lucy, you of all people deserve this and we decided a long time ago that this is our only course. To be frank we should have done this a long time ago. Leave that miserable life you lead and make a new start. Mary has more than she will ever need to live her life out so no arguing, it is decided. We thank you for the sunshine you brought into our family's life Lucy and it is time you got a break. God bless you Lucy," Bill smiled and getting up pulled Lucy to her feet embracing her warmly.

Lucy sat for some time, absolutely overwhelmed, never realising the depth of feeling Liam's parents had for her. All her life she'd been belittled and looked down upon but here she sat before two wonderful human beings who had always adored her, as had their son.

Returning home she placed her few groceries into the cupboard and made herself a coffee. As she looked around at her home she knew that the Walshes were right. Enough of her life had been wasted and, although she had no idea how much, she knew whatever she inherited, combined with her own reserves would be enough to make a new start. It was now or never!

Lucy decided to spend the weekend with Sheridan before she embarked on her trip around Australia. Then she would make plans for herself. Rex would hardly miss her. Sex had been missing from the marriage for over fifteen years as the alcohol and nicotine had long robbed him of his libido. She mused, shaking her head, how their sex life had always been a quick one-minute job anyway and mainly just to relieve him without any thought of her needs. Lucy had no idea how dramatically her life would change in the next few weeks and how it would come to chart her future.

Chapter Two

Over the next few days Lucy cleaned the house ready for Sheridan's arrival. Acutely aware that since leaving home to attend college she'd not come home very often and when she had it was only for an overnight visit. This was no doubt because her father made no bones about the fact that he blamed her for everything that had happened in his life, instead of looking at his own shortcomings.

Lucy decided not to mention her forthcoming inheritance, something that was constantly on her mind. She had no idea of the amount involved, although she did know that the Walshes had once owned one of the most prestigious properties in the area. Her expectations were not high but she felt honoured they thought so much of her.

Lucy struggled to sleep at night, kept awake by the thought that her life to date seemed determined by circumstance. The house she lived in had belonged to her parents and because none of her other siblings had wanted it the property was transferred into her name following her mother's death. Now it was old and neglected because of her husband's unwillingness to carry out any repairs. The lack of funds had been another huge factor while raising her daughter and of course her reluctance to spend the minimal savings she had so carefully scrimped together over the years.

On the Saturday Sheridan arrived. Although they spoke daily on the phone it was always a high point in

Lucy's life when her daughter came to stay for the night. Rex had as usual gone off with one of his mates for the afternoon, so mother and daughter sat around chatting, one of Lucy's favourite times, they were incredibly close. Whenever Lucy felt desperate and trapped the thought of Sheridan kept her sane, and motivated her each day to get up and persevere, "I have something really exciting to tell you but please keep it in confidence" said Lucy looking solemnly at Sheridan.

"Mum, if it's about the Walsh Will, I typed it up so I already know," Sheridan replied.

"Why didn't you tell me Sheridan?" asked Lucy, startled that her daughter would withhold such information.

"Mum, client confidentiality. I risked losing my job if my bosses found out I told you. Even they didn't realise that the beneficiary was my mother," Sheridan replied smiling.

"I suppose you're right but you surprised me. That's all. I had no idea Bill and Mary thought that way. It's probably not worth much, but really I never expected anything anyhow," Lucy replied.

"Well, I'm not sure of the exact amount after costs but it is a substantial amount and far more than you realise," said Sheridan.

Shocked Lucy replied "You can have most of it. I think it may be too late for me."

"Mum, don't be crazy! You are relatively young and with a whole new life ahead of you if you want it, but only you can make the decision to change your life. For years I've begged you to come and live with me to do just that" said Sheridan passionately.

"I would never impose my miserable life on you, besides I can now travel around Australia with you by phone! Just ring me whenever possible and it will give me something to look forward to," said Lucy.

They finished their meal and talked into the night. Rex staggered in about eleven o'clock and went straight to bed, grunting at them both as he slammed the bedroom door. That night Lucy slept in the spare room, her first step in the separation that she knew was inevitable and when she felt that the time was right.

Mother and daughter bid each other a fond farewell when Sheridan's friend Carmen picked her up in the campervan the girls had bought for the trip. Sheridan had sold her car to a local buyer and he was to pick it up on the Sunday.

As they drove off and she waved them goodbye, Lucy felt very alone. Her daughter had always been within travelling distance. Tears welled in her eyes and she stood for some time feeling exhausted and confused.

Returning to the house Lucy experienced an unexplained hatred for it and without really knowing why, began to go through all her belongings. She packed her most treasured possessions, which really were only a few photos of herself and Liam happy in love and laughing, of Sheridan growing up and of her parents on the farm at Tunnack all those years ago, the only truly happy times in her life. Carefully she placed them in the bottom of a suitcase then packed the few decent clothes she had including two pairs of jeans she had hardly ever worn because Rex had chided her on her 'fat arse'. She placed the case in the spare wardrobe with no real plans to do anything, but the action gave her a sense of achievement. The second phase in unwittingly changing her life!

That evening an excited Sheridan phoned and informed Lucy they had loaded the campervan onto the ferry. They were having a meal while watching the land disappear. Lucy felt overjoyed by her daughter's happiness at the start of her great adventure. The two girls intended to take as long as they wanted and work occasionally to supplement their savings. Lucy secretly hoped that Sheridan would meet a nice young man and fall in love. Another 'Liam' must await her daughter somewhere! Lucy knew Sheridan had had a few dates but nothing serious. Like her mother, she was a little plump but had a beautiful face and a bubbly personality.

For the next two weeks life settled back for Lucy. She continued to visit Mary and Bill who both now seemed to have lost their zest for life. Bill moved into full-time care at the hospital and Mary spent most of her time sitting at the side of his bed. It was as though they were waiting for the inevitable. Bill began to slowly slip away and life without the man she had dedicated her life to was beyond Mary's imagination.

Each evening Sheridan and Carmen would phone Lucy, informing her of the day's events. Lucy almost felt that she was on the trip with them, checking the map as they journeyed along the Great Ocean Road. They stopped in several towns before entering South Australia with its beautiful wine regions and the stunning Murray River.

Lucy followed the girls by marking her map each day as they weaved their way to Adelaide and then onto the Yorke and Eyre Peninsulas.

Several weeks passed and Lucy received a call from Sheridan in Ceduna advising that they were preparing to cross the Nullarbor and into Western Australia.

Then she phoned again one morning to tell Lucy of her incredible news! She had met a man on the jetty provisioning his yacht for a trip to Perth and eventually up to Darwin. At first Lucy felt elated but then began to worry when Sheridan's behaviour and attitude changed. Carmen also informed Lucy that she was alarmed that Sheridan was talking about going with her 'newfound friend' and in fact the two girls had argued several times about it. Carmen told Lucy that Sheridan had accused her of being jealous but it was in fact because she felt something was not quite right with the story Con Wilson, a half-caste Aboriginal, had told them. Carmen sensed that far from just delivering the yacht to Darwin there was much more involved.

To her absolute horror, the phone calls from her beloved daughter ceased and a sad Carmen informed her Sheridan had sold her her share in the campervan and sailed off with Con. Carmen said she had decided to stay in Ceduna for perhaps a couple of months in case Sheridan changed her mind. Lucy felt pangs of fear for the safety of her daughter, it was so unlike her to make such a rash decision, especially as she had only just met this man and known him for a few days. For another two weeks Lucy waited for a phone call and when none eventuated she told Rex.

21

He just laughed it off and told her not to be ridiculous. Three weeks later, in a complete panic, Lucy told Rex that she was going to look for Sheridan and as usual he gave her no support, only abused her for being stupid.

Sadly, Mary and Bill Walsh both passed away within two days of each other and were to be buried in a dual ceremony. When Lucy heard of their passing, she booked herself with the ute onto the ferry. She phoned Carmen, asked her to wait in Ceduna for her and planned to join her after the funerals.

Having witnessed Bill and Mary being laid to rest, Lucy felt that it marked the end of her long connection with Liam. She felt free now and would pursue her search to locate the last remaining person she really loved, her daughter Sheridan.

Lucy phoned the solicitors acting for the Walsh family and advised them of her plans. They in turn advised her to seek her own solicitor and get him or her to act on her behalf. Lucy did so the following day and leaving the bank and other details as well as authorisation to act on her behalf she returned home and packed the few remaining things she felt she might need. Her old ute had a canopy and she threw a double mattress into the back with bedding, ready to depart the next morning. Having never in her life been north of Oatlands she felt a pang of fear about her imminent venture yet her profound love for her daughter heavily outweighed any concern she had for herself.

That night when Rex returned home late she told him of her plan. Predictably he flew into a rage, threatening her as he had done many times before but Lucy retaliated for the first time ever and so ferocious was her response, he meekly went to bed. Lucy felt empowered now and decided to leave at once and sleep in the ute somewhere north of Oatlands. Even though she owned the house, Rex was welcome to it, her time had come to leave and it had to be done now. Starting the vehicle she backed out of the drive not even looking back as she made the short trip to Oatlands and north into the unknown on a quest to find her darling girl.

With her mind racing and adrenaline pumping, Lucy felt liberated and gave a yell as she drove north, not really knowing where Devonport was but she was filled with determination and felt free for the first time, the shackles at last had been removed from her life.

At Campbell Town she decided to park in the rest area. Even in the dark it seemed peaceful by the river. Climbing up into bed she lay awake for some time until finally the stress of the last few days seemed to ebb from within her and she dropped off into a deep sleep.

Lucy awoke with a start. Her heart was racing in the few seconds it took her to realise where she was. Her stomach knotted as this was the first time she had spent away from her home in over thirty years, ever since her parents had moved there when she was just a child. Sitting up in the dark, a sweat broke out on her brow, then she remembered what had happened and her determination set in. She just had to continue her search and to try to locate her daughter even though she had no plan or any idea of how to start. All she could think was to head to

Ceduna in South Australia to obtain as many facts as she could and then make a plan from there.

Dressing while laying in the back of the ute was far from simple, particularly as she had even decided to wear jeans. Having successfully completed that task and combed her hair she went to McDonalds for some breakfast since the ferry wasn't leaving until that evening. Knowing she had some time to kill Lucy checked the road map again and decided to buy some gear in Devonport before leaving. She needed a portable gas stove, some camping gear and a GPS to help her find her way out of Melbourne when she disembarked the ferry. The thought terrified her but she felt strong and, after a hearty breakfast, she freshened up in the restrooms and set off.

It was a beautiful day, traffic was light and Lucy enjoyed the drive. She turned off at Perth and headed to Devonport arriving well before midday. After buying her items she filled a container with water, pleased that now she was able to at least make herself a drink. A helpful shop assistant helped her fit the GPS and showed her how to set and operate it but looked aghast when she told him she was off to Ceduna. He looked at the old ute she was driving, shook his head and wished her all the best!

At four o'clock she found her way to the waiting line at the ferry terminal and since she was a little early decided to stretch her legs and wander around. Others had already lined up and to her pleasant surprise several of them entered into conversations with her which made the waiting time fly by. Finally, undaunted by this new experience, Lucy boarded and found her way to the cabin. She collapsed onto the bed and was asleep within twenty minutes. She was awakened by an intercom call to inform everyone that the ferry had docked in Melbourne. Lucy leapt out of bed and had a quick shower. Her heart racing, she made her way below decks to the vehicle, planning to stop for breakfast once she had left Melbourne.

Seated in her ute she set the GPS for Mount Gambier. Having looked at the map again, she decided not to drive quite as far on her first day. After what seemed an eternity, the bowels of the vessel opened and vehicles of all shapes and sizes streamed out. Her GPS picked up a signal and a reassuring voice guided her out over the West Gate Bridge.

Lucy had to really concentrate, as she had never driven on a four-lane highway before, but before long felt confident and discovered it was far easier than expected, especially with the guidance of the GPS. Stopping at a service centre along the highway Lucy had a good breakfast, happy that her ordeal seemed less traumatic than initially anticipated. Her quest had begun and so had a new chapter in her life.

Although alone, she didn't feel lonely and didn't miss anything from her previous life. Finding her beloved daughter was her task at hand. Was she truly prepared for such a trip? Who knew? All Lucy knew was that nothing would prevent her from searching for Sheridan and that determination was her greatest asset.

After eating, she filled the ute with fuel and pulled out onto the highway. She was ready.

Chapter Three

Lucy drove at a steady speed of ninety kilometres per hour. So what if some of the other road users and large trucks did not appreciate it! She drove at the speed 'she' felt comfortable with and only stopped to boil the kettle for a coffee and to stretch her legs. The weather was lovely and she settled into a routine rather quickly, surprising herself how capable she actually was, her confidence growing with each passing hour. Although it was not that dark, Lucy wanted a hot shower and an early night so pulled into a caravan park near Blue Lake in Mount Gambier. Booking in, she decided on a cabin and, after phoning Carmen who had nothing to report, cooked a meal and retired, ready for a longer drive the next day.

Feeling more confident, Lucy began to make plans. She knew Carmen didn't have much information, even the name of the vessel, so intended talking to the yacht broker in Adelaide to glean as much as possible, then ask the relevant authorities to help her track the progress of the yacht. Perhaps knowing its name and how much time had passed, they could assess how far ahead the vessel might be. She wrote down all the necessary information and questions she needed to ask just so she wouldn't forget anything.

Waking early, Lucy made a coffee and studied the map again carefully. She would eat later in the morning. Aware of her appointment with the broker the following day she decided to stop overnight east of Adelaide so as to arrive as planned at about 10am. Lucy had not informed the broker why she wanted to see him and just let him assume she was a potential buyer.

Driving through the wine-growing regions, Lucy regretted not having escaped her mundane life years before. Since Sheridan had left home Lucy's world had been one of loneliness, trapped in an environment that was slowly destroying her. Now however she was on a journey of discovery not only to find her true self but more importantly to find her daughter. Lucy was determined to locate Sheridan and nothing would dissuade her from doing so, no matter what the road ahead had in store for her or what obstacles she encountered. It was this thought that became so entrenched in her mind that the past simply faded into history. 'Did she miss her husband?' 'Definitely not,' the thoughts made her smile and finally she felt clean and free.

Although she made several stops along the way, to her surprise she arrived at the caravan park mid-afternoon. She felt tired. Perhaps it was the adrenaline slowing down now that she had settled into a routine. Lucy booked into a cabin but knew that for her money to last she would need to start sleeping in the vehicle. Browsing the map, she became aware of the large stretches of highway still ahead of her and which would determine her luck in catching up to the yacht. Hopefully they would have to stock up on provisions before reaching Darwin, but in any event that would be her destination based on the knowledge she had at this stage.

The following morning she arrived before the appointed time at the yacht brokerage and was immediately ushered into the office. She noticed immediately how both partners looked at her dilapidated ute.

"Now Mrs Jacobs, what can we do for you today?" the salesman almost sang, in an oily voice.

"Well," Lucy replied, "to be honest, I don't know much about yachts but recently an acquaintance of my husband, an Aboriginal chap from Darwin by the name of Con Wilson bought a yacht here and we were so taken with the vessel that we decided to try and purchase something similar." Lucy was surprised at how easily she lied.

Both men frowned and looked at each other before one salesman replied, "Sorry, we haven't sold a boat to anyone by that name but we did sell a ketch to a Nic Augustus about six weeks ago. Barry knew him from Darwin and he is of mixed race" the spokesman said as he glanced around nervously.

"Oh how stupid of me!" Lucy replied "Con was one of the crew he had when we spoke to them in Ceduna."

"Well, our sales are confidential Mrs Jacobs. How long have you known Nic?" the 'oily' one enquired.

"To be honest, our daughter lives with him in Darwin and we want to go sailing up north also, and please, call me Lucy," replied Lucy coolly, aware she had to be careful in order to get the information she now knew Barry had.

Barry replied, "Oh that's no surprise! Nic is a real woman-chaser, has over twenty kids from various Aboriginal women. Your daughter must be some gal to keep him under control."

Lucy's heart skipped a beat. "Yep Barry , let me tell you our daughter is a tough one, learnt it from her father who is a wharfie in Darwin."

Barry quickly settled. Lucy knew that she had his confidence and the tension in the room eased.

"I'm surprised they went up the west coast, a much harder trip. I suppose that's why they called into Ceduna for fuel. Although, with the cargo he had on board" Barry laughed and winked at Lucy, "the less ports they called at, the better!"

Again Lucy took a deep breath. She was now beyond her depth and chose to play cagey so as not to display her lack of knowledge of what might be happening.

"Perhaps Barry, the less said about the cargo the better. Now, what do you have that might suit us?" asked Lucy, acutely aware that Sheridan could be in grave danger.

Lucy certainly did not want to arouse suspicion. If Barry and Nic, not 'Con' as she believed, knew each other then perhaps it would be better not to let him know she was looking for her daughter. Keeping up the pretence Lucy looked at several yachts, writing down prices and showing great interest, all the while gleaning bits of information from Barry.

Once he felt he had gained her confidence and thought she was fully aware of Nic's 'cargo' he stopped at the end of the pier, "Now listen Lucy, not prying into your business, but one trip can pay for one of these yachts. I have the contacts and, right now prices for dope are low because of supply, just ask Nic. As no doubt you are aware, up north in the remote communities you can make heaps. He used to take it up the Stuart Highway by car but some of his drivers got caught so that's why he bought the yacht."

"I'm aware of all that Barry, but will need to talk it over with my husband. I'll be in Darwin next week and will let you know. I am to deliver this old ute from his brother in Tasmania, it had broken down here and hubby wants it for his farming activities in Darwin," she winked at Barry who was sold with this information.

Lucy did not realise until she'd left that sweat was pouring out of her profusely, and her heart was pounding wildly. The information she had obtained was mindboggling because her only knowledge of drugs was from TV programs! Now she was involved in the seedy business by way of her daughter. Her top priority was to find Sheridan and get her away from this Nic. With her mind racing she tried to concentrate on the GPS guiding her through Adelaide. Spotting a bank to her right she stopped and withdrew five hundred dollars. Checking her balance she was pleased to see she still had eighteen thousand and that at least for the time being money was not a big problem.

Once Lucy settled on the Port Wakefield Road, she travelled awhile then stopped for a break at a roadhouse. Not terribly hungry she sat drinking a coffee, her appetite supressed by the latest information. Lucy at first was hopeful that things would turn out okay thinking her daughter had had a meltdown and just made a stupid decision but now she was worried that the affair was far more sinister. Driven by fear for Sheridan's welfare and knowing time was of the essence Lucy drove non-stop to

Ceduna, arriving late in the evening. She decided not to disturb Carmen as it was approaching midnight so parked at the town jetty and lay in the back of the ute, but sleep evaded her.

Lucy got up at daylight and freshened up in the nearby toilets. Locking her vehicle she made her way to the local caravan park and located Carmen's campervan. Taking a breath, she knocked on the door.

A sleepy Carmen opened the door, "Shit Lucy, you look bloody awful! Come in," she whispered. Lucy stepped inside the van as Carmen put the jug on the gas stove, and filled her in on what she knew. Carmen looked worried.

"I knew something was not right. He was so keen to get her on board and Sheridan withdrew ten thousand dollars, nearly all her savings!" informed Carmen.

"Carmen, this can't get much worse. Now we know why he poured on the charm and why they needed the money. Barry told me they would be sailing mostly into headwinds and currents at this time of year and that would be pretty heavy on fuel," Lucy replied.

"Listen, Lucy, I've decided to go home, this has ruined my holiday. I only stayed on until you arrived. If you like, you can take the camper on and pay me back later for it. I'll fly home and go back to work" announced Carmen.

"No! I don't want to spoil your adventure, it wouldn't be fair," Lucy replied adamantly.

"Listen Lucy, my trip is fucked anyway. It's turned into a nightmare. With the two of us it was fine but on my own, no way. I went to the police but they laughed at me and actually one even muttered something about me being jealous of Sheridan. So it's you who will have to find Sheridan and this is comfortable and much cheaper to run than your heap of shit," said Carmen. I will take your ute to Adelaide, sell it for whatever, and fly home."

Lucy knew she was right, the old ute was burning oil and it would be a miracle if it lasted to Perth, so they both transferred their belongings and gave each other a comforting hug before driving off in opposite directions.

After exchanging receipts for the sale of the vehicles to each other, Lucy discovered that the camper was more responsive and easier to drive and even more importantly, the fuel consumption was so much better. Plus, she now had a mobile home. With all the information she had to date Lucy knew the yacht would be far north by now but would make enquiries at Fremantle and then at each little town before Broome. Lucy knew too that it was best not to involve the authorities as her real priority was to protect Sheridan.

That evening Lucy parked at a camp on the Nullarbor. She was delighted she had listened to Carmen, the bed was large and comfortable and with the van lockable, she felt safer. There were many other caravans parked around her so she took advantage and chatted to the many grey nomads making the big trip around Australia. Lucy gathered some vital information from the other travellers and charted her course to Kalgoorlie, then on to Perth, saving a lot of travelling by cutting straight through to Fremantle.

Regarding herself now as a seasoned traveller, Lucy pulled into the Fremantle Warf two days later. Despite making numerous enquiries she turned up nothing. The thought crossed her mind that the yacht would most probably be deliberately kept away from major ports and fuelled at some of the fishing villages north, when and if necessary.

As luck would have it, a couple on one of the yachts in Fremantle invited her aboard for coffee and having confided in them, they became interested in her plight. They had just sailed down from Broome so the three of them studied charts. Their information and suggestions were crucial to Lucy's plans. It was suggested that the yacht might be fuelled at Port Hedland, a busy port where the iron ore facility ran twenty-four hours a day and the appearance of a yacht would hardly be noticed. So thanking her new friends Lucy decided to continue north, skirting Perth, and make enquiries there. Lucy sensed something. It was as though her daughter's presence was getting closer and this encouraged her to complete the large distances. Not many vehicles passed her.

Eventually arriving at Port Hedland, Lucy was surprised by the chaos of the traffic caused by huge trucks and equipment clogging the roads. She was only used to the slow spasmodic traffic in Tasmania but she was now gaining experience daily and, weaving her way between the traffic, parked on The Esplanade.

Her first thought was to turn on her mobile phone to see if she had any messages and to her absolute delight she had a voicemail from her daughter! Listening intently she heard, "Hi Mum, sorry for not making contact sooner but have been at sea. No doubt Carmen has filled you in on what's happened. It's okay, it was my decision and I'm fine. Hope to be in Darwin later in the week then on to The Gulf of Carpentaria. I'll make contact later."

Lucy sat stunned. She knew deep inside her that all was not as it should be. Perhaps Sheridan was too proud to admit to a mistake or maybe she was in a position where she was trapped at sea, unable to get help or leave the yacht. Lucy dialled Sheridan's mobile but got the automated message that it was turned off or out of range.

She was alive! Lucy fuelled the van and pulled out onto the Great Northern Highway. She would never make Darwin by the end of the week, as it was already Tuesday, but the only thing she could think to do was drive.

Chapter Four

The steady hum of the engine and warm weather hypnotised Lucy and she found herself dozing at the wheel. Shocked and angry with herself, she was slapping her face to wake up when she spotted the Sandfire Roadhouse up ahead. She pulled up at the roadhouse to spend the night, making a mental note to stop for intermittent rests if she was to arrive in Darwin safely. Killing herself she decided, or some other innocent motorist would not help her cause.

After parking the van Lucy took a shower in the amenities block then cooked a delicious meal using some of the meat she had in the fridge. She knew she had been drinking too much coffee and noticed when she looked in the mirror just how tired and haggard she was becoming.

Lucy ate her meal in the van because of the ever present annoying flies, and watched some television. She contemplated again the change in her life and knew she would embrace all that was offered. To return to her past was not an option.

The next day Lucy passed the Broome turnoff, bitterly disappointed she hadn't time to explore the old pearling town she'd read so much about but promising herself to repeat the journey again and do some more sightseeing. Fuelling at Willare Bridge Roadhouse, Lucy headed towards Fitzroy Crossing. It was a warm day and Lucy, concentrating on the road ahead, hadn't noticed the engine heating until steam hissed from beneath the vehicle and the engine began to seize. Something like this was not on her radar. She panicked and pulled off the highway. As she stood on the side of the road in shock, a massive road-train pulled in ahead of her and the driver, a short man in shorts, jumped down.

"Are you ok matey?" he asked.

"No! Even with all the shit things happening in my life at the moment I can't believe this, it just came out of the blue," Lucy replied, her voice trembling.

"Let's check her out. By the way matey, name is Lyndon Savage, truck driver extraordinaire," he reported holding out a hand for a firm handshake.

"Lucy Jacobs, damsel in distress," she responded, still in shock and unable to really focus.

After examining her vehicle Lyndon announced, "Yep, it's seized alright. No way can we get that going. Where are you heading?" he asked.

"To Darwin" Lucy replied.

"Your lucky day Lucy, that's my destination! Pack your gear into the truck if you like and we'll get someone from Fitzroy Crossing to come out and tow the van in," suggested Lyndon.

"Are you sure? I really don't know what to do, this came out of left field!" muttered Lucy.

"How long since you checked the oil and water?" Lyndon asked casually.

"Oh no," cried Lucy "bloody hell, in my rush to get to Darwin I didn't give that a thought."

"Next time old girl perhaps you'd better, now come

on, get the stuff you want to take and let's go, I'm late already," Lyndon chuckled.

Lucy followed Lyndon's instruction and packed her suitcase, her mobile phone and handbag. She locked the still steaming van and, having helped her into the truck Lyndon set off east, with Lucy still in a daze.

Pulling into Fitzroy Crossing they called at the only towing service in town. Lyndon suggested Lucy pay for the tow and have the vehicle stored until she was in a position to retrieve it or even sell it later. The tow truck operator set off straight away advising a still stressed Lucy that, even in that short time the van could be stripped.

Lyndon insisted he buy her lunch at the roadhouse but Lucy hardly ate a thing. She was still in shock at having not given any consideration to the maintenance of the vehicle

On the journey north, her barriers came down and Lucy opened her heart up to her saviour, feeling so much better for doing so. She found Lyndon a good listener and he in turn told her about his life. He was divorced and owned a home in Darwin. Two more trips and it would be paid for. After that he intended selling his truck and getting a job in Darwin. He had had enough of life on the road, plus costs had skyrocketed in the last few years and new Government Regulations and customer expectation made for diminishing profit and longer hours.

Lucy relaxed, she felt comfortable with her knight in shining armour. He was an easy-going soul and they discussed her current dilemma at length. He was aware of the drug trade operating in remote communities, along with alcohol issues. Even admitting that on more than one occasion due to financial pressures, he had been tempted to run alcohol just like many of his acquaintances. He promised he would help her gather information about her daughter's 'boyfriend' once his load had been delivered. His sister, he told her, was married to a Northern Territory Police Officer. This news was calming to Lucy and feeling tired from the day's events, began to doze off.

Lucy awoke to a gentle nudge from Lyndon. It was dark outside and he had parked in a truck stop with several other trucks surrounding them.

"I'm going to have a few hours' sleep in the back Lucy. You can too if you want, it's a large bed and I promise to be good," Lyndon chuckled.

Lucy looked in the back at the bed. She had not even contemplated anything with Lyndon and agreed that they both needed sleep. Lyndon made hot drinks and they shared the sandwiches he had bought at the roadhouse, before slipping into bed. Lucy remained dressed in her jeans as she drifted off to sleep, aware that Lyndon slept soundly beside her. Despite having only met him that day, feeling his body close to hers gave her a sense of security.

Waking a few hours later she needed to go to the toilet and tried to slip out of bed quietly but woke Lyndon up.

"Are you alright?" he asked.

"Need to go to the toilet, like right now," Lucy replied giggling.

"Here, take the toilet paper and cover the seat in the toilet block. I'm getting up anyway so I'll stand guard for you," he replied.

Lucy stumbled out of the truck. Lyndon took her hand and showed her the way with his torch. It was inky black. Entering the drop toilet, Lucy nearly gagged from the smell but trying not to think about it, finished her business as quickly as possible.

"God that was awful," she laughed stumbling out of the toilet.

"Get back in the truck and wash your hands in the small sink. I'm heading off now but sleep for a few more hours if you like," Lyndon replied.

Assisted by Lyndon, Lucy climbed back into the cab and finding the small washbasin, washed her hands vigorously. The door was still open and she smiled as she heard a splash as Lyndon peed outside before getting back behind the wheel. He started the big rig, letting it idle for some time before heading off and although she tried to sleep, Lucy couldn't so she made two cups of tea and joined him in the cab. They kept each other company as they wound their way east towards Katherine.

For the first time in many years, Lucy began to enjoy conversing with a man. She was so used to her husband hardly communicating at all, except to criticise and deride her, that it was a novelty chatting to Lyndon. Their topic centred on the bureaucracy and of the red tape strangling the country and free speech being curtailed because of political correctness.

It was four o'clock when they pulled into a freight yard in Katherine.

"I need to drop off one of the trailers here then have a shower, some food and a few hours' sleep before we head to Darwin," Lyndon told Lucy.

Lucy knew from previous conversations with Lyndon that he was over his allotted driving time and that if he had been pulled over he would've copped a heavy fine for not complying with his log book rest periods.

While Lyndon was unhooking one of the trailers Lucy showered in the depot's amenities and although tired, she felt refreshed. Lyndon followed her soon after and they stored the dirty clothes in the truck then walked to a nearby cafe where they enjoyed a hearty meal, the first in several days.

Returning to the truck in the dark, Lucy this time stripped to her undergarments as had Lyndon. They climbed into the cab and curled up falling into a deep sleep.

During the night Lucy woke up realising Lyndon had his arm over her and also felt the hardness of his erection against her buttocks. She froze and then slowly began to turn over, coming up against his face. He too was awake and without saying anything, they began to kiss. Their kisses were at first gentle but suddenly they responded with passion and began to tear each other's undergarments off. Lucy automatically opened her legs as he rolled on top and entered her in one wild thrust, taking her breath away.

Never in her life had she experienced such prolonged and wild sex! Slamming into each other she felt something rise within her, not recognising an oncoming orgasm. He felt huge as he rode her like a raging bull and they shuddered, climaxing simultaneously, their bodies covered in sweat.

Neither spoke for some time until Lyndon slipped out of

her and rolled over on to the bed, "Sorry for that. Believe me Lucy, I never planned it. Just the feel of your bottom was so inviting, I couldn't sleep. Have to say though, that was one wild ride," he chuckled.

"Don't be sorry Lyndon. That was the best sex I've ever had! In fact, it was my first ever orgasm! I too never thought about it, but am I sorry? Hell no! It's the best feeling I've had for a long time. I had no idea sex could be so satisfying," Lucy replied sighing.

Lucy lay wide awake, her sexuality awakened. She felt Lyndon slowly and gently caressing her breasts and then turning towards each other again, they kissed passionately, his erect penis pressing against her. Throwing off the blankets they embraced and wrapped themselves in ecstasy as he drove deep inside her. They rose higher with each thrust, engaging in a marathon of powerful sex, oblivious to everything, both lost in the passion and fire they shared until eventually reaching a crescendo of moans and groans before Lyndon shuddered and ejaculated inside her. They then slipped on some clothes and went to shower, their lust, for the time being, sated.

Returning to the cabin they changed the sheets before snuggling up and dropping off into a deep sleep. No words were exchanged. There seemed no need.

Lucy woke late. She became aware that the truck was moving and after dressing made her way to the cabin. Lyndon smiled at her and squeezed her hand. Lucy returned the smile and it was then she knew she was hopelessly in love, for the first time since the death of her first love, Liam. She sensed that Lyndon shared the same feelings, those of two people accidently meeting on life's pathway and forming such a strong bond in so short a time.

They arrived in Darwin mid-afternoon. Lyndon dropped off the remaining trailers at the depot and they drove to the outskirts of Darwin where he had a small acreage. Lucy fell in love with the tropical trees surrounding the small cottage and large shed.

"Sorry the house isn't that big, the divorce cost me a lot of money," he smiled, but sadly.

"Lyndon, it's lovely! You should've seen the heap of crap I lived in! Gosh, everything just confirms that my life has been on hold in so many ways and ironically I owe my daughter for breaking me free of it. I just hope she's safe. Once I'm sure of that I can begin a new life," Lucy told him as she stood under the shade of a large tree.

"Look, I have a few days off before the next trip to Adelaide and back. It's already booked, so let's spend the night here then take my car into town and find out what we can. I'm sure all will turn out fine," he said to comfort her.

"To be honest, I was a little upset with her for running off like that but now, really, who am I to judge? First chance I get, here I am bonking a man I've only known a few days," giggled Lucy.

"Blame it on circumstance but, same here I never planned on another relationship. Actually Lucy, I hope we can keep it going as I think you are a really nice person," Lyndon smiled at her.

"First time in a long time I've heard something positive about me Lyndon. No promises. Life is strange isn't it? Let's see what eventuates and don't forget I'm still a married woman," Lucy reminded him.

Entering the house Lucy laughed, "You might be a good truckie but as a housekeeper, bloody hell Lyndon, what a mess!"

Lyndon blushed, "Yep, not my strong point. I'll let old Kevin know I'm home, he feeds the chooks. Then we can get some food, there's heaps in the freezer."

Lucy replied, "Go on then, I'll clean up a bit and get some food happening."

"Change the bedding, there's heaps of new stuff in the wardrobe. I suggest we have an early night tonight as we are both bushed," Lyndon yelled back as he walked across the paddock.

"Typical man, I am fully aware of your intentions, Lyndon Savage!" Lucy yelled back, laughing and shaking her head.

The house was only small and Lucy was surprised how quickly she cleaned it up. After giving the floor a sweep, she headed to the kitchen and to her delight saw that the freezer was full of food and the cupboards were also packed with food items. Taking out some T-bone steaks she placed them in the microwave to thaw and then broke open a packet of mixed vegetables into a saucepan. Filling it up with water she placed them on the stove.

One thing she noticed was that no washing up had been left in the sink. While the meat thawed in the microwave she walked to the door and, looking down the paddock, understood why the freezer was full of meat, several cows with calves grazed on the land below the house. Impressed, she returned as the microwave finished thawing the meat. By the time Lyndon returned, the place looked tidy and the smell of food permeated the air.

"Wow old girl! Best thing that has happened to me in a long time, finding you," he casually smiled at her, patting her affectionately on the buttocks as he passed.

They chatted over the meal before retiring to the couch to catch up on the news. More manufacturing jobs had been lost, dominating the broadcast and after a while Lyndon turned it off, "Sorry I turned it on, all bad news it seems" he said, "we've overpriced ourselves and cannot compete, plus we've lost our freedom of speech and gone all 'politically correct'! Maybe it's just me, but I think our nation has gone mad. Let's go for a walk."

Lyndon pulled her to her feet and together they wandered past the paddocks below, watched by the small herd of cattle swishing their tails against the myriad of flies.

"Right, first thing tomorrow we'll go round to my sister's place and see what her husband can tell us. Then we'll decide the next move in locating your daughter. My only worry is that I'm committed to leave in two days' time and have no choice but to fulfil the contract," explained Lyndon as they walked hand in hand back towards the house.

"Maybe I can drive over to the community Nic lives in and take it from there?" Lucy suggested.

"It's not that easy I'm afraid old girl. First, you need a permit and second, it's one hell of a drive down to Mataranka on to Roper Bar and then Numbulwar. You'll need a better reason than that to get a permit also," said

Lyndon as they sat in the twilight on the porch.

"What permit?" asked Lucy.

"To enter Aboriginal land, you need a permit," answered Lyndon.

"They come onto white man's land with no permit," retorted Lucy frowning.

"That is the way things are unfortunately. Let's wait and see what Kevin the cop reckons, we'll work something out," replied Lyndon assuredly.

They continued talking together, aware they would have to be parted for some time. Cuddling up in bed, they fell fast asleep with their arms wrapped around each other, unsure of what lay ahead.

Lucy woke first as daylight crept over the bed and as she looked down at the sleeping form next to her, she felt herself wanting him. Slowly and carefully, she eased forward, kissing Lyndon as his eyes opened slowly. They embraced and began to make slow and passionate love, each wanting desperately to please the other. After climaxing they lay replete in the afterglow, savouring the moment.

Neither wanted to get out of bed and face the uncertainty of the day but both knew that Lucy would never rest until her search was successful and she found her daughter.

Chapter Five

After showering and dressing and a light breakfast, Lyndon opened his shed and backed his car out. Lucy was surprised to see that he had a relatively new Toyota.

Seeing her look Lyndon laughed, "Ok, this is my one extravagance. I work long hours and live rough but I love my car."

"I really can't blame you, for what you go through you deserve it," Lucy replied climbing in the passenger side.

Already the day was heating up as they wound their way through the morning traffic towards the city.

"I always thought Darwin was a small town," said Lucy as the traffic slowed to almost a crawl.

"It was once, but in the last decade it has boomed and is now a large city by Australian standards. The old days are long gone," Lyndon sighed.

Turning right he drove to an inner suburb, one of the older housing areas near the city centre, and pulled up outside a neatly kept, middle-class home.

"Let's see what happens. I love my sister Lucy but to be honest, we've never really got on. Kevin too is a bit of a tosser in my books but treats Joyce well, so that's all that matters," commented Lyndon casually as they got out of the vehicle.

Joyce opened the front door and greeted her brother warmly. After introductions were made she invited them in for coffee and the four sat around the table.

"Ok brother of mine," she smiled cheekily "tell us more about this nice lady you've found, and not before time?"

"I'll let Lucy tell you her story and boy, is it a story! That's why we're here. We are hoping that Kevin can point us in the right direction" Lyndon replied seriously.

Lucy felt nervous telling her story in some detail but she was glad she had written down all the information to date. When they had first sat down, Kevin had shown little interest but as the story progressed his mood changed. Checking names, dates and other facts, Kevin waited until Lucy had finished. No one spoke. Then Kevin Peters looked straight into Lucy's eyes and spoke, "Lucy, you've told me nothing we are not already aware of. In fact, a large illicit trade in drugs, mostly marijuana and alcohol, exists in all Aboriginal communities, mainly because of the location of many of the communities. Attempting to stop this trade is almost impossible. To be honest, the community you mention is one of the more isolated and we rotate two police officers, in the main single, for three-monthly stints. This in itself creates problems as the officers often lack the experience to gather information or the time to obtain the trust of the locals," Kevin informed her.

"Is it possible for Lucy to travel there and speak to Nic and her daughter?" Lyndon asked.

"A large white community exists there delivering all the services but you need a police check and a bona fide reason to visit. The other problem is that there is no accommodation for visitors, only for workers. I might add that it is a 'politically correct' situation at this time and so sensitive that the truth and facts are distorted to follow the approved mantra," Kevin replied.

"What am I to do then? All I want is to find my daughter. Can the police help?" Lucy responded, her voice wavering.

"Lucy I must be frank. Your daughter is with this man of her own free will. Something else you should be aware of is that he has a house in Darwin and several wives. I think he has had over twenty-five children with these women. They've avoided Darwin for obvious reasons, and sailed on to The Gulf. Why don't we intercept them, you might ask? Truth is, the Federal Government is fully stretched with illegal arrivals and we have limited resources. Nic and his crew are experienced and know the area well. It would be like trying to locate a needle in a haystack.

When they ran drugs by road from Adelaide we intercepted and virtually stopped the trade but now we are informed they are bringing the drugs from Papua New Guinea, hence the new and larger yacht. They also have several smaller boats with large motors and are skilled at navigating the shallow waters in The Gulf and its treacherous reefs. They can operate at night without any lights. The new yacht will be a mother vessel to sleep and cook meals on. Sorry Lucy, this is the world your daughter in her innocence has entered," Kevin explained, shaking his head, knowing his advice would create stress and worry for Lucy but recognised her as a lamb trying to locate a pack of wolves.

"What do you suggest? How does he afford houses at Numbulwar as well as here and keep so many women and children? The drug trade must be incredibly lucrative," asked Lyndon as Lucy, stunned and devastated stared blankly at the table.

"Simple, the government supplies houses at a small rent and the allowances for twenty-five children would be in the thousands weekly. Then there are the tens of thousands of dollars exchanged weekly in the illicit drug trade but as for what to do? To be frank, I can offer no advice. Oddly enough, down south and in Darwin proper, the drug trade is run by cartels or gangs but in the Aboriginal community it is mainly run by their own kind. They are more organised than you think although they do dob each other in from time to time but, even if they are aware of those plying the trade, mostly a code of silence exists amongst them. It is a game for them to outwit white authority. Suicide and boredom are rife and unfortunately very few work so the illicit trade gives them not only excitement and money but strangely enough, for a proportion of the population on the communities, respect from many," Kevin remarked. Then he looked directly at Lucy and concluded, "Sadly Lucy that is all I can help you with."

Lucy stood up to leave. She was overwhelmed by what she had been told. Her task to locate her daughter had just hit a major hurdle.

"Thank you Kevin, at least you've been honest. I must admit my life has been very sheltered and in fact, every day on this journey I am learning how different my perspective about life in Australia has been. I had no idea," she said quietly, even forlornly.

Lyndon did not speak until they bid farewell to his sister who seemed genuinely upset at Lucy's plight. Joyce knew by Lyndon's reaction that he and Lucy had become close but having been married to a police officer for two decades, knew all was often not as it seemed.

Lyndon drove south, and without speaking turned into a large truck depot. "One last shot Lucy," Lyndon said, "Jimmy Black is a truck driver who often drives to Numbulwar with supplies in the dry season. That's his truck parked by the loading bay. Let's see what he reckons," he suggested enthusiastically.

"Oh Lyndon, if Kevin can't help, what can this bloke do?" Lucy asked, sounding despondent. "Sometimes Lucy, when the law cannot help us, we have to take things into our own hands," Lyndon shot back. They located Jimmy supervising the loading and Lyndon explained the situation.

"Your lucky day Lyndon, take this flyer. I met a convoy on the road going in last week. One had broken down and the guide they had gave me this after I helped get them on the road again. Sorry I'm late and must go, but this is your way in!" Jimmy said as he passed them the flyer he'd had in the truck and started the motor, waving as he drove off.

Upon returning to their vehicle Lucy and Lyndon both read the flyer then looked at each other in stunned silence. The heading stated: *'For the first time ever, Cape Barrow in Arnhem Land will be opened to tourists by the Indigenous owners. Participants will be supplied permits and be escorted in from Roper Bar Store.'*

"Let's phone the number! You'll need to go on your own I'm afraid, but at least you'll be in the company of fellow tourists and a guide," Lyndon told Lucy.

"I'll need to buy a four-wheel drive and a camper trailer," said Lucy looking wide-eyed, a semblance of hope returning.

"Yes, look! Bickerton Island and Groote Eylandt are off the coast. They both have large communities so at least that puts you in the vicinity and you might get into Numbulwar for fuel or groceries. When I get back, I'll fly in to meet you," continued Lyndon looking at a map he had unfolded.

"Look, before we ring, can I go to the bank and see what money I've got left and perhaps look at a few vehicles?" Lucy asked, feeling her adrenaline rising as she looked at Lyndon.

"No problems old mate, I've about seven thousand spare if that helps," he replied.

"No! I already owe Carmen twelve thousand for her camper! Better not ring up any more debt. I think I may have about sixteen thousand left, let's just see what happens," explained Lucy.

They drove into the city where Lucy found a NAB Bank and placing her card into the ATM, read the printout. She collapsed onto the footpath. Lyndon ran to her side and pulled her to her feet, her body shaking all over.

"Good God woman, what happened?" he asked loudly.

"Look ... at ... the balance," Lucy stammered.

"Holy shit Lucy! Large numbers! If I'm right, it states that you have over five bloody million! For fuck's sake, what's going on?" enquired Lyndon in amazement.

Lucy told Lyndon about her first love, Liam Walsh and how he had died in Vietnam. About the friendship she had maintained with his parents and how they had told her they intended leaving her their Estate. Lucy explained that she knew the property was large and one of Tasmania's most prestigious wool-growing estates but never in her wildest dreams did she think it was worth so much! In fact, judging by their frugal existence Lucy told him, she genuinely thought her inheritance would only be a few thousand dollars and in her quest to locate her daughter, had even forgotten about it completely.

"Wow!" said Lyndon, standing speechless, "I suggest a strong coffee to steady our nerves, then we'll phone and book you into the next trip to the Cape and, after that buy a Toyota Troopy camper. We saw one on the way in at the hire company. They're still in excellent condition and about forty five thousand but old fruit, you can afford it."

That afternoon they returned home with Lucy driving her Troopy and with a booking to The Gulf in nine days' time. Once back home, Lyndon opened his map again and they scoured the area intensely. With all the information to date, Lucy felt strongly that Bickerton Island was where she would find Sheridan, or as Lyndon suggested, "At the head of the Walker River where," he remembered "an old prawning mate used to anchor his vessel at times."

Turning to her, Lyndon said, "Listen Lucy, I hope your sudden inheritance makes no difference to us. I really like you and we get on so well together. I would like to think we can continue our relationship once you locate your daughter. We make a good pair."

Lucy replied, "Lyndon, I'm the same person you picked up on the side of the road. Admittedly, since I left home to find Sheridan, I've changed. I'm no longer the old Lucy, thank God. I now have confidence in myself for once. As for the money, I intend to go into town this afternoon to invest most of it for the time being," adding "and there are a few other matters I need to attend to."

"Ok, sounds good. You go into town. I need to service the truck, ready to roll tomorrow arvo. I had planned a BBQ with a few friends so perhaps you can get a few snags and some beer. I'll get some money," said Lyndon, getting up.

"Sit down silly! If we are going to be partners, let me at least start to pay you back, after all I can afford it," she chuckled.

After lunch Lyndon disappeared into his shed to work on the truck and Lucy drove back into town in her Troopy. She had to admit she loved it! Her first call was to the supermarket where she bought enough food to fill her cupboards for over a month and finished with her purchase of sausages and beer for Lyndon. Then she visited the bank and placed most of her money in a short-term investment account. After that was sorted, she called in at a Solicitor's office to keep an appointment she had made earlier.

She had instructed the firm to contact her husband and transfer the house she owned to him, with her covering all the necessary costs. She also requested that they send him a cheque for fifty thousand dollars and a letter stating she was starting divorce proceedings at once, the money and transfer of the house subject to him not objecting to the divorce. Lucy knew her husband would accept. He'd have a roof over his head and enough 'drinking' money for a few years. He had never thought anything of her but 'useless' and 'a nuisance' and as she left the office she felt really free for the first time in her life. She promised herself to make her own decisions from here on and that included keeping Lyndon in her life. She just needed to find Sheridan safe and happy and not as she suspected, trapped in some mad dream gone horribly wrong.

Stopping at the post office on the way home, she sent off a cheque to Carmen for the van and a letter with rego papers to the tow man in Fitzroy Crossing gifting him the van to keep or to dispose of as he wished. Now, her debts paid, she could pursue her own agenda.

When she got back to Lyndon's place she put the snags and beer in the fridge, made a coffee and walked over to the shed to find him under his truck. Bending over she tickled his buttocks. Sliding out, he beamed, "Twenty-four hours to cut that out old girl!"

"Listen Lyndon, I just know in my heart of hearts that you are the one for me. Can I pay off your house before we head off? I would love to pay you back somehow," she said earnestly.

"No not now! Wait until we both have time to think it over and you find your daughter. Two more trips till I finish and the place will be paid for anyway. Let's not put pressure on each other but, to be honest, I'll miss you like hell, though absence is supposed to make the heart grow fonder! We'll be free sooner than later but both need to attend to unfinished business first," replied Lyndon wisely.

"You're right of course. I'm rushing things. I'm still trying to adapt to my new sense of freedom and true, until I find Sheridan I'm better off having no other commitments. I am genuine about the money though Lyndon," said Lucy.

"That's my girl! I wouldn't want to place any pressure on you at this stage but if you need me at any time, I will come. You can count on that," said Lyndon.

"You are indeed my 'knight in shining armour', the only one in the world I know of who would help me at the moment. It's so good to have such a dear friend and lover," said Lucy fondly.

The conversation seemed to settle things between them and that evening when they went to bed they had a new hunger for each. In their nakedness, the thrashing of their writhing bodies culminated in sating their sexual passion.

Lucy woke up to the smell of breakfast cooking, in itself a new event in her life. Rolling out of bed still naked, she smiled as she inhaled the aroma of sex permeating the air of the bedroom, something else she had discovered with the right partner, was immensely satisfying and uplifting.

After she showered and dressed, Lyndon placed breakfast on the table. They exchanged a kiss, but sat at the table in silence knowing it could be their last day together for some time. Lyndon had already moved his departure back as far as he dared. His business had been built on delivering on time and even though it had been sold, he wished to keep up his good reputation. If things did not work out as hoped, he may have to return to trucking.

Being a Saturday, they had arranged a midday barbecue so set about cleaning up around the property until the first of the guests began arriving and Lucy was stunned at the large number of friends Lyndon had. No doubt the bush telegraph had been flat out as most of his friends appeared anxious to meet Lucy, particularly the women, but it wasn't long before everybody was relaxed and sitting beneath the large, shady trees as they started the barbeque. Lucy soon gathered this was a common event as she watched Lyndon sipping his stubby and mingling with everybody. Lucy was unaccustomed to standing amongst such a throng of people all wanting to know her story so she was rather relieved when, out of the blue Kevin appeared, indicating to her that he wanted to talk.

Walking a short distance from the crowd, he turned, "Listen Lucy, I heard you are joining the camp ground lot at Cape Barrow," he said.

"Yes, Lyndon found out about it from a friend," replied Lucy.

"I must admit I didn't know, this is a first. The couple running it used to work in the area years back apparently, and they are trying to get some business going for the locals" advised Kevin.

"All I can do is but try. Cape Barrow, I understand is not far from Bickerton Island," continued Lucy.

"You are lucky. In some ways the Aboriginals are not like the white or Asian gangs involved in the drug trade. There's little chance of you being harmed by them, most are happy-go-lucky and don't take anything too seriously.

Even Berrimah Prison they regard as a holiday camp," smiled Kevin.

"Here, take my card and if you need me try to ring, you'll have mobile phone coverage at all the communities. Be aware, they operate under the cover of darkness and know the area backwards. It is very isolated so make sure you take plenty of food and water with you if you leave the main camp," he warned her.

"I've no idea what I can do but at least I'll be in the area. I just hope somehow, I can find her," Lucy replied.

"Perhaps going in with no pre-conceived plan might just work. To have come this far will show how resourceful and dedicated you are, so it'll be interesting to follow your progress. I've phoned the local police at Numbulwar and informed them of your imminent arrival but perhaps you should call in and touch base," Kevin suggested.

"Thanks so much for your help," responded Lucy, shaking his hand.

"Just one final thing Lucy, if your daughter is involved in this, there's not much I can do to help her. You see, a white woman involved in supplying drugs to Indigenous communities would cause a media frenzy in this politically correct world. She would be treated far more harshly than her Indigenous cohorts, believe me," warned Kevin as they slowly walked back to the main crowd.

Lucy frowned. Perhaps this whole venture was far more serious than she thought. She was glad in many ways that it would be a week before she left as it would give her more time to do some homework and perhaps get hold of a satellite phone.

That evening, Lucy and Lyndon lay in each other's arms. It had been a long day and they knew that daylight would see the pair parted for some time. Something neither wanted, having just discovered a compatible mate, lover and partner.

Lucy waved sadly to Lyndon as he drove off at sunrise. She went back to bed and curled up tightly, feeling all alone. More alone now than ever, since leaving Tasmania, which seemed like an eternity ago.

Lucy knew that Lyndon's neighbour would take over caring for the property on her departure. She had met him several times and liked him immensely. He was a true Territorian and a real character.

Chapter Six

For two days Lucy moped about the house feeling lost and alone even though for most of her life she had been a loner. She knew money would not buy love or happiness and having met Lyndon now felt wanted, she actually had someone who really loved her for what she was.

That evening he phoned. She knew that being on the Stuart Highway he would most likely be out of phone range so she was thrilled when he told her that he really missed her more than he had anticipated! She was then taken aback when he proposed over the phone and without thinking, yelled, "Yes!" After she hung up, Lucy cried tears of happiness for the first time in many years. She was smiling and crying at the same time and told herself that it was the happiest day of her life! Only one thing remained – to find Sheridan!

Lucy now had a new sense of purpose. A future with a man she knew was a rare find, quiet and unassuming. She missed him terribly. After cleaning the house and checking her Troopy several times, she went into town and bought a satellite phone. She then found an internet cafe and 'googled' all she could find on The Gulf and about the Aboriginal groups living there. For three days she browsed the internet, quite surprised at all the information available. She planned to join a safari group but knew she would have to play the cautious card so as not to tip anyone off as to her true intentions. Lucy even bought a fishing rod and gear, learning as much as possible about using them from the salesman at the sports store.

Two days prior to pick-up at Roper Bar, Lucy locked the house and drove to Bitter Springs Caravan Park. Once settled, she joined some of the other campers for a swim in the warm pools. The weather was hot and she enjoyed chatting to other tourists. One group was planning to join the safari trip she had booked so they agreed to leave together the next day and to stay overnight at Roper Bar. Lucy was invited to join some other campers for dinner that evening. The caravan park was full of tourists but no one had been further than Roper Bar. When casually asking about permits, she was surprised to learn that quite a few had become available to enter eastern Arnhem Land in The Gulf. Some of the campers had heard complaints about that camp being isolated and Lucy wondered why the hell they had gone there in the first place! Surely they would have checked to see where it was and realised it was extremely isolated.

That night Lucy went to bed late, satisfied that she had taken every precaution for her forthcoming trip. Every nook and cranny was filled with food, a first aid kit was in the glove box and her satellite phone was safely packed. She had used it twice in order to learn how to operate it and its presence gave her a sense of security.

Lyndon had left her a text message advising that he had reached Adelaide and would load the following morning for the return trip. He then gave her some news that made her smile. The new owner had agreed to do his final load for him, and so on his return he would fly into the Walker

River airstrip and she could pick him up sometime the following week.

Lucy woke up early. She was now a seasoned traveller and shook her head as she remembered how in the past she had been unable to leave her husband and the dilapidated house they shared, too afraid to leave what she considered 'security'. All those years of her life, just wasted.

Lucy showered, ate breakfast and was just about to leave when her travelling companions pulled up alongside. She had formed a friendship with Roz and Ken Baker from Sydney. Ken was a retired Solicitor and Roz had been a stay-at-home mum but with their two children now married, they had hit the road like thousands of other 'Grey Nomads' looking for adventure.

The previous evening over a few glasses of wine, both parties told their life stories. Lucy had held nothing back and was pleasantly surprised when Ken and Roz took more than a passing interest in her story. In fact they offered to help in any way possible.

Lucy enjoyed the tandem drive along the Roper Highway. Although the road was narrow in many places, they had plenty of time and pulled over for trucks and bigger vehicles. The weather was hot and uncomfortable for southerners and Lucy got her first taste of 'dust' as the last section into the Roper Bar Store was unsealed. They arrived just before midday and paid at the store for one night in the park.

Once at the park Ken suggested they go for a drive to an Aboriginal community which he had heard was about forty kilometres from the Roper Bar crossing. Although it was on Indigenous land, the locals apparently encouraged tourists to visit the Art Centre. They all agreed and Lucy left her vehicle and joined her new friends in the air-conditioned comfort of their vehicle. The road was corrugated and they met several carloads of Indigenous people travelling to the Roper Bar Store. They were a little mystified as to why, since they had been informed that a well-stocked shop existed on the settlement of Ngukurr, or 'Nooka' as it was pronounced. For Lucy, who had never really shown any interest before, this was something new and despite some trepidation, was looking forward to the visit. She had heard so much in the press about the shocking living conditions of Indigenous Australians that she was more than a little fearful as to what she would encounter. Lucy knew her home state of Tasmania had an Aboriginal population but they were mainly 'white blood' and looked like the mainstream population. This would be a first for her, meeting large numbers of full blood Aboriginals.

On the drive they passed the turnoff heading north to Numbulwar hitting a sealed road for the last couple of kilometres as they entered the settlement of Ngukurr. They were all taken aback, especially Lucy. The housing was far better than in her home town. There was a large school on the right and on the left, one of the best sports ovals and associated facilities she had seen, complete with several swimming pools! Finding the store they were again pleasantly surprised. An elderly Aboriginal man opened the door, letting them into the modern, air-conditioned building full of everything, more than many of the stores in the country towns that Lucy had passed through on her trip. The prices were fair so they took advantage and stocked up with more food. Obtaining directions to the Art Centre from one of the store workers, they drove the short distance to the Gallery where the Gallery Manager was more than helpful, showing them some of the local art. Lucy didn't buy anything, but her two companions bought two paintings which the Gallery Manager agreed to keep for them until their return trip from Cape Barrow.

It was late afternoon when they returned to the park. Several other campers were sitting beneath a tree and they too were intent on being escorted the following morning. Lucy and her friends together with their newly acquainted fellow adventurers all hoped to begin the trek at eleven o'clock the next morning.

Lucy was unable to get a signal on her mobile but decided not to use the satellite phone as it had only been a day since she'd chatted to Lyndon. It was rather late when everyone went to bed after having made the most of the last of the alcohol. The area they would be visiting did not allow alcohol under the new intervention laws.

At nine o'clock Lucy was awake and dressed and looking outside saw a Landcruiser parked where a young couple were handing out pieces of paper to fellow campers. Lucy introduced herself to the couple, whose names were Laurie and Sylvia Tuck. They told Lucy they, in conjunction with the Aboriginals, had for the first time ever opened up a large area of eastern Arnhem Land. Lucy paid her money and was handed a permit, then Laurie informed all those present that they could, if they wanted to, depart and travel slowly to Policeman's Point River which was not far from the turnoff to Cape Barrow. He also informed them that if any wished to visit Numbulwar they would need to meet at the turnoff at one o'clock.

Everyone agreed, it sounded a good idea as some had not yet arrived and breaking up the convoy would allow those ahead to spread out to avoid the choking dust and to choose their own speed. Lucy and her friends Roz and Ken, with Ken leading the way, set off immediately. By way of their two-way radios Ken warned Lucy of any possible road hazards or of oncoming vehicles. Lucy was glad Lyndon had talked her into the Troopy, it was solid, compact and suited the conditions she had to face. Ken and Roz had a Landcruiser and camper trailer. The camper, built in Australia, was solid and had already been tested on several outback treks.

At first the road was corrugated and rough but as they continued they were surprised but pleased to come upon two graders at work. The road then panned out wider and was a great deal smoother which allowed them to pick up speed, reaching the river by midday. Stopping for a coffee, it was unanimously agreed that the journey had been far easier than anticipated. Ken had maps of the area and Numbulwar was shown as being not that far ahead. The return trip to the meeting point was only five kilometres from there so with the weather being hot and humid they decided after visiting Numbulwar to return to the turnoff and wait for their guides.

Lucy was astonished when entering Numbulwar to see all the new, two-storey houses and by the amount of people wandering casually everywhere. At the store they bought some takeaway and sat on a step to eat it but the sorry sight of the starving dogs upset them. The animals were covered in fleas and ticks. Roz commented to Lucy and Ken that the store was far from the standard of the one at Ngukurr and were relieved they had plenty of stock on board for the upcoming trip.

Noticing a police officer over the road Lucy walked across and introduced herself. The officer knew of her predicament and advised her that Nic had just left town, in fact he had been in the store just before they themselves arrived. He told Lucy that he had not seen her daughter but didn't want to tip him off about Lucy's arrival by enquiring about the girl, for obvious reasons. The officer suggested the yacht might be well north of the town in one of the rivers or on the western side of Bickerton Island as there was a settlement on the eastern side.

Lucy knew the two police officers on duty were stretched to the limit maintaining order in the town due to its size and would have no chance of offering her any assistance. Already they were heavily engaged, she was shocked to see, dealing with several of the women who seemed drunk or suffering from hangovers, despite the community being 'dry', meaning 'no alcohol allowed'.

The officer she spoke to appeared tired. Apparently he had been working late the previous night dealing with the alcohol fuelled fighting, a daily occurrence which only ceased at daybreak.

Lucy passed the information on to her friends. The trip for her had been far different to what she had envisaged and her friends agreed she was on a journey to hell to try and locate her daughter. Returning to the turnoff, they sat and waited.

On schedule at one o'clock, Laurie and Sylvia Tuck arrived with the last two members of their group. Although one other group had not turned up at the scheduled time the trip organisers refused to wait any longer at the pick-up point, concerned about the others waiting in the hot sun. Their objective was to get everyone settled before darkness fell, informing the assembled convoy that travelling on the tracks ahead was going to be extremely difficult and challenging.

Lucy waited until most of the convoy had left before she, along with her friends, the Bakers, followed, hanging back to avoid the choking dust. The pace was slow on the single vehicle track, rough and corrugated with sand patches making progress difficult as anticipated. Springs had broken on two of the camper trailers ahead of them and as they passed saw the owners making repairs, helped by friends. Lucy soon began to feel drained. Several hours later they crossed an enormous salt flat, barren and shimmering in the merciless heat. Lucy thought the salt flat would never end and that she would never make it to the camp. However she eventually came across a red mound of sand and as she hit the open country she was in awe of the panorama that opened before her.

In the distance she could see two houses with outbuildings. Finally they had reached the camp headquarters. As she pulled up, Lucy was met by the guides who pointed out suitable camping areas up and down the coast or behind the houses. Laurie recommended a camping spot in amongst some high shade trees. It was ideal, next to the water tank that supplied the water for the houses and operated by a solar pump. Lucy and her companions agreed to set up in this particular spot for the time being and check out the rest of the area later.

As Lucy settled in for the night, the enormity of what she had undertaken hit home. Tired and dusty in one of the most isolated places on the planet, a sense of dread embraced her. Her two companions, themselves exhausted by the day's events, showered under the overflowing tank, too tired to walk to the shower block up at the two houses then crashed into bed.

Lucy slept fitfully, woken by crazy dreams of her daughter drowning and the face of Lyndon smiling at her. Several times, covered in sweat, she lay in bed wondering if she had stepped outside her capabilities. She knew defeat was not an option but acknowledged that her quest was not going to be as simple as she had hoped or anticipated.

The sun's rays pierced the tree canopy and the wind blew onshore, as it had all night. Lucy and her companions made some breakfast while discussing the 'sand blasting' those who chose to camp on the open dunes would be experiencing. Lucy and the Bakers had managed to escape the strong wind as it roared overhead, agreeing that it just added to the eerie atmosphere!

Having planned it the night before, they met at the main camp for a guided trip down the coast to an estuary. Many of the travellers wanted to catch barramundi, a fish famous in the Top End. Having set up camp next to Lucy, Ken suggested she accompany him and Roz in their vehicle. Lucy agreed and grabbing her fishing rod, handed it to Ken who placed it on the roof of his car alongside the boat he carried on top. They made sure they took plenty of drinks and snack food as they joined the others, ready for the day's adventure.

Everyone remarked about the scene before them as soon as the trip began. Kilometres of stunning, uninhabited country, much the same as it had been for thousands of years. Unfortunately, as their guides pointed out, the dumping of rubbish in The Gulf from trawlers was rife and it wasn't long before they noticed thongs, nets, plastic and a myriad of waste material along the shoreline.

Not far from the camping area they crossed an estuary populated so they were told by several crocodiles and, as if on cue, one could be seen coming in from a night's hunting on the reef. This, along with several herds of wild buffalo and pigs wandering back to the jungle after a night foraging on the coastal dunes, confirmed for Lucy just how wild and untamed this country was and how magnificent.

The small convoy stopped at a place called 'Turtle Beach'. Their guides informed them that years before people had lived in the derelict buildings making a living from turtle shell, used for button making and other decorative purposes. Lucy marvelled at the isolated existence of the turtle hunters. Some of the local Indigenous people stopped to collect turtle eggs, considered a delicacy she was told, by the locals. They came up here during the dry season as most of them had homes in the community and in the home lands. The group later stopped at a large Tamarind tree, as it was known down that area of the coast. They learned that early explorers from the Island of Makassar, about eight hundred years before, had planted many of such trees in order to supply 'Vitamin C' to long distance sailors.

Lucy and her friends were in awe of the untamed features of the landscape as they journeyed south and contemplated in wonder, the lives of the early Aboriginals who had travelled the area for centuries, living on the bounty of the land. At mid-morning they stopped at a river mouth and Laurie invited those who wanted to fish to walk inland to the many isolated pools to try for some barramundi. Lucy and her companions rigged their fishing lines with lures and set off to find a quiet spot. It wasn't long before they settled and landed two excellent-sized fish which they knew would be enough to feed them for a couple of days. They marvelled at the quiet beauty of such an isolated and harsh area of Australia, seen by so few and mutually agreed with other campers just how lucky they were to have had the opportunity to discover a part of the country not many had even had the privilege to enter.

However it had become apparent that this area of The Gulf was too shallow for a large yacht to enter. Some campers reported hearing boats as late as three o'clock that morning but Ken was sure they would have been much smaller vessels than the one Lucy was chasing.

Over the next four days Laurie and Sylvia guided them through areas which surprised them all, discovering several abandoned or never lived in houses. On the fifth day they backtracked to the huge open sand flats they had crossed previously, the guide informing them that due to the low wet season, for the first time in years, most of the area was inaccessible. The travellers were advised to stay on the tracks of the previous campers warning them that if they broke through the surface it would be almost impossible to pull them out of the blue, sticky mud, which earned it the name of 'Blue Mud Bay'.

The journey north was spectacular. Dozens of buffalo stood on the edge of the salt flats, many of the old bulls with huge horns! They eventually reached the river after several kilometres, and stopped to do some more fishing. They noticed a number of large crocodiles slide past them on both sides of the river and that the tide was coming in at a fast pace.

As the others fished, Lucy noticed Laurie sitting in his vehicle reading, waiting for his guests, and taking her chance went over and started chatting to him. She learned that he had actually worked at the township of Numbulwar years earlier and knew the area north of the Cape reasonably well and even the area further inland from their current position. During the conversation she edged the subject towards 'yachts' and asked if any would be sailed near Cape Barrow. He told her that many yachts did sail that way but not in the immediate area of their camp. Instead they anchored, along with the prawn and fishing trawlers, just to the north in the Walker River. She learned that if a small dinghy was to be launched from where they were now, it would easily make it to Blue Mud

Bay and the Walker River which she knew was not far north from the exit of the river they were now fishing in. Finding him amicable and friendly, Lucy diplomatically enquired if he knew of the existence of any drug trade around their present area.

Laurie smiled immediately and replied, "Yes" and went on to tell her that a large and lucrative trade in alcohol and drugs, mainly 'gunja' as the locals called marijuana, certainly existed and that if she ever saw a large, aluminium dinghy left at the settlement it was because the traders often camped there and came and went late at night. If she hadn't heard them by now, she would hear them in the future.

Lucy voiced her concern about their safety and Laurie laughed it off, informing her that the Indigenous people fought amongst themselves but basically treated the 'whites' well, because if not the hundreds of whites delivering services to the communities would leave and they certainly did not want that to happen. He told Lucy from his own personal experience, having dealt with Aboriginals for years that it was extremely difficult to ever really know what they were thinking. In most cases they gave the impression they agreed with all that was said, even though they had absolutely no intention of carrying out their promise.

It was at this point that Lucy decided to confide in Laurie and see his reaction. Time was marching on and she was getting worried as Lyndon had not answered his mobile or returned her calls. Laurie sat and listened to Lucy but, halfway through her story she began to doubt herself and wondered if she was right to place her trust in him. He sat quietly, his face devoid of emotion and did not answer until she had finished. There was a long pause.

"Yes. I know the man you mention. He is half Greek and his mother was a full blood Aboriginal. I can even tell you that a few days ago the yacht was anchored in an inlet just north of here and I'm sure it's still there," said Laurie.

"Can you take me to it please?" begged Lucy.

"At the moment I'm in the middle of helping one of the Elders get a tourist venture going here, but to be honest, it's almost impossible. They want the money but the majority show no interest in helping. Normally I try to keep out of their business but in your case I'm prepared to make an exception. It's too late today, but in the morning we'll come back with a dinghy and I'll take you out to the coast. Hopefully we'll come across the yacht, it's called 'Tradewinds'," replied Laurie.

Now Lucy even had a name for the yacht! "Thank you so much," she said, grateful for his support.

"You might not thank me later. Nic has a heap of kids from several Aboriginal women but thankfully he's a charming rogue and I'm sure he would do no harm to your daughter. He also has a large following amongst the young fellas in the communities as most of them are bored and looking for adventure. We'll make it look like a coincidence that we came across them but after that it is up to you and I suppose, your daughter," Laurie explained.

"Do the police know all about this business?" asked Lucy nervously.

"Well, yes but this isn't an isolated incident. Every community across the Top End has its smugglers and suppliers and even spending millions on intervention won't stop it. Make something illegal and worth money and people will supply it. Every major city has crime gangs supplying sex, drugs, firearms and anything else illegal that has a monetary value, it'll never stop. The law can only try to contain it. These young fellas and Nic are smart. They know The Gulf like the backs of their hands. I really believe the authorities have put it all in the too hard basket," answered Laurie.

Much to her disappointment, the others started to drift back ready for the return trip to camp.

"Let's keep this confidential, I don't want these busybodies gossiping about it," Laurie whispered to Lucy.

Lucy understood completely but did, on the way back, tell Roz and Ken who agreed that it be keep quiet and not made a major event, enough gossiping and complaining about 'nothing' went on as it was. Lucy was aware that a story like hers would make every major newspaper in the country if it were to be leaked and her friends agreed that a slow and steady approach was necessary.

That evening Lucy packed a small backpack. In the outer pocket she put her satellite phone and a spare, fully-charged battery, carefully wrapped to avoid being damaged. It was decided that if she had to go on the yacht or, for any other reason was unable to return with Laurie, Roz would follow Ken out the next week with her vehicle and park it at the Bitter Springs Caravan Park. They were to then tell Lyndon who in turn would inform his police officer brother-in-law of Lucy's last known position. Laurie undertook to let them know what transpired in the event Lucy remained on board the yacht.

Chapter Seven

Again that night, Lucy was unable to sleep. 'When would this nightmare end?' she thought.

She was up, dressed and waiting when Laurie appeared at daylight with the boat and trailer. As previously arranged, Lucy left her keys with Roz and Ken who both gave her a big hug and waved them off as Laurie set off for the salt flats and to hopefully find Sheridan.

Neither of them spoke much, knowing it was a long shot that Sheridan would be on the yacht. Laurie had phoned a friend in Numbulwar, one of the Elders, asking him if Nic had been seen in town with a white girl. The Elder advised that if that had been the case the whole community would have been alive with the news but that as far as he knew, Nic was still in town.

Launching the dinghy, Laurie and Lucy reached the coast in half an hour. The entrance to the sea was so low they had to drag the dinghy a short way over a bar to the open sea. Laurie was disappointed the yacht had been moved from where he had seen it but, on a hunch he headed north to the mouth of the Walker River. Lucy admired the stunning coastline and it felt as though she and Laurie were the last two humans on earth, nothing but wild coast and open sea out into The Gulf.

The entrance to the Walker River was wide and they saw two trawlers anchored a kilometre down the entrance. Laurie pointed to a yacht that lay at anchor close to the mangroves and alongside it was the dinghy from the camp. Pulling up parallel to it, Laurie recognised Joseph, one of the local boys. Lucy had seen him at the camp on her arrival.

"Hi, is Sheridan here?" Laurie asked him.

"Na, she out on island," replied Joseph, obviously confused.

"This her mother, she come to see her hey," Laurie replied .

Seeming satisfied, Joseph smiled back extending a hand to help them on board. Lucy was surprised at how he seemed to trust Laurie and the fact that she was Sheridan's mother settled the situation. 'At least,' she thought, 'my daughter is alive.'

"When is Nic going up to the island?" asked Laurie casually, "perhaps Lucy go and see daughter."

"Nic on Groote Eylandt getting fuel and doing the business. Back tonight and then we go maybe," answered Joseph.

"Fuel is only one dollar a litre on the island," Laurie told Lucy, "by way of a deal the Indigenous owners struck with the mines, as well as royalties." Turning to Joseph, Laurie said, "Maybe you take Lucy to see her daughter. I am sure Nic won't mind, she will pay her share if you want."

Joseph was more than happy with the arrangement. It was lonely caretaking the yacht and Laurie knew she would be safe. Nic might not welcome the visitor but Laurie knew he had no other option than to take Lucy with them when they departed for Torres Strait. Lucy also knew, as did Laurie, that this was her only chance of contacting her daughter.

When leaving, Laurie advised Lucy to keep quiet about having a satellite phone with her, but to tell Nic she had left her mobile in her vehicle. Thinking she was unable to contact anyone would make him feel easier about the situation.

Now on their own, Lucy suggested to Joseph that they go fishing for some fresh food. Joseph agreed happily as he had been sitting on the yacht for two days and this new company was more than welcome. As Lucy stored her bag below, she noticed how unkempt the yacht was, it was a real mess. She told Joseph that on their return from the fishing expedition they would start a major clean-up.

Throwing some fishing gear into the dinghy, Lucy felt relaxed and not at all alarmed. She knew she had to be strong as her actions would be relayed to Lyndon and others. She was now overjoyed and relieved that Sheridan was safe. The whole adventure gave her an adrenaline rush.

As Lucy and Joseph sat quietly in the dinghy pulling in the fish, Lucy began reminiscing. She found it hard to believe that since leaving home she had found love, become a millionaire and aware that she was capable of far more than she ever thought possible. Joseph was great company and the two chatted together like old friends. Lucy learned from Joseph that he and the others now travelled to New Guinea to Admiralty Island where there was a small island inhabited by a Chinese man who grew and supplied gunja very cheaply. In fact he was much cheaper than their old contacts in South Australia and it was far safer and further from the police, Joseph revealed. Lucy smiled, a little surprised at how open he was with her.

When they returned to the yacht Joseph cleaned the fish, while Lucy picked up all the scattered clothes and scrubbed the galley. She was surprised how quickly the small space seemed to come to some type of order. They ate a huge meal of fresh fish and some rice Lucy had found. She'd found plenty of tea bags too so huge cups of sweet tea followed. After cleaning up, Lucy lay on one of the bunks and soon drifted off to sleep, content she was getting closer to being reunited with her daughter.

Lyndon Savage shook his head and rubbed his eyes. It had been an arduous trip and meeting Lucy had changed his life. Since leaving her several days ago he had been unable to get her beautiful smiling face out of his mind. He knew that through a set of strange circumstances he had found his one, great love. Their lovemaking was incredible and her aroma still wafted through the cabin of his truck. He chided himself for not telling her, after he had proposed and she had accepted, just how much he loved her and that, in fact he loved her more than life itself. Why did he let her go on this dangerous quest by herself? Now that new owner had agreed to take over earlier than the contract stipulated there was no reason why he couldn't join her. Driven by guilt and by the belief he should be at her side, he drove day and night, aware he was pushing the boundaries.

As he peered into the night, he thought about her gorgeous, smiling face. Although she was a little chubby, like himself, her personality and smile had stolen his heart. Nothing else mattered now to Lyndon, he had to get home and go after her.

For two days he had been unable to sleep and rest eluded him. Now two hundred kilometres from home, he squinted into the darkness, following the highway that he had driven many times before but never with the underlying desire to get to his Lucy. He had let her down in her moment of need. Glancing to the right, he saw a mob of cattle meandering across the road and he braked heavily. The huge rig jack-knifed and the last thing he remembered was the cab spinning, then darkness.

Lyndon Savage was found some time later and, when the ambulance arrived, grave fears were held for his survival. A week later he remained on life support in the Darwin Hospital. None of his grieving friends considered informing Lucy, as they simply thought she was someone who had just recently entered his life and regarded her as a passing acquaintance.

Lucy awoke to voices and checked her watch. It was midnight. Going on deck she saw two males in the dim light.

"Hi. I'm Lucy," she introduced herself, "Sheridan's mother. Hope coming along was okay."

"No problems. I'm Nic," one of the men replied.

Lucy understood immediately her daughter's infatuation. Nic was dark, swarthy and handsome.

"Did you tell anyone you came here?" Nic asked ever so casually. "Now Nic, as if I'd be so stupid. I don't even have my mobile," laughed Lucy.

Nic smiled, obviously satisfied with her answer, and replied, "Okay, let's get underway. The sails aren't too good so we will need to use the motor."

Lucy observed that most of the equipment was in disrepair and needed maintenance. Most of the vehicles she saw in the communities were run down and dilapidated. Maintenance was not a priority within the Indigenous community nor it seemed was food. They had loaded plenty of fuel but very few food supplies.

The old yacht shuddered as it headed into open sea and the motor seemed to be running roughly and blew smoke. Luckily the night was calm, and they made slow but steady progress. Lucy made some tea but would have preferred coffee. There was only some tea and a few tins of bully beef in the galley. The atmosphere on board eventually settled and even became jovial.

Lucy was surprised to learn Sheridan was on an island, living in a small hut. She was extremely shocked though when Nic told her she was pregnant and expecting his twenty-eighth child. He was proud of the fact that he had sired so many children from a variety of women. Lucy was at a loss to understand how her well-educated daughter had turned into a breeding cow for Nic but then this trip so far had taught her to expect the unexpected. She after all had found Lyndon and hoped above all else, her feelings for him were mutual. Before then her attitude in life had been to never expect a great deal from men.

To her absolute surprise, Lucy began to enjoy the journey. She knew they deliberately avoided coming into contact with people and the islands but the weather was balmy and life on board was pleasant enough with her companions sharing everything with her, even information on the 'business', as they called it. They were all on some type of government payment through schemes set up to employ Indigenous Australians and although turning up for work was not an option to them, payments appeared fortnightly into their bank accounts.

On a few occasions other yachts glided past, with nothing exchanged but a cursory wave from the crew.

Another defunct item on the Tradewinds was the radio. Like most items on board, it had been pulled to pieces and had wires protruding everywhere, a sure sign someone had attempted to fix it. Lucy was unable to find any life jackets but relaxed because of the dinghy bouncing along behind. One such dinghy had been left in the bush at Walker River.

On their fourth day, at daylight Lucy spotted land on the horizon and she could see several people waiting, having sighted the yacht. Drawing a deep breath as they neared land, she recognised her daughter but her heart leapt into her mouth as she saw that she was dirty. Her hair was a mess and she was wearing an old dress. Other women and children stood nearby.

As they anchored, Lucy climbed into the boat with Nic and Joseph. At any other time the palm-lined sand would have been a sight for sore eyes but now Lucy sat stunned as they motored into shore. This was her worst nightmare. What had her daughter been thinking? As they approached the shoreline Lucy decided to play it cool until she was fully aware of Sheridan's situation.

Several of the younger men on the sand ran into the water and pulled the dinghy ashore. As Lucy rose to jump out Sheridan recognised her at once and, with a little cry fell into her arms. Mother and daughter had found each other.

They walked a few steps away from everyone and stood looking at each other both sobbing, Lucy unable to comprehend how a trip around Australia could end on a tropical island in Torres Strait.

"God, Mum! I am so sorry, really I am! I never thought it would turn out like this, ever. I was smitten. It's the worst mistake of my life," blurted out Sheridan between sobs.

They were ignored by the others, too busy returning to the yacht and unloading boxes for which, Lucy noticed, money was being exchanged.

"Now, tell me the full story so we can get you out of here," said Lucy looking through tear-stained eyes at her precious girl.

"Mum, to be honest, when we met on the wharf in Ceduna he was so friendly I went on board for a couple of drinks. We got carried away and had sex, the best sex ever, he's a real stud. We talked and talked and had sex over the next couple of days and when I told him I had money, he asked me to come on the trip and said he loved me. I knew they had run out of money for fuel and for some stupid, ridiculous reason, being so infatuated, I gave him all my money. He never hits me Mum but he made it obvious very quickly that he was the boss. He never let me leave the yacht and then my pills ran out and I soon fell pregnant. I found out from the others that he has many women and children. He will not let me leave the island either and my biggest fear now is that neither of us will ever leave this place. The Chinese man who runs this island has several women too and he knows that my knowledge would cause him a great deal of harm. He took my phone but even so there's no signal here, so we are trapped," wept Sheridan, covering her face in her hands.

Lucy was speechless. This was far worse than she had imagined and thinking quickly, remembered the phone in her rucksack. Looking back at the yacht, Lucy noticed the others were all too involved in their various chores to watch or worry about her and her daughter, and why should they, they too were prisoners. To the left was thick jungle growing along the beach and Lucy guided Sheridan towards it, whispering to her, "I have a satellite phone in my backpack. No one knows."

The look of surprise on Sheridan's face said it all and Lucy continued, "Keep walking towards the trees. We'll hide it and return when it's safe."

Sheridan took her mother's hand and continued talking as they walked, trying to act as naturally as possible. Lucy glanced back again and saw that no one was watching. Racing into the thick jungle, she hid the pack under a log, covered it with leaves and then quickly returned to the beach, as if nothing had happened. Nobody seemed to notice anything, all still heavily involved with offloading the yacht, its arrival on the island a major occurrence and a welcome break from everyday life.

Lucy approached Nic on their return. "Can we both get a lift back with you please Nic?" Lucy asked.

"Not this trip, maybe later. We have big business to do on our way back and it's too dangerous. You stay here with Kim, he'll look after you, no problem" replied Nic.

Lucy knew then that the island was to be their prison and to plead any further was a waste of time. Not to upset her hosts or Nic was in their best interests. She looked at Sheridan, knowing she too understood the situation they faced.

Sheridan led Lucy to her small one-room hut that they would share. It was basic but comfortable. Lucy assured her daughter they would escape but that they had to remain calm, cool, patient and display no anger or frustration.

That evening the villagers roasted a pig for the guests and it was late before they retired. The little hut contained a table and two beds. Lucy froze when Nic entered shortly after they had got into their beds. She heard Sheridan's bed squeaking and low groans coming from her daughter. Wide awake and staring at the ceiling, Lucy appreciated that it was futile for her daughter to resist. She was actually a sex slave.

Lucy was disturbed twice more in the night as the sounds of sex woke her. Rather than offending her, it actually made her think of Lyndon. He too was a real stud and she missed their lovemaking sessions more now than ever.

The next morning when Lucy awoke Nic had gone and her daughter slept soundly. Turning over in bed, she decided to remain calm, have a lay in and recharge her batteries. Nic would not be back for a few weeks and she had found her darling daughter alive. They were together again but she would need all her cunning to get out of this one!

Nic had no need to harm either of them, of this Lucy was positive but she knew they had no choice but to remain where they were until he chose if ever to take them back to the Australian mainland. Oddly enough Lucy did not feel threatened. She knew Nic wanted her daughter's money and having sex with a white woman and owning her was to him a power play, but Lucy knew too that her daughter was addicted to the powerful sex they shared.

While still resting in bed, Lucy made a decision not to tell Sheridan about the inheritance she had received from the Walsh family as it could certainly endanger their lives if Nic or the Chinese man learned that one of their captives was extremely wealthy.

When Lucy got out of bed, she looked around and saw that there was no electricity. Instead, a small gas stove sat on a table out on the porch. She made herself a cup of tea, minus any milk as there wasn't any, added some sugar and went back inside the hut just as Sheridan woke up.

"Sorry about last night Mum but Nic isn't very private when it comes to sex. Despite everything he still has this incredible power over me and that is why I'm pregnant. As I told you, my pill supply ran out and he just kept going! He seemed really pleased when he got me pregnant," Sheridan told her mother rather sheepishly. "I must confess, I cannot judge you on that. I had a rather torrid sexual affair myself and I miss him greatly," replied Lucy, slightly embarrassed.

"You're joking Mum! What happened?" Sheridan asked, wide-eyed.

85

Lucy relayed her whole story since leaving Tasmania while Sheridan sat listening intently, never having thought her mother had the strength and passion to come all this way and endure so much in search of her wayward daughter.

"Dear Mum, I'm so sorry for all the anguish I've caused you! I've got us into a situation that could cause us both some danger although I do feel safe and have made up my mind not to try and escape while I'm pregnant. In my heart I know this will never work, he has several women, one in each community he supplies and one in Darwin," Sheridan tearfully told her mother.

"Okay, let's not fret sweetheart. We've come this far and we will get out of here. Wait a couple of days until the dust settles. What's the Chinese man like?" asked Lucy.

"His name is 'Mr Kim', he's Chinese/Korean and is the only man here. He has four women who do all the work. He is the father of all their nine children. Each month he takes his boat to the main island to buy supplies but no one else, including me, ever leaves," Sheridan explained.

"Do you talk to him at all?" Lucy asked.

"No, he and his women ignore me, as they will you. Another boat often calls, I think from Cairns, and they cook up tablets of some kind for them from chemicals they supply. Two of the boys run the 'cookhouse' as it is called, back in the jungle. The rest of us are banned from going there," Sheridan explained.

"Would they help us?" asked Lucy.

"Hell no, Mum! They're Islanders, and ignore me completely! They'd be afraid of us dobbing them in," said Sheridan seriously.

Chapter Eight

Lucy and Sheridan went fishing together in the lagoon which was relaxing, but Lucy was filled with anxiety so decided to just sit beneath a pandanus and watch Sheridan fish. She planned to phone Lyndon when the opportunity arose and so kept a lookout down the beach for anyone approaching. She was sure he would have an answer and, with the help of his sister and her husband, would find a way to rescue them.

A deep frown came over Lucy's face again when Lyndon didn't answer his phone. She was sure he'd be home by now. In fact, according to her calculations he should have been home for at least a week! 'Why wasn't he answering her calls?' she thought, but left a short message informing him of her position, giving him the GPS coordinates she got from the satellite phone. Switching it off to save battery, she again hid it, this time taking exceptional care to hide all trace of her backpack as the other women often allowed the children to play in the area when they came to the lagoon to fish with their cast net.

As they left the lagoon with a few fresh fish for the evening meal, Lucy and Sheridan noticed a large runabout parked on the beach and stepped back behind some palm trees when they heard people arguing. Suddenly several shots rang out and they saw one of the women drop to the ground. Mr Kim lay on the sand begging not to be shot when two bursts of rifle fire came from the jungle causing two men to run towards the runabout with bullets kicking up the sand behind them. A loud scream rang out as one fell, blood streaming from his leg. The other turned, grabbed him and dragged him into the boat, managed to get the outboard motor to start at once and sped off.

Two young men ran to the shoreline, still shooting at the boat. The female who was shot wailed in pain and without thinking Lucy ran to her and stemmed the flow from the gaping wound in her shoulder using her sarong, leaving her nude.

Sheridan ran to her hut and got the first-aid kit she had taken from the yacht. Having cleaned the wound and applied a pressure bandage she made the poor woman comfortable on a bed in front of the main house.

Lucy went to clean up and find some fresh clothes. Despite all the drama, Sheridan managed a laugh when she gave Lucy a mirror. Lucy was horrified at the sight of her naked body covered in blood. Wrapping herself in a clean sarong, she made some fresh tea and cleaned the fish before checking on the patient.

She was sitting up and in pain but was alive. Mr Kim took an immediate liking to Lucy, believing she had saved the life of his favourite concubine. Life for Lucy and Sheridan changed from that moment. Lucy cared for the patient while the other women cooked and washed for her.

Life was definitely more comfortable for them both now but Lucy did notice that one of the young men, who had come to their rescue and had driven off the assailants, was always on guard scanning the horizon for boats during the daylight hours, and at night listening for the sound of any approaching vessels.

Attending meticulously to her patient, Lucy used disinfectant to clean the wound and always fresh dressings but knew antibiotics would help, if only they had some. To her great surprise however, her little patient recovered quickly, although sadly she would carry a visible scar. Lucy learned her name was 'Prue', which seemed to her a surprising name for a local until she found that many of the women had English-type names. Mr Kim pronounced her name as 'Missy Pluey'.

During this period Lucy had noticed new women and children appearing without any introduction. Sheridan explained when asked about this that she had never noticed because she herself had not mixed with them all. The only woman she'd mixed with was 'Moe' and then only in the evenings after the others had gone to bed. Mr Kim she said only put in an appearance occasionally but never slept in the dilapidated shacks on the beach that made up the small settlement.

Bit by bit Lucy won his trust and one day she questioned him about the altercation. In his broken English he explained that a new buyer, who was part of a large bikie gang in Cairns, had found out about their supplier and through him learned all about the details of Mr Kim and the island. That day he and his companion arrived unexpectedly, demanding to be supplied exclusively or else! Of course Mr Kim had declined and that was when they shot one of the women. Fortunately, two of Mr Kim's older sons had heard the shots and come running. Mr Kim told Lucy he had lived on the island for thirty-odd years and paid bribes to police officers and other officials to leave him alone. This incident was the first of its kind and had upset Mr Kim greatly.

After his long conversation with 'Missy Lucy', as he now referred to her, Lucy was confident Mr Kim considered her trustworthy. He told her too that he was in his late sixties and extremely worried about his extended family, becoming more nervous every day, knowing full well that the wounded man and his companion would return with a larger force and seek revenge. Lucy could see that his island paradise was under threat and that Mr Kim was uncertain how to protect it.

The following morning Mr Kim appeared early with two of his sons. The young men were both armed and one carried an extra rifle which Mr Kim handed over to Lucy! Initially she was shocked but then realised that it was not such a silly idea and it certainly made her feel safe to be able to protect herself. Lucy had learned to shoot as a child on the farm, shooting rabbits for the table. She inspected the SKK assault rifle with a twenty-shot clip and then one of the youngsters gave her a demonstration on how to load and fire the weapon.

Mr Kim watched as Lucy shouldered the weapon and with mild satisfaction thought, 'This woman can also handle a firearm'.

"Missy Lucy, you and Missy Shelidan, you come alonga now. We go to safer place maybe," Mr Kim instructed as he marched off towards the jungle. The two sons made a chair with their arms and scooped up Missy Pluey.

Lucy and Sheridan looked at each other bemused.

'Just what was Mr Kim up to?' All the time the women simply sat around the campfires seemingly uninterested in the procedure happening before their eyes, with three children playing amongst them.

With the rifle safely over her shoulder and two spare clips of ammunition in her shoulder bag, Lucy looked at Sheridan and both moved off in single file, following Mr Kim onto a small jungle track.

After several hundred metres they came across a large iron hut which Lucy guessed was the 'cook house' as empty drums of chemicals lay scattered everywhere. Many of the drums had been burned over time and two men were busy working over large copper pots, cooking whatever it was they manufactured.

No one looked up as they approached but Lucy spotted some rifles on a table nearby and ammunition. She assumed that a lookout would have been posted out of sight but Mr Kim told her that the front lagoon was the only visible entrance to the island. The west side he explained had enormous cliffs and a rocky shoreline caused by centuries of pounding seas.

As they entered thick jungle again it began to rain, a soft patter of warm rain. No one slowed or talked, there were no visible tracks. They must use various ways to traverse inland so as not to form them. The last hundred metres saw them pushing through heavy undergrowth which then broke out onto a beautiful and stunning lagoon. Lucy and Sheridan stared in awe. The main camp was paradise but this was beyond belief. Gently placing Missy Pluey onto the soft sand, the two young men strolled down the beach a small distance and uncovered a dinghy hidden in the undergrowth. Picking it up, they carried it to the beach and placed it into the warm water, gently lapping the shoreline. Lucy saw hundreds of fish darting through the crystal clear water.

One boy held the boat while the other picked up Missy Pluey and set her down carefully into the boat. Mr Kim smiled and indicated for Lucy and Sheridan to get in. He then sat in the bow as one of the boys started the small outboard and they slowly crossed the palm tree-lined lagoon. Both Lucy and Sheridan sat stunned as they quietly glided around the headland into the lagoon proper. Rounding the headland Lucy grabbed Sheridan, there in the bay sat a large modern motor vessel tied to a jetty and then, gobsmacked and speechless they stared at a magnificent house sitting on the rise above the jetty.

Lucy's heart was pounding. This was out of a movie. Never in her life had she seen such opulence. Further up the rise several smaller homes sat all neatly placed facing each other, surrounded by the most well-kept gardens, bananas, fruit trees and acres of what she would learn was marijuana or gunja, all carefully tended by the islanders. Behind the village stood a sheer cliff covered in misty cloud. Alighting onto the jetty Lucy frowned, there was no exit visible to the sea. 'How will Mr Kim get the fifteen-metre motor vessel out of the lagoon?' she wondered.

Walking to the main house and glancing about in absolute wonder, Lucy and Sheridan saw the fantasy Mr Kim had created for his clients but they were confused as to just why he had allowed them to enter his domain. 'After all these years, why would two strangers be allowed enter this sanctuary?' Lucy's mind was working overtime 'but then he would not have armed me if he hadn't had bad thoughts as to the future'.

Two almost naked women met Lucy and Sheridan. Indicating for them to follow they ushered them into a large bedroom with the biggest bed Lucy had ever seen! Silk curtains waved gently in the breeze and opulent furniture graced the giant room. One woman glided past them and gently pulled aside a heavy velvet curtain to reveal a carved pool into which water gently cascaded from a beautiful statue. Two luxurious towels were draped over a bench seat beside it, with a range of exotic soaps and perfume. Lucy and Sheridan were speechless.

They looked at each other's matted hair and dirty appearance and without speaking, dropped their dirty sarongs and sank into the warm pool, sighing as they let the water caress their bodies. One of the women returned with two beautiful Chinese dresses and matching sandals and placed them on the seat, then quietly glided out and left Lucy and Sheridan to wallow. It was all so surreal. "Mum, is this a bad dream or what? To think I have been on this island for all these months, living in virtual filth and yet this paradise exists! The crafty old bugger! All that shit on the other side of the island is one bloody big front!" exclaimed Sheridan splashing herself, already the lustre coming back to her skin.

"I'm afraid I'll wake up and find all this is a dream! My mind is working overtime, what is he up to and why would he reveal this to us? He must have some motive. Just to succeed and survive so long here would take a lot of cunning and planning," said Lucy soaking up the perfume of the soap, and closing her eyes added, "Perhaps I'll pinch myself and wake up back in bloody Parattah!"

Then, breaking into her thoughts, the two women reappeared with large platters of food placing them on the side of the pool and leaving as silently as they entered. But an even bigger surprise shocked them when Mr Kim entered in a white dressing gown and sat down on the seat. Lucy and Sheridan hurriedly tried to cover their breasts.

"Please, no worry. Mr Kim have plenty women, we need talk, maybe here good place, relaxing what?" he smiled.

"Mr Kim, Sheridan and I are confused as to why you are treating us so well, what's going on?" Lucy asked, dropping her hands back into the water. How ridiculous were they to try covering themselves when there were bare-breasted women wandering all over this gigantic house!

"Ladies, Mr Kim velly worry. Big ploblem coming soon, first time big ploblem not know what must do. Perhaps Missy Lucy, clebber lady, help," said Mr Kim slowly.

Lucy then saw how shattered he was. For decades he had quietly been building an empire and now it was at risk. Lucy was fascinated as to how he had done it.

"I can see Mr Kim that leaving all of this is not an option. Can you not get help from other customers? I'm sure no one told the bikie gang on purpose, it must be one of the workers who was given a bribe maybe," suggested Lucy.

"Ah Missy Lucy clebber lady, me know straight away. You see all my family here, not able to help me, always boss man. Only five young sons capable to fight and need leader, not much big world experience maybe," Mr Kim replied.

Lucy and Sheridan understood that after decades of hiding his paradise, his trust had been shattered and he was confused and frightened, the recent incident had changed his world. Lucy remembered him screaming for mercy when the two men had held a gun to his head, far beyond anything he had considered in the careful plans he'd made.

"Perhaps we can phone your other client in Cairns and tell him what happened? He can help can't he? I assume you are aware that Con would not be much help," said Lucy munching on the fresh and delicious food. Now that she was needed she felt empowered.

"Ah ploblem, no phone on island," said Mr Kim sadly.

"But there is a phone on the island. I've hidden a satellite phone in a backpack on beach. Have you his phone number?" asked Lucy smiling.

Mr Kim jumped up yelling to a young girl who was standing quietly observing. A sigh of relief came as he said, "Me know Missy Lucy one clebber lady! We go straight back and phone. See if Mr Kline man help with ploblem."

As if on cue again the young lady glided in with a pair of shorts and a shirt while scooping up one of the beautiful dresses at the same time.

"Better clothes plobbly. Missy Shelidan she wear dress,

95

stay here, no more walk, much baby on way," smiled Mr Kim.

Mr Kim left quietly. Lucy reluctantly rose from the water but knew this matter was urgent. She dressed quickly and found Mr Kim and the two heavily armed boys waiting at the jetty. Before Lucy left, Sheridan had dressed in the beautiful sequined blue Chinese dress with splits up both sides. Lucy noticed how regal Sheridan looked with her thick luscious hair held back by a beautifully carved hair slide and smiled at her small baby bump.

Chapter Nine

As promised, Ken and Roz Baker delivered the Troopy to Bitter Springs for storage. Laurie had assured them that Lucy would be safe with Nic, although he was a drug runner he would never harm anyone. Nic was a lover, not a killer, he assured them.

Before heading back south they decided to visit Darwin and inform Lyndon personally of what had transpired. Knowing Lucy had not been able to contact him, they wanted to pass on the information themselves.

Arriving at the address Lucy had given them, they drove up the drive and after stopping, knocked on the door. They stood for some time and then turned to leave. Just then, an elderly man appeared from around the back.

"If you're looking for Lyndon, he's still in hospital and he'll be there for some time yet," the old man informed them.

"What happened? We've a message for him from Lucy," Roz explained.

"Shit lady! Big accident when he was getting back to Lucy. He proposed you know. Lovely lady, don't blame the man for wanting that," replied the old man sighing.

Thanking him they left and drove straight to the hospital. When they eventually located Lyndon they both gasped. He looked gaunt and was covered in bandages with one leg still in plaster.

They introduced themselves, "Hi! We're Roz and Ken,

friends of Lucy."

Immediately Lyndon's eyes lit up and he became so emotional he started sobbing.

"What happened? Is she okay?" he asked.

"Yes, we saw her a couple of weeks ago or more. She found the yacht her daughter had been on and then hitched a ride to an island she was apparently staying on," said Roz holding Lyndon's hand, she too becoming emotional at his reaction.

"My phone was lost in the crash. Can you do me a favour? I didn't ask my sister or her policeman husband in case I got Lucy's daughter into trouble. Can you get me a new phone with my old number so I can check for messages? She must need me," asked Lyndon panicking.

"She was phoning you often and leaving messages. She still has her satellite phone so why didn't we think of that Come on Ken, let's go get a phone. What's your number?" asked Roz.

"There's money in my wallet. I was out to it for two weeks, only came out of the coma last week and still feel shit," said Lyndon rubbing his eyes.

"Our shout, can you sign a form authorising us to get your old number on your new phone?" asked Ken as they got up to leave, realising they were now becoming involved in the saga.

Roz wrote a short note of authorisation for Lyndon to sign and Ken witnessed it, returning two hours later with the new phone.

"We had some luck, got a young girl who must have thought Ken was you Lyndon! She was most cooperative.

Try it and see if any messages remain, I think they get deleted after a couple of weeks," Roz, all enthused now, told Lyndon.

Lyndon searched for messages and found there were two. Listening carefully, he smiled, "She seems okay, and still loves me," beamed Lyndon. "Can you get a pen and write down the coordinates of the island she is on for me please? God knows what she must think of me," he replied sounding exasperated.

Roz listened intently, replaying the message several times to write down the exact location of Lucy's whereabouts and passed it to Lyndon.

"I'll leave a message for you on her Sat phone to tell her of the accident and that will at least explain why you have not been in contact," said Roz dialling the number. Instead she got an enormous shock when Lucy herself answered!

"Lucy! What is going on? We are with Lyndon, he had a rather bad accident racing back to you, silly man," Roz informed her passing the phone to Lyndon, whose hand was shaking.

"Lucy my lovely, sorry I didn't answer your calls but I lost the phone in the accident. Are you alright?" Lyndon blubbered.

"Lyndon, my darling man, please get better and don't worry. It's a long story but we are fine. How long before you're out of hospital?" Lucy sounded alarmed but relieved knowing now why he hadn't made contact.

"Doctor told me I can go home in a week. You do what you have to and I'll keep the phone on. If you need help, let me know," Lyndon replied.

"No. We're both fine," Lucy assured him then added, "Lyndon, look after yourself. I really miss you and hopefully we'll be back together soon. Take care, need to save battery so I'll just say 'love you', goodbye!"

Lucy hated to hang up. She'd just talked to Mr Kline and the news was not good. He apologised to Mr Kim several times but admitted that he had also supplied the bikie gang with amphetamines for many years and as the gang grew in strength and numbers, they decided to do without him. Apparently one of his couriers was intercepted and tortured into revealing his supplier.

Mr Kim was shocked at the news and felt alone and vulnerable. On the way over to the beach settlement that he used as a front, Mr Kim confessed to Lucy that he had once been the cook for a wealthy German who had built the hideaway. Mr Kim also confessed that the German had been a Nazi and had escaped with a large amount of gold after the war, disappearing into the Pacific and eventually building his shangri-la on the island. Most of the building material had come from Sydney. He had a small ship along with false papers. He had been educated in Britain and spoke perfect English. Mr Kim had joined him in Rabaul along with several other servants and over the years, had slowly built his empire. Mr Kim indicated that he still had some of the gold.

The German died of a heart attack before completion and so Mr Kim simply took over and carried on the project. At first he grew marijuana for the local market and over time made a contact in Cairns. The contact, Mr

Kline, had requested a few years previously that he start producing amphetamines. This was a lucrative proposition but Mr Kim now regretted it as money here was not of great importance. Now his paradise was possibly going to be destroyed. Lucy found it strange that, faced with a problem he was unable to come up with a plan to resolve, Mr Kim had turned to Lucy for help.

Lucy had to make a decision. She could head back to the house to Sheridan, although that was risky. If the bikies took over the island, they would eventually discover it and then what would happen to all those innocent people. She knew that some of the women had been purchased like chattels by Mr Kim from outer islands and the mainland. They were now older with grown-up children who knew nothing of the outside world and if they left, they would be destroyed. Even Mr Kim knew this and that his power was slipping away. He was unable to think of a way out of this predicament.

"Have you any explosives?" asked Lucy, unsure as to why she even asked such a question.

"Yes, gelignite at settlement used to blow up reefs, make entrance to lagoon," Mr Kim enthusiastically replied.

"Right, we'll go back and get a heap of it. Can the boys set detonators up?" Lucy asked, a plan forming in her mind.

"Yes, yes clebber lady," Mr Kim beamed.

Lucy raced up the beach deciding to hide the sat phone back in her well-disguised spot. They returned to the main village as night descended.

While Mr Kim and the boys loaded the explosives, Lucy

felt exhausted and went to her room promising herself she would explore the large home and surrounds as soon as possible. It intrigued her. She guessed all up, that about nine women of various ages inhabited the island with a few young men and about ten children, all of whom looked as though they were fathered by Mr Kim. She thought it strange that he had managed to remain hidden for so long. Not many places on the planet could give protection to such an undiscoverable hideaway.

Lucy found Sheridan sound asleep, and looking quite angelic, when she entered the room so slipped quietly into the luxuriously soft bed, falling asleep immediately. This was the first night she had enjoyed absolute comfort for months and slept soundly. In fact she couldn't remember ever having such a sound night's sleep, somewhat amazing when she considered the dangerous situation they now faced.

A light tap on the door startled her and the small face appeared of a young woman beckoning her to get up. Quietly, leaving Sheridan sleeping, she slipped out of bed and dressed quickly. Mr Kim was pacing nervously on the jetty. Without a word she climbed on board and they motored around the point to where Mr Kim's three sons and two daughters were waiting to be taken aboard. They crowded onto the little boat, all armed and Lucy sensed they were bewildered and nervous. Arriving at the beach they disembarked, each one carrying a box of explosives and padding along silently with Lucy showing the way. She had become the leader in the war ahead and in some way felt committed to the cause, although unable to explain even to herself how this had been manifested.

Arriving at the settlement they were met by two women and Lucy instructed them to place the explosives in both the larger buildings. She told them to hide them in the sand floor and replace the mats and beds over them, making sure the fuses were not exposed. Lucy was surprised how a plan came to her at each stage of the operation. When they had finished Lucy and Mr Kim stayed with the women while the others returned to get more explosives to place in the remaining two smaller huts, one which Sheridan had lived in for some weeks. Lucy figured it would take them three hours by the time they loaded and returned, or even longer.

Lucy decided to go down to the beach and phone Lyndon. She had promised to phone him back and knew he would be waiting for her call. Shouldering her rifle she sauntered down to her spot and sat under some shade. She unwrapped the phone and held it up, waiting for a signal. Then she heard them, two high-powered speed boats rounded the corner at top speed. Quickly and silently she melted into the undergrowth and watched in horror as five heavily-armed men from each boat jumped out onto the sand firing randomly at the building. Mr Kim ran out, a look of horror on his face and went down in a hail of bullets. Two young children ran from one house and died writhing in the sand. The women ran screaming, only to be caught by some of the men who, like wild animals, ripped their clothes from them, threw them to the ground and raped them, punching them viciously if they resisted. Lucy was thankfully camouflaged but sat trembling and terrified as she witnessed the horrific scene unfolding before her.

Three men ran off into the jungle and soon after a plume of smoke erupted from the direction of the cookhouse. Luckily both the boys had gone back for the remainder of the explosives but the thought of them returning sent a chill up Lucy's spine. Somehow she had to stop them. Despite them being armed, Lucy was certain they were innocents. She watched as new equipment was placed inside Sheridan's old hut and assumed it was now the new cookhouse. It was more sophisticated than the old building. Lucy understood clearly that the island was now controlled by a bikie gang, some members of which were of Island origin. There was no doubt in her mind that they planned stay on to run the island and keep the women as slaves.

Glancing right, Lucy worked out that if she wound her way north of her current position she would be able to cross the open sand without being observed. Slowly she made her way, a feeling of loathing coming over her, those men were no better than animals. She saw their treatment of the two women who now lay in foetal positions on the hot sand. The last one to rape the older woman drove his boot into her with a sickening crunch, as he pulled up his trousers.

It took two hours for Lucy to circle the old track and break out onto the lagoon, just in time to meet the three young men returning. The girls had stayed back at the main village having seen the smoke rising in the distance from the burning cookhouse. Lucy recounted what had happened. Now late in the afternoon, she chose to quietly return on the trail she had come in on. Everyone was frightened and reluctant but followed Lucy without question after having hidden the dinghy.

Two hours later just on dusk, with adrenalin pounding and sweating profusely, Lucy and the three terrified youngsters clutching their rifles, peered down the beach at some men standing around a large fire all drinking. The two boats sat on the sand and it was evident to Lucy that the head of the bikie gang was planning to stay overnight to supervise the setting up of his new drug empire. Little did he know that a paradise awaited him on the other side of the island!

Slowly, as darkness enveloped them, they inched toward the buildings until they dared go no closer. Lucy was glad in one way to see the women moving about in the light of the fire although they were obviously in pain as their movements were slow and stiff. They were completely naked. Even from a distance Lucy could see blood caked on the older woman's face. Lucy's companions stared in terror and she reeled back in disbelief at the sight of small arms and legs appearing in the dancing flames. They were burning Mr Kim and the children and forcing the women to transport firewood to carry out the gruesome task! Lucy was unsure what to do and felt helpless.

Voices were raised and shouts of encouragement rose as one of the men grabbed the younger woman in a headlock while another parted her legs and pounded her roughly, screaming like a mad animal as he climaxed and collapsed onto the ground.

Lucy saw that her companions were still trembling in fear and slowly raised her hand indicating to them to be careful. Whispering, she explained they would wait until the exhausted men eventually went to bed, hopefully in the two houses where they had placed the explosives. Lucy had no doubt the young men wouldn't have either the expertise or the inclination to rush in and shoot the drunken animals.

The time dragged slowly and it wasn't until after midnight that Lucy saw the leader limp into one of the two houses. The whites of her young companions' eyes were so bright in the dark through fear that she knew they would run rather than fight. With Mr Kim gone, who'd always looked after them, guiding them daily in their tasks and shielding and protecting them from the savageness of the outside world, their quiet paradise was being brutally shattered.

Lucy rubbed her eyes. She had dozed off as had her companions. It was all quiet and only the embers remained of the fire. Looking around her, Lucy realised that the men were in the huts asleep and only the two women remained outside, laying by the fire. Lucy shook the young men quietly telling them to cover her. The time had come to set off the explosives. Like a cat, Lucy stalked the edge of the jungle looking for the fuse and knew she had to get the two women away from the fire. Lucy then cursed, "No bloody matches to light the fuse!" Placing her rifle down, she crawled slowly to within a few metres of the women and picking up a pebble, threw it at the nearest one who woke with a start. Lucy put her finger to her lips indicating to remain silent and to wake her companion, then move to where she was. Silently and stealthily the woman walked over to her friend, nudging her gently. All that could be heard were a few coughs and some snoring in the main building.

The women crawled over to Lucy who whispered to one to go back and get a hot coal. She walked cautiously to the fire and finding a metal cup, filled it with hot coals and returned to Lucy who then made her way back to the fuse. She was again soaked in sweat with her heart pounding heavily. Waving the women away, she placed the fuse into the cup and immediately it spluttered to life. Lucy grabbed her rifle and cocked it. She watched in trepidation as the fuse ran silently to the building.

After what seemed an eternity she dropped her head, the plan was not going to work. She felt totally defeated. 'This is it,' she thought, 'we are all going to die!' Suddenly the place erupted in a deafening roar! Flames shot into the air, bits of timber and iron rained down like a picture from hell.

Lucy stared in shock but was brought back to reality when the bikie leader and his buddy ran out of the second building just as it too exploded, knocking them forward. As she watched, one staggered to his feet but she heard the bark of rifles to her left and both men died instantly. Her gentle companions had come through. An eerie silence hung heavily over the scene of carnage.

Lucy shakily got to her feet. The reality of what she had done hit her like a sledge hammer. Inexplicably she knew that her life had changed forever. Gathering her senses she couldn't help but notice the eyes of the three young men before her. Blazing, pleading and seeking some sort of guidance. Their innocence was lost here tonight and she now looked into the faces of three killers, quite capable of repeating the deed at any time on her command.

Lucy had metamorphosed from a quiet, softly spoken, downtrodden wife into a violent killer in the matter of a few months. It then dawned on her that this was now her island. If she left the inhabitants would soon be taken over, perhaps by more sinister forces so to return to her old life was now impossible. Having summed up the situation she ordered the women to build the fire as quickly as possible. The smell of burning flesh was sickening. All those inside the main building had been blown to pieces. Only two bullet-ridden bodies lay intact.

Lucy ordered one of the boys to return to the main camp to bring back all available help and he immediately ran off into the night without question. She knew that from here on she was in total charge. With the rifle still on her shoulder Lucy stood staring at the roaring fire, covered in dust and soot, making an imposing sight. She ordered her followers to collect all the bodies and after removing any rings or other identification to throw them onto the fire. Using the timber from the building, now strewn over a large area, the fire grew into an almost pagan-like ritual as sparks flew into the air with each handful of splintered timber and body parts. She assumed the leaders she had killed tonight would have for security reasons kept the location of the island from all but the selected group who now lay roasting on the fire! Lucy began directing the difficult clean-up and despite their exhaustion and fatigue, not one of them faltered.

With the clean-up continuing, Lucy inspected her two new boats. The boats with powerful twin motors had been especially purchased for the new venture. It had obviously been carefully planned and Lucy gave a little shriek when she saw all the weaponry. Apart from two rifles that had been picked up at the destroyed building amongst the bodies, it appeared that all the rest had been placed back in the boats ready for departure that morning. She found a suitcase containing a large amount of cash and a revolver which she took possession of, plus a pistol, belt and holster. Strapping it around her, Lucy Jacobs had just become the leader of a large drug operation and the owner of an island and all its riches.

Chapter Ten

As daylight broke, everyone from the village arrived and stopped still on the sand when they saw the carnage before them. Sheridan appeared clutching her rifle, wide-eyed and shocked. Every member of the island community was there except for the young children and the wounded Prue.

Lucy immediately arranged work parties to collect all the twisted iron, along with that from the old cookhouse and to wrap it in bundles. They transported it all out to the reef where it sank slowly from sight. Already rusty, it would soon disappear into history. After three hours they dragged palm fronds over the sand and, apart from some charcoal, no visible sign remained of the battle and the killing that had taken place such a short time earlier. Lucy removed the new equipment they had placed in Sheridan's old hut and hid it back in the jungle, covering it from the elements. The women then tidied up the remaining buildings. Satisfied, Lucy instructed two of the older men and three women to remain in the camp and act normally if anyone arrived by sea. She told them to inform any newcomers that Mr Kim was away but that he would be back fairly soon. Lucy also instructed that one of the villagers must contact her if this in fact happened. It seemed the standard practice would continue.

Lucy and the three young men boarded the two boats, keen to find the hidden entrance to the lagoon. Having checked the fuel level they set off around the island while Sheridan and the others faded into the jungle preparing for the return trip back the main village. From a distance, Lucy was satisfied the outpost looked just like any other but decided to build another main building to make life more comfortable for those manning the fake village.

The two new boats certainly impressed her young commandoes. She grinned as she watched them expertly put the boats through their paces, each boat about seven metres and very fast as they were powered around the island. Lucy was rather surprised at how small the beach was they had left, soon replaced by towering rocky cliffs. She wondered how they would manoeuvre their way into the quiet and placid inland lagoon amid the enormous waves crashing onto the rocks, making the entrance appear treacherous. One of the boys standing at the controls pointed to the cliff face and headed straight towards a cave mouth. It was quite high but from a distance almost undetectable, and as he eased back on the throttle Lucy saw that the entrance was also quite large. 'How on earth did the German ever find the entrance and indeed the island?' she thought but would never know. Mr Kim was dead and whatever had taken place had died with the old Chinese man.

The boats roared out into the lagoon and raced over to the jetty. Lucy stepped onto the jetty, deciding to inspect her new empire beginning with the large motor vessel gently rocking in the wake they had created.

Climbing aboard, she entered the wheelhouse and found it equipped with sophisticated state-of-the-art controls.

One of the staterooms had been turned into a cool room! She was told by Tom one of the boys, that Mr Kim kept the island supplied, making visits to Port Moresby on a regular basis for the supplies and he added, for banking. Tom used to accompany Mr Kim and Lucy questioned him about the location, if any, of Mr Kim's office and stores. More than happy that the new 'boss woman' seemed to place her trust in him, he eagerly told her what he knew and then helped her from the vessel back into the runabout.

Bypassing the village, Tom headed towards the sheer cliff behind the village and to the main house. Behind a large boulder was a small entrance and with her enthusiastic guide padding ahead, Lucy entered the main cavern. Light came from above. Tom stopped abruptly in front of a large iron gate, and reaching into a crack covered by ferns he retrieved a key and opened it.

Lucy stepped inside and, looking around as he lit some candles, gazed in awe at the huge shelves weighed down with gold, silver and jade plus hundreds of other vases and items she knew were gold and every type of gem, together with carved ivory and elephant tusks.

Lucy was not worldly but knew she was looking at some of the plunders of Europe and Africa from the Second World War. Her enquiring mind now wondered 'who exactly had this mysterious German been and just how did he end up here in his own paradise?' 'Even more pertinently, how did he do it undetected from the outside world?'

Fatigue suddenly embraced Lucy. Lack of sleep and the stress of the last few days now began to take their toll.

After locking up they returned to the main house to do a quick search of the palatial residence, marvelling at the old paintings and beautifully carved furniture in every room. The kitchen and pantry were stacked with food and other supplies. She did note however that there was no power and that the refrigerator was run by gas. Climbing the sweeping staircase she opened the door at the top and gasped. The master bedroom was enormous with a four-poster bed and canopy sitting in the centre of the room. A view of the lagoon was visible and in one corner sat a carved wooden desk. Admiring all the books stacked neatly on shelves above the desk, she saw a large ledger and was captivated by a neatly written note in English:

'*Missy Lucy,*

If bad thing happen to me, you please take care of business and people, instruction on private bank vault in Port Moresby in envelope, no bank account only safety deposit boxes in four banks.

Mr Kim'

It then dawned on Lucy why Mr Kim had befriended her. He had a premonition of his impending death and not only wanted his little world to continue but for his people and women to be protected. She knew too that Mr Kim did not like confrontation and violence and in her, had seen a saviour. Just as his German employer had done to him, he passed the continuation of this little part of the world on to her.

Lucy left the room and went to Sheridan's. She was soaking in the pond. Lucy joined her and they talked for some time before exhaustion forced Lucy out of the soothing water. She wrapped a towel around herself and climbing the stairs, fell into the large bed and floated into a deep sleep.

As light crept into the room and woke Lucy she glanced around at the grandeur, becoming aware that she was perhaps now one of the world's richest people. She became committed too to keeping the little island paradise going, the incidents of the past few days making it impossible for her to turn back. There was order on the island and everyone knew their responsibilities, no doubt due to Mr Kim's original teachings and influence. Lucy decided that today she would have a good look around to see what she had inherited.

Lucy sat up in bed and froze. Someone was on the other side of the bed! She recognised a small head and realised it was one of the island women. Lucy watched as she slid out of bed silently, went over to a large commode chair beside the huge window, lifted up the lid then sat down and urinated. Standing up, she wiped herself with tissues from the box on the dressing table and then closed the lid. Lucy realised the woman had been so indoctrinated that she came to the bed last night as though Mr Kim were still alive. Lucy noticed she was shaven, 'One of Mr Kim's fantasies?' she mused.

"What is your name?" Lucy asked.

"My name Moe," she replied, "I go gettum breakfast

now."

Lucy was surprised at her English, although pidgin, and as she went to leave, called her back. "No need for you to do that or to sleep here now Mr Kim has gone," Lucy told her.

Moe appeared to be intelligent and educated but seemed surprised and sad at this news, so Lucy at this stage would maintain the status quo until Moe got a proper handle on the situation.

"Moe Toosday here, other women come alonga tonight. Moe get breakfast Missy," she replied, somewhat relieved as she hurried downstairs.

Lucy sat up in bed and it wasn't long before she heard the patter of feet returning. Moe placed a tea tray, upon which sat a large plate of fruit and a glass of juice on the bedside table for Lucy, who by now was ravenous and very appreciative.

Moe turned to leave but Lucy asked her to stay. Moe looked confused as she sat on the bed. "Here Moe, you eat too, then you take Missy Lucy and show her round gardens maybe," suggested Lucy.

"Moe show you later on maybe. Moe wash clothes today and clean house," she replied.

Lucy knew that the order and timing of each day was paramount in their lives, recognising that was why everything was so neat and organised. "Perhaps you ask Tom come and talk to Missy Lucy," she suggested.

"Tom he gone long beach, take some out and bring some in maybe, me tellum come back," Moe replied scuttling off ready to start her day's work.

Lucy ate all her breakfast. The heat was beginning to rise and she knew the monsoon season was not far off. As she was dressing, one of the men arrived unannounced! Lucy stood watching as he changed the toilet receptacle without even seeming to notice her. "Where you take bucket?" she asked him, now inquisitive.

"Belonga garden," he replied casually.

Again Lucy was stunned. Complete order and innocence, the man was wearing only a penis sheath. Nudity here was natural and Lucy had to learn to get used to their traditions. She noticed too, the violence that had taken place appeared wiped from the minds of the island people and their daily life returned to normal, as it had no doubt done for decades.

As Lucy watched them all working happily and chatting amongst themselves, it seemed to her their only break was the days on duty at the beach village. To a passer-by the scene was one of a few locals living traditional lives.

Sheridan came running upstairs as Lucy dressed in her shorts and skimpy top, glowing with her newly acquired tan.

"Come on Mum! Let's explore the village. I've made up my mind to stay here with you and my baby, if that's alright?" she beamed.

"That would be my dream but are you sure? On the surface it looks great but we are mixed up in a horrendous business, made patently obvious by the violence and bloodshed some will go to in this unsavoury trade," replied Lucy solemnly.

"Mum for heaven's sake! Haven't you been listening

to the news? There's blood shed every night in our capital cities back in Australia, the unions and labour members are fucking corrupt, as is most of society, come on. I worked for lawyers for years and after rent, saved ten bloody thousand dollars for shit sake! Take a look around Mum and think back to the shit hole you lived in for the greater part of your life," said Sheridan passionately.

"What about Nic, Sheridan? To keep this as it is we have to use caution. I've even wondered if I can completely trust my Lyndon, but when I see him I'll know," said Lucy.

"Look, reality has set in. Nic was an adventure and a great fuck but that's all. He can go on the backburner, it's over. He was only ever after money and sex and to parade me as a white trophy. This has woken me up. If you hadn't turned up, I would have been shot on the beach and that's a fact, so let's get real Mum!" Sheridan fired back.

Lucy knew her daughter, like herself, had succumbed to money and power and that turning back now was most certainly not an option. Sheridan still had over three months to go in her pregnancy so before that they would need to have everything worked out. Lucy thought about living in Lyndon's place and Sheridan having the baby in Darwin. That way the baby would be an Australian citizen. Neither had Passports and being outside Australia's territorial waters would be classified as foreigners. They had to think carefully and logically. Lucy and Sheridan left the main house and passed the wing where Mr Kim's women lived, he had one for each night of the week.

"Dirty old man," Sheridan laughed.

"That may be so, but he treated them well and they all seemed happy. Far more than I can say for women like myself whose lives passed daily in complete boredom and misery," remarked Lucy.

"Sorry Mum. I must admit I hated coming home and seeing you like that, but never thought you would have the guts to leave," Sheridan replied.

"I break out in a cold sweat when I think that if you hadn't left on your trip my life would have continued on its shitty way with me being totally dependent on government handouts. I would die before I ever went back to that," Lucy said in a determined voice.

For over three hours, mother and daughter inspected pens of fat pigs, goats and poultry running amongst the banana plantations. There were tropical fruit trees including mangoes coming up to picking time and vegetable gardens bursting with produce! Lucy was impressed at how ordered it all was and understood exactly why no one had any spare time. In order to protect his empire Mr Kim had deliberately kept numbers to a minimum knowing that the fewer people the fewer security risks. They then encountered large enclosures full of marijuana growing abundantly and healthily, and the sheds in which it was being dried.

"I wonder how he got all his women. He must have bought some," Lucy suggested to Sheridan as they passed islanders working away happily, some singing and all obviously very healthy.

"Good heavens Mum, you're an innocent! He buys them from families on the surrounding islands, the others are their family members!" laughed Sheridan out loud.

"Oh Lucy, you idiot, of course, Missy Pluey was no doubt his last buy," said Lucy, cursing herself for being so naive.

"Poor Missy Pluey is a bit homesick. She only came in when I did. She adores you Mum and thinks your powerful medicine saved her life, they all do," said Sheridan.

"I will take her to a proper doctor for a complete check-up when we go to the main island and she can visit her people then too," announced Lucy.

"Careful Mum, although it seems that all births take place in Port Moresby, Mr Kim had many Chinese friends who took care of his women when they were waiting to give birth," Sheridan replied.

"How do you know all this?" questioned Lucy, surprised at her daughter's local knowledge.

"Moe made friends with me and was kind to me. She was the most trusted of Mr Kim's women and her parents are here because of that. We talked for hours of a night when it was her turn at the ocean village. Tom is the one who knows how things operate but Moe told me that planes fly the drugs right around The Gulf. An Aboriginal airline is available all the time to take the Aboriginals to funerals, appointments for health and to visit relatives, so other light aircraft are not noticed flying in to bush airfields," Sheridan told her surprised mother.

"Good God. Really! Where are the planes we use?" Lucy asked.

"On the main island, you actually own them Mum. Moe told me that Mr Kim bought the first plane in Port

Moresby. A young German had set up a business but it collapsed and Mr Kim was tipped off by the German's Chinese bankers who purchased the business. It now has three planes," Sheridan replied.

"Why didn't you tell me this before?" stammered Lucy.

"Look Mum, we were looking to escape and who cared? I would have told you later, but until the 'incident' it didn't seem to matter," Sheridan replied casually.

"I suppose not but tell me, what else should I know?" Lucy asked looking at Sheridan, stunned at all her new revelations.

"Ok. In the warehouse, there is enough produce to meet this month's deliveries, which by the way is tomorrow. After that, if we don't get a move on with manufacturing, we may lose face and clients. I checked the store out last night while you slept," answered Sheridan.

Lucy was gobsmacked. "How do you know so much? You amaze me!" Lucy gasped.

"Mum, I worked for a bunch of slimy lawyers for years so, say no more. I came into your room and got the books to check on deliveries, thought it might help you. By the way, now we only have Nic actually coming to the island, everything else is delivered. My view is that this should stop. They are careless and will eventually get caught," advised Sheridan seriously.

They checked out the warehouse finding it stacked with building material and chemicals, fertiliser, pallets of food and drums of fuel. A petrol generator was still in its crate.

"I wonder why Mr Kim never had a telephone to the outside world," Lucy pondered out loud.

"Phone and radio signals can be traced now Mum. He was paranoid about that and only provided a service on certain dates in the month, always as ordered and on time according to the books. He was meticulous with his bookwork" Sheridan explained.

Tom arrived back with the changeover. Everyone was more than happy to finish the shift as they were understandably fearful of the place after the shock killings.

Lucy knew that in order to continue in Mr Kim's footsteps she needed to act decisively and quickly. "Tom," she said, "I want you to load the boat and fuel it for tomorrow. Sheridan will keep the books from now on and tell you what to load. Get two of the others, send them around in one of the new boats and bring all the equipment back to the warehouse here. We've lots of room to set up here and start cooking" instructed Lucy.

Tom nodded and walking back to the beach met two others coming in from checking the fishing nets. The lagoon fed them daily with fresh fish and that, along with rice formed a large part of their diet. Combined with goat, pork and the fresh fruit and vegetables, theirs' was a healthy diet. No alcohol was brought to the island.

Sheridan agreed to do the bookwork, setting off immediately to make a list of who they were to see and pay and also who supplied the products they needed in Port Moresby. The names of the products were all neatly written in Chinese but Mr Kim had taught Moe to read the language and so she happily translated for Sheridan, loving being needed and relied upon.

Lucy decided to go with Tom and two of the other men

to pick up her phone. She now had a way to recharge it but was mindful that any transmission would be monitored. On arrival she was pleased to see the clean-up had been successful. With Tom's help they chose a fresh, clean site to build two new huts to make life more comfortable for those on duty at the island village. They would be on the beach, opposite the main area but protected by a well-hidden cave entrance.

Returning late that afternoon, Sheridan met them at the jetty. She had a book with all the relevant details they would need, including a key and a letter from Mr Kim stating that he was 'ill' and that 'Missy Lucy was his representative and would henceforth conduct his business.' There was even a seal in Chinese on the authorisation documents. Mr Kim had indeed been meticulous, professional and thorough in his business and dealings right up to the end.

Two of the men began to set up the new equipment in a corner of the warehouse, far from the storage area. Lucy nodded and concluded that this was far safer and offered better security than the main beach area. The drums that were needed for the cooking process were stored in the warehouse, saving many man-hours transporting workers and equipment to the other side of the island. Lucy and Sheridan had other plans for that side of the island! They were going to turn it into a quiet and peaceful village for the workers in which they could fish and live traditionally during their rest periods.

That night, Lucy and Sheridan ate a tasty dinner of curried fish and rice, washed down with freshly squeezed orange juice. They retired early as they knew the next day would be a day of learning and that they would need to proceed with care. It would be a few days before they returned but were confident the island community would stick to their schedule and way of life, instilled over many decades.

Chapter Eleven

Lucy woke as the first rays of light appeared. Her new room was facing the lagoon and because the sun wasn't shining directly through the window it was kept cool by the gentle breeze off the water. The curtains swayed softly, creating a peaceful and tranquil ambience. Lucy was living the dream and loved having her daughter with her. She intended to live it as long as possible.

Glancing to her side Lucy smiled, another of the women slept soundly. Slipping out of bed she dressed quickly and headed downstairs with Sheridan's crocodile briefcase, Mr Kim's seal emblazoned on the front. She was anxious to start the day and ready for anything. She also had the case of cash she had found in the boat and taken possession of, after the incident.

Keen to get underway, Tom and another of his brothers already had the diesel motor of the cruiser throbbing, and as they stepped aboard Tom cast off and returned to the cabin. The water churned up and they were off into the unknown, a first for Lucy and Sheridan.

Missy Pluey sat patiently on the boat. Lucy smiled, knowing she had probably been waiting for hours. When Lucy told her she was taking her to a doctor and then to see her family, Missy Pluey replied, "Missy Lucy 'Number One Doctor', no need," but indicated she was thrilled to be going to see her family on the main island, their first port of call.

Crossing the lagoon again reinforced to Lucy and Sheridan that they had indeed found their shangri-la but they were unhappy to now be ensconced in the world of drug running and all its consequences, some of which they had unfortunately already experienced. Neither wanted to admit however that she had become addicted to such a lifestyle, just like those poor devils to whom they eventually supply.

Entering the cave entrance the boat surged dangerously close to the wall as a large wave rolled in. Tom was experienced in the manoeuvre and thrust the throttle as they surged forward, before shooting out into the open ocean. Lucy breathed a sigh of relief but felt vulnerable leaving the sanctity of her hideaway as they headed out to sea with the island fast disappearing behind them. Within three hours the outline of the main island came into view and being a master of this trip, Tom deftly settled the boat alongside a small wharf. Only one other barge lay at anchor near the wharf and Tom told them that it came weekly from Port Moresby with supplies.

While the boys were securing the boat an old Landrover pulled up and a local Police Sergeant got out with two others. Lucy and Sheridan glanced at each other but stood at ease as Tom, and Leo his half-brother, started passing boxes to the two locals. They then stacked the boxes of drugs into the police vehicle, while the Sergeant leaned against the vehicle smoking and casually looking around for any prying eyes.

The noise of an approaching vehicle broke the silence and it pulled up near the police vehicle. A young man with blonde hair alighted and approaching the boat he introduced himself, "Hi, I'm Hans. Is Mr Kim on board?" he asked cheerfully.

"My name is Sheridan and this is my mother Lucy, a very trusted friend of Mr Kim's. He is unwell and Lucy is conducting his business at this time," Sheridan explained.

"Fine, can we go then? Mr Kline will be landing soon and we have business to discuss. The police officer here will put your cargo safely into the warehouse," Hans replied, holding out a hand to help them down the gangplank.

"Really Hans, a police officer transporting narcotics?" said Lucy in shock.

"Lucy, this is Papua New Guinea, one of the most corrupt and lawless countries on the planet. When you're in Port Moresby please let Mr Kim's Chinese friends take care of you both. They will arrange for a gang of rascals to guard your boat. Tom knows the particular wharf to tie up to, take my advice seriously," Hans warned.

Lucy and Sheridan glanced at each other. What had they got themselves into? It appeared that in order for them to continue their lifestyle, they now had to enter a jungle of corruption and danger at every turn. Tom and Leo were used to the procedure and sat relaxed in the shade of the rear deck. Watching Lucy and Sheridan drive away from the wharf, Missy Pluey had already made a hasty exit, happy that she would soon meet up with her loved ones.

They followed the police vehicle as it made its way to the airstrip. Lucy noticed the town village was basic with about fifty-odd dwellings and one shop but no other facilities. Hans pointed out that life here was rudimentary with the locals fishing and growing coconuts, the majority living a very hand-to-mouth existence. Except that is for the Police Sergeant who made more from Mr Kim than his annual wage, simply for turning a blind eye and arranging transport to the airport warehouse every two or so weeks upon his arrival.

The road to the jungle airstrip was more like a track and full of potholes. New tracks were simply made whenever the old ones became impassable. Pulling up at an office near the hangar, Hans invited them in and made coffee using a small gas stove. There was no power or refrigeration and the room was stuffy and humid.

Sheridan asked, "How come you ended up here in such isolation Hans?"

Hans laughed, "Good question. I started up a small one-man show in Port Moresby unaware of how one does business here, soon losing my meagre savings and going broke. I know now that one of Mr Kim's Chinese bank friends told him of my plight. Mr Kim set me up here and I will always be grateful to him. We have three planes and, apart from his work which keeps us going, there are two other pilots who also fly for us."

"Thanks for being honest Hans. I hope we can carry on the relationship," Lucy replied.

"We must be honest with each other Lucy. Mr Kim trusts nobody so I know you must be being honest with me," Hans responded.

Lucy relayed to Hans her full, horrific story since arriving on the island. Hans frowned deeply and shook his head in disbelief.

"Remind me not to trifle with you Lucy! I assure you that you may be confident and secure in what we do and I too trust we can keep the relationship going. No doubt you are aware of my business deal with Mr Kim, it has worked well and long may it continue to."

Sheridan opened her briefcase, "I see here that you get thirty percent of turnover for delivering and that includes bribes etc. to the police, plus all costs associated with the airline owned by Mr Kim. Am I correct?" asked Sheridan.

"Excellent Sheridan, that is absolutely correct. Now here are my books for the month. As per usual, the money after my percentage is in the case on the table. I have your supplies in the warehouse ready to load for your return journey," smiled Hans, pleased that the formalities were over. Lucy noticed him smiling at Sheridan.

"Hans, would it be possible to land the seaplane I see outside on our lagoon?" Lucy asked.

"Certainly, although Mr Kim was always afraid someone might see us taking off. Landing isn't so bad, as we can circle and make sure the coast is clear. I'm sure too that no one would suspect a thing if we spoke like the other islanders here, now that there is some type of communication" suggested Hans.

"I have a satellite phone. If you give me your office phone number we can keep in contact more efficiently," Lucy replied as they heard an approaching plane.

"One last thing, before Mr Lynch arrives. My pilots do not know the contents of our freight. The sensitive orders into The Gulf, I personally fly," Hans informed them as he walked out of the small office.

128

They watched as the plane came to a halt and its passenger stepped out. A short, bald man approached Lucy with his hand out, "Adrian Lynch, you must be Lucy," he introduced himself.

Hans turned and winking at Lucy said, "I have some refuelling to do, perhaps you and Sheridan could take Mr Lynch into the office for a little chat."

"How was your flight?" Lucy asked him as they sat in the tiny, stuffy office.

"Fine thanks, I've always loved the beauty of the Australian coast, coming north," he replied.

"Okay. Our time is limited so let's get down to business. Have you heard anything in Cairns?" Lucy enquired.

"Well, it's strange really, the bikies have been my clients for over a decade but suddenly some newcomers arrived and forced my offsider to name our suppliers. He was the only one apart from me who actually knew how to locate Mr Kim. Usually we met the plane south of here and picked up our orders. I am so sorry Mr Kim had problems because of me. We had been doing business for many years and there was never any trouble before. Having said that though, the bikies seem very quiet and some even approached me recently asking if we could re-establish our old relationship. I've also heard that the newcomers may have left town or something," Mr Lynch replied.

"Mr Lynch, ten of them left the earth permanently," Sheridan replied, waiting for his reaction. "We also believe our location died with them, as again only a few trusted men and those who stayed to run the island would have known it."

Mr Lynch was obviously shocked at this news. "I know we're involved in a violent trade and that times are changing, and I knew the leader had returned to Cairns wounded, but I had no idea they had returned. I think though Mr Kim would have known they'd come after the call you made from your phone Lucy. He instinctively trusted you," he remarked, suddenly appearing very old and exhausted.

"It appears you also seem to trust us Mr Lynch and so I am sorry but must inform you that Mr Kim was killed when they did return. Unfortunately I was not on the beach at the time of the murder. However that evening, after Mr Kim had been killed together with two of his innocent children and the shocking rape of two women, I did return and without going into too much detail, disposed of the perpetrators," said Lucy.

"Lucy, I know I'm what you call a 'crook' but I'm from the old school, so what you tell me makes me feel sick! Despite his trade Mr Kim brought many people a lot of joy and good lives, except of course those who ended up addicts. I can hear the irony in what I am trying to say, but if I stopped supplying, someone else would quickly fill my shoes," Mr Lynch replied.

"Yes I hear what you are saying. Drugs are an addiction but so are the lifestyles, money and power they yield. Do you want to continue to work with us?" asked Lucy.

Mr Lynch sighed, "Lucy, my path is charted as no doubt is yours. Of course I'll continue, it'll be a pleasure, but a word of caution, do not be as open to others as you have been to me. One very important thing Mr Kim taught me was that information is best kept to a very few, only to those who need to know. We live in an ever increasing violent world of corruption and killing and the old days are gone forever. We started off with marijuana but this new trade brings more money and money equals violence and killing as you learnt recently."

Lucy rose and responded, "Thank you for your insight. I am glad we're to continue to work together but best keep our exact location between ourselves and your offsider."

"Lucy, my offsider is dead. No matter what happened, he should not have broken my trust. He would've known the bloodshed and mayhem it would cause," said Mr Lynch as they walked to the plane, now refuelled and loaded, ready for take-off.

Lucy watched as the plane taxied and lifted into the sky.

"All went well, hopefully?" queried Hans cheerfully, holding the car door open.

"Yes, very well. He was quite a surprise," Sheridan replied.

"Bit of a strange one. A family man who attends church and gives money to charity, he must loathe himself for what he has become," said Hans.

They arrived at the boat but Missy Pluey was not yet present so they decided to pick her up on the way back. Tom cast off as Lucy hid the money under one of the galley seats.

Sheridan and Lucy enjoyed lunch as they sped towards Port Moresby and whatever revelations were soon to be uncovered. They were pleased they had met Mr Lynch although it had been a rather sobering experience that certainly made them wonder at their own involvement. Ironically the lifestyle was more addictive than the drugs they peddled and to return to any other way of life, even with all the money Lucy now possessed, would never make up for the adrenalin-charged set of circumstances they now embraced in their new lifestyle.

Chapter Twelve

Lucy and Sheridan retired to the luxurious cabins they had each claimed and lay on the soft beds. Soon the rhythm of the boat had them drifting off to sleep. It had been a long and stressful day with them virtually entering the unknown. Sheridan agreed with Lucy that meeting Mr Lynch made them feel more confident with the situation and their now more measured and cautious approach seemed wise.

Lucy woke with a start. The cabin was in total darkness. Looking out the porthole she saw flickering lights in the distance, 'Port Moresby' she thought. Immediately she freshened up and called into Sheridan's cabin to find she had already gone on deck. Lucy joined her in the wheelhouse and together they viewed the approaching city. As Tom brought the vessel alongside, several figures appeared and assisted with securing the vessel to large pylons on the jetty.

Suddenly two vehicles swept into view. The lead vehicle was a Mercedes Benz and as it came to a halt the driver jumped out and opened the front passenger door, allowing an elderly Chinese man to alight.

The Chinese man approached Lucy and Sheridan waiting on the jetty and as he bowed he introduced himself. "Please allow to introduce Mr Haan, velly good friend of Mr Kim sadly deceased." Mr Haan again bowing, indicated for them to get into the back seat, saying "Mr

Hans he phone, tell me unfortunate business."

Lucy was pleased to know this information had reached Port Moresby. Obviously Hans had as in the past, arranged for their reception on arrival, for men to guard the boat and to transport them into the city. Lucy also knew from Hans that the Chinese man would take care of them whilst in Port Moresby and that the loading would actually begin that night for their return journey. It was just as Hans had said, 'all taken care of by Mr Kim's Chinese friends'.

Lucy and Sheridan enjoyed the sights as they sped along, closely followed by another car which was no doubt security personnel for themselves and Mr Haan. The car began to slow up in Champion Road where several Chinese restaurants fronted the street. Security guards stood at the entrance to each one. Gradually they came to a halt in front of two large wrought-iron gates decorated in Chinese emblems. As if on command they slowly parted and the convoy slipped inside and along a palm-lined drive that ran straight towards a magnificent residence. Servants came to meet them and took their luggage. Mr Haan gestured for Lucy and Sheridan to follow.

"Perhaps velly late. Me send nice meal to bedroom, speak in morning after breakfast, then take to bank," said Mr Haan, bowing and scraping.

Lucy and Sheridan agreed it had been a long day and both felt hot and sticky. Despite their sleep on the yacht, a relaxing bath and then sleep would indeed be graciously accepted.

The bath was one of the biggest either had ever seen! Then a young Chinese girl wheeled in a large trolley laden with an array of the most delicious food either had ever tasted and they washed it down with green tea. Climbing into their beds, they looked forward to the next part of the giant puzzle that was the world of Mr Kim.

The following morning found Lucy and Sheridan anxious to find out the intricacies of what they had inherited. They were guided into a beautiful dining room and to a table laden with food. A smiling Mr Haan was there to greet them.

"Good morning Missy Lucy and Missy Shelidan," he smiled as the servant ushered them both to sit down.

"Good morning Mr Haan. Thank you for making us so welcome last night, it was very late and we must apologise," said Lucy gratefully.

"Ah, Missy Lucy no ploblem, Mr Kim number one velly good customer. The letter you give me last night Missy Sheridan, it say you, Missy Lucy is number one clebber lady, so now you big boss," said Mr Haan, nodding and smiling. No doubt Mr Haan was referring to the way Lucy had taken control of the whole saga in order to protect Mr Kim's island even if he himself had been killed. As a banker, he was relieved that the business from the island would continue.

After breakfast Mr Haan guided them to two waiting vehicles where, seated in the back were the most horrendous looking individuals, quite obviously security men. Moving out onto Champion Parade they made a quick journey to a secure carpark of one of the banks, moving to the rear of the building before alighting. Mr Haan ushered Lucy and Sheridan into his office which was an elaborately furnished room with the smell of incense wafting in the air. Seating himself in his red leather chair, Mr Haan gave instructions to one of his staff who then slipped out of the office and soon returned with some files. Mr Haan wasted no time in getting down to business.

"My supply orders and arrangements in Port Moresby all kept in this book," said Mr Haan opening a large black folder.

Lucy was relieved Sheridan was with her as she would take responsibility for the bookkeeping. Sheridan opened her briefcase and walked over to the desk studying figures and taking notes as Mr Haan sat, smiling graciously.

"Perhaps Missy Lucy let girl count money for account," Mr Haan pointed towards the case that Hans had given her.

Lucy lifted the case onto the table and gasped when she opened it. It was full of one hundred dollar notes in Australian currency. Two clerks then sat at an adjacent table and started counting with calculators rattling away as they bundled the money into wads, encasing it in rubber bands. Mr Haan looked on contentedly. His expression could not disguise his banker's delight in seeing so much money pouring into his bank.

'No wonder he was so accommodating, thought Lucy' watching the procedure while sipping a glass of juice. A few months prior to this, two hundred dollars to her was a small fortune!

Sheridan eventually returned to the table and sat down, indicating that it was now all in order. The accounting had been meticulous. One account was in kina, worth about two dollars to one Australian dollar. Mr Kim had also kept a US dollar account. It was all rather overwhelming for Lucy. With the inheritance, she was now one of the richest women in Australia.

When the clerks had finished counting the money Mr Haan gave Sheridan a receipt and ushered them to follow him to the main bank vaults. Opening a heavy steel door he directed Sheridan to use one of the keys she was holding and asked her to return to his office once they had inspected the contents of the safety deposit boxes inside.

Sheridan opened the first of three steel boxes. The contents of the first box were a mix of bundles of cash and gold. The second box contained the same but the third box contained titles to several buildings in Darwin and the name of the real estate agent who rented them out. One apartment in a complex on The Esplanade was marked as vacant and Lucy and Sheridan realised that Mr Kim must have kept this particular apartment for his own use. The thought had already crossed their minds as to how he went to and from Australia, doubting that he would take the boat into Australian waters. Maybe Hans would know the answer.

Locking up they returned to Mr Haan's office as requested.

"Mr Haan velly busy, driver take you other banks, check safety deposit boxes," he told them. "Mr Haan thank you, but why did Mr Kim use other banks and not stick to yours, his good friend?" asked Sheridan. Mr Haan grinned, "Ah Mr Haan he also have safety deposit other banks clebber lady, not all chickens one basket hey."

Lucy and Sheridan grinned back. Mr Kim had certainly been cautious in hiding and hoarding his treasure. It had almost been an obsession, even using the caves back on the island in case he was ever found out and had to flee his paradise.

Lucy and Sheridan checked out the other banks which all held different amounts of cash and gold. Two had pouches of diamonds! Indeed, Mr Kim had a large and far-reaching hoard of money and valuables, yet when first seen on the island at the beach village no one ever considered he had such a fortune behind him. He was quiet, yet cunning and although he had been lucky for the last few decades, the careful planning in the end had not saved his life, a lesson to be learned at their peril.

It was mid-afternoon when they returned to the boat. Tom and Leo were thrilled to see them. The last supplies had been loaded below and the deck was full of material for the warehouse and to build the new homes on the beach. Sheridan calculated they had more than enough for the job. The priority was to maintain the facade of the village in order to shield it from enquiring eyes and to protect their 'lagoon paradise'. Once aboard Tom pulled in the gangplank and Leo reversed slowly. Lucy sensed that neither Tom nor Leo were too comfortable with the locals who'd guarded the boat and that they were more than happy to be on the return journey. It occurred to her, having noticed Tom waving to one of the local girls, that the three boys on the island had no female company and decided to question Tom about that later.

Lucy and Sheridan chatted animatedly about the Port Moresby experience, still in awe at their good fortune. Lucy knew Sheridan was right when she said Mr Haan would be happy to keep the status quo. Although Mr Kim was no longer around, his Port Moresby associates who had been doing very well in the business and banking scene did not want to upset the proverbial 'apple cart' and so it was in their best interests to maintain the flow and order. Lucy and Sheridan both emotionally exhausted made their way down to their cabins and slept soundly, lulled by the gentle thudding of the engine.

Chapter Thirteen

Lucy woke several times during the night, her body soaked in sweat, as she tried to escape nightmares of the shocking images of men screaming in pain and of the dreadful smell of burning flesh that had filled her nostrils.

She lay awake trying to understand but knew that like any addiction, she was hooked and would never return to her former life. Her addiction was not so much for the physical wealth but for the power she now had and was sure Sheridan felt the same. She was aware this new life could end horribly and quickly too but living out her life in an old-age home, sitting and dribbling in a chair, was not an option. Now a stalking tigress unable to stop or retreat, Lucy's future was charted except for one problem, Lyndon. She really loved and missed him and was determined to visit him as soon as possible. She would keep her cards close to her chest and play it by ear when the time came.

Lucy was in the shower when she noticed the vessel had stopped. After dressing she went on deck to find Sheridan chatting to Hans, the two of them laughing and obviously enjoying each other's company. The loading of chemicals was already underway and being supervised by the portly Sergeant of Police studiously attending to his duties.

A small group of locals approached Lucy who immediately recognised Missy Pluey. She slowly came on board as her parents and a younger brother stood on the jetty sadly watching her leave.

Lucy went up to Missy Pluey, "Are you sad to leave your family?" Lucy asked.

"Little bit sad but parents have hard times here, no work," Missy Pluey replied quietly.

"What does your father do?" continued Lucy.

"He build and fix house," Missy Pluey replied.

"Tell your family that if they want to come and live with you at the beach village they can help build the new houses and Missy Lucy will pay good money."

Missy Pluey did not reply but ran back to her parents shouting and laughing. They all turned tail and ran back to the village. Lucy sat watching happily as they disappeared down the dusty track to get their things in order.

Hans came up to her laughing, "You've started something there Lucy, but he is a good builder in a local sort of way, and his son also. Where they live now is pretty rundown and they have hardly any income."

"Truth is that we are short-staffed and, being Prue's parents, I assume they are trustworthy," Lucy replied.

"Lucy, they'll love you but you might find it hard to return them after the

building," warned Hans.

"I see no reason to return them. There will always be plenty of work on the island" Lucy explained, as she watched them coming back up the track with a few possessions.

"Tell me Hans. How did Mr Kim get to his apartment in Darwin?" asked Lucy as they all climbed aboard.

"We would deliver goods to an isolated station airstrip west of Roper Bar. Mr Kim had a car stored there and he simply drove into town. A huge amount of local air traffic transporting Aboriginals operates all over The Gulf, we simply join the parade" Hans laughed, now at ease with his new partners.

"When do you go next? I would like to go too if possible as I have some business in Darwin," she said.

"Monday if you like, I'll fly down Sunday night and stay the night, then we'll fly back here early Monday and go down to The Gulf. I can pick you up the following Monday and if Sheridan has any problems she can always phone me," said Hans. It then struck Lucy that Hans was concerned about Sheridan and her pregnancy, and smiled inwardly.

Lucy walked up to Tom behind the controls and he smiled as she approached. He was always anxious to get back to the sanctity of the island after each trip.

"Tom was that your girlfriend back in Port Moresby?" she asked.

He looked sheepishly at Lucy, "Yes Missy Lucy but Mr Kim not let Tom take her home and Tom have no money to pay father," replied Tom.

"Look Tom, next time we're in Port Moresby, you let Missy Lucy pay father and you bring girl home for wife if you want." Tom broke out in a huge beaming smile and Lucy knew she had made a staunch friend for life.

As Lucy left the wheelhouse, she turned back to Tom and said, "Boys your age should have a woman."

Tom casually announced, "We sleep old women, they

show us how to please woman."

Lucy shook her head in disbelief. Each day was a revelation but she did wonder about the younger women back home, what hope did they have of finding a man? It was something she would consider later.

Sheridan was seated in the galley eating.

"Sit down Mum, try the fish curry I cooked. I'll take some up to Tom later." Sheridan happily pointed to a plate of steaming, aromatic food.

"Tell me love. You seemed happy chatting with Hans. Did he ask about the baby's father?" Lucy asked curiously.

"Yep Mum, I told him the truth. He laughed and asked me if we had an ongoing relationship, but I just told him I had been young and naive," Sheridan grinned at her mother's expression. "No seriously Mum, I told him that Nic has several women. I also admitted to getting hooked on good sex and adventure and that if I hadn't, none of this would have happened. Strangely Hans has asked me if he can come and see me and I said 'yes'."

"Life goes on Sheridan. My stance from hereon is 'face to the wind' and to just live each day as it comes. My only problem is not seeing Lyndon. I really want him but do wonder what his reaction will be to all of this," Lucy replied, deep in thought.

"Listen Mum, go and see him, but play it cool. By the sounds of it he's sold the truck so he can come to The Gulf to help you and that speaks volumes for the man!

He sounds great so keep him if you can Mum but, the bloody problem is, even if you decide to only meet up in Darwin monthly he will wonder what you are up to."

said Sheridan.

"Now I know why Hans wants to come down on Sunday," laughed Lucy.

"My own German air ace Mum!" giggled Sheridan.

"The bugger had better get out of the lagoon safely," smiled Lucy nervously.

"Mum, I've been thinking about Nic. Basically he is our only loose cannon. If he gets caught he would blab for sure, they all do. Somehow we must convince him we are leaving the island and cut him off. He's a small player but will be trouble in the long run," Sheridan told her mother.

"Yep, I agree. Perhaps we can deliver to him in some safe drop-off on the mainland and convince him we are moving. He thinks the settlement on the beach is it, so we should show him the burnt buildings and scare the shit out of him about the killings, make out we are terrified and that Mr Kim has moved to another island." replied Lucy deep in thought.

"Brilliant Mum, tell him that Mr Kim is taking us home, then there'll be no need to see him again. Hans can drop off and collect for us. I know several small air strips in The Gulf at abandoned homeland settlements. The one at Walker River is not far from where you found the yacht. I've heard that the odd plane lands there," Sheridan replied enthused.

"Done, let's ask Hans on Sunday and when Nic comes we'll act frightened and put the fear of God into him! If we tell him we had to kill some of the men, he'll be a bit wary of us too and can pay you the ten grand back!

Cheeky bugger," said Lucy, feeling happy with the plan.

Tom slowed down, waiting for the light of dawn to help locate the entrance. Although he had made this trip many times caution was always needed when negotiating the entrance. Any mistake could have serious consequences for the vessel and all on board.

As daylight streaked over the horizon, Lucy felt as if she were coming home. Tom expertly entered the small opening, finally shooting out into the clear crystal waters of the lagoon and tears welled in Lucy's eyes. If seventh heaven was what most people aimed for in their lives, she had indeed arrived.

Several of the islanders were waiting on the jetty and waving happily, mindful that the vessel held a few special treats for them as Mr Kim always ordered the necessary household items, new clothes, sunglasses and sweets.

Missy Pluey proudly took her parents to one of the homes she lived in. Lucy told Tom to arrange for some of the men to unload the boat and to hold off taking the building material around to the beach camp until Nic had visited, as he was due to arrive any day. Lucy's eyes again brimmed with tears as she entered the main house. This was now her sanctuary and after her visit to Darwin she would share all duties with Sheridan although she was more than capable of coping without her. If Lucy never had to leave this place again she would be more than happy, but the prospect of meeting up with Lyndon awoke her sexual drive, and she felt wet.

After a hot, perfumed soak in the spa, Sheridan and Lucy went to the office where Sheridan explained to

Lucy the set-up and the workings of the business. Lucy was very impressed but more than glad she did not have to do it on her own, quite aware that with her limited education and knowledge it was far beyond her capability. It was here in the office the two women agreed on their respective responsibilities. Sheridan would be in charge of the bookwork and visit Port Moresby every two weeks while Lucy would run the day-to-day life on the island, supervising the locals who were now steadily growing in number. Sheridan would go to Darwin to give birth to the child so he or she would be documented as an Australian citizen. It was agreed to get Passports as a backup in case something untoward happened and they had to flee the island by boat to the Australian mainland.

That same afternoon Lucy showed Sheridan the hidden treasure cave. This time, even Lucy who had a quick look a few weeks earlier, was amazed. Sheridan found the Nazi emblem on some of the gold bars, cementing the view held that the original owner of the island was a Nazi of high order and they knew what lay before them were spoils of war. They agreed as a precaution to move some of the bars to a more isolated spot further from the village with only themselves being aware of the location. Looking back at the cliff face behind them as they left the cave they noticed several little caves higher up and determined they'd explore those at a later date.

When they got back to the village it was mid-afternoon and they could see one of the main beach men waiting on the jetty. Nic was coming in as he left. Lucy and Sheridan boarded the dinghy but then suddenly Lucy jumped back out.

"Wait Sheridan, I have to get something first," Lucy told her as she ran to the warehouse, returning with the pistol on her side and shouldering an SKK.

Sheridan grinned. Lucy looked a fierce sight, like a deranged Amazon! They glanced at each other and burst out laughing.

When they broke out of the jungle Nic was waiting at the shack Sheridan lived in and looked extremely confused. Joseph smiled as he saw Lucy approaching with Sheridan at her side.

"What happened here?" Nic asked.

"Some really bad men came and killed several people before burning the houses down," Lucy replied glancing about, "so Mr Kim moved to another island after we killed many of the men."

Nic looked terrified. "Better get gunja and go bloody quick! Maybe they come back!"

"Listen Nic, it's not safe for you to come back here. If they catch you, you'll be killed for sure!" Lucy warned dramatically. "I'll phone and we'll deliver by plane for you to pick up" she informed Nic, who was now looking really worried.

"Sheridan want to come back? I can drop her off at Groote Eylandt," said Nic looking at Sheridan and getting horny at the sight of her.

"No thanks Nic. Mr Kim will take us off tonight, so let's do business and you can get away quickly," Sheridan replied grimly.

As Nic opened a large bag of money Sheridan pondered

on how insignificant this deal was compared to the other transactions she knew of and considered it strange that Mr Kim had allowed Nic to come and go despite deliberately hiding it from the other clients. 'What had been his motive?' she thought.

Now frightened, Nic was confused and flustered and readily agreed. He grabbed the bag of gunja, and as he took his leave, looking pleadingly at Lucy explained, "Joseph in big trouble. Have to hide on boat, he get killed if he goes back to community" and asked "Can he go with you?" as he pointed to a forlorn looking Joseph.

"What did he do?" asked Sheridan sighing.

"Silly bugger fuck another woman and her husband big boss, kill him for bloody sure," Nic replied.

"He must take after you then Nic, shoving your dick in every fanny you can find. Oh, and another thing, when can I expect my money back?" confronted Sheridan. She was a changed woman now that she had power and money.

"Shit! How about one thousand each time we buy off you. What about Joseph?" he whined.

Lucy knew that as far as the money was concerned it was useless. Maybe over time he would repay it but did it really matter? As for Joseph, he was a good-looking young chap and she had got on well with him on the initial trip. She thought of the lonely young women and turning to him said, "Joseph we will be moving a long way away and you won't be able to go home."

"No problem Lucy, if I can stay with you that is good," Joseph replied smiling.

"Okay then Nic. You had better go now, big problems

and killing here soon if you stay," warned Lucy. Nic needed no reminding and he soon pushed off. They watched the dilapidated yacht leave and Joseph looked relieved as he saw them disappear over the horizon. Lucy and Sheridan smiled knowing he would never want to return.

As they stood gazing after Nic themselves, Sheridan looked at Lucy. "Mum, I have it worked out. Nic was a way off the island so if all else failed for Mr Kim he knew Nic was good at navigating The Gulf and would be able to land Mr Kim and all his money anywhere in The Gulf. From there he could make his way to Darwin to a little nest egg of real estate as a last resort. Cunning old bugger, he had most bases covered but in the finish it was an unexpected source that ended his life," said Sheridan looking pensive.

"Ok Joseph! You come with us and the others will stay here. We'll send one of the boats back with building material in the morning," Lucy informed Joseph and the islanders.

Joseph looked perplexed. "Come on Joseph, you're safe. Look after us and we'll take care of you my boy. As for your wandering dick, I am sure we can keep you fully occupied," said Lucy as he followed them into the jungle. He was a little uncertain but kept close to Lucy who still looked menacing with her pistol and rifle.

Chapter Fourteen

As they broke out onto the lagoon Lucy watched Joseph's face. She smiled as she saw his mouth open in astonishment. It hit home that she now wielded power over other people's lives but promised herself not to use it in any detrimental way on those who lived under her wing. Mr Kim had looked after those who relied on him and he had done it decently. Having seen the living conditions of the Aboriginals and Islanders she began to understand the great divide separating the two cultures. The Islanders surrounding her new home had no government support or income at all, while the Australian Aboriginals had everything provided from birth until death. They were now well and truly a dependent society with Australian workers providing all the services.

Lucy was so glad to be home when they landed at the jetty. She escorted Joseph to the living quarters aware he was unused to any discipline or work, a person with a completely different culture to the subsistence lifestyle of the Islanders. Lucy told Tom to start loading the boats with the building material the following morning and to show Joseph the fishing boat. From here on he was to catch fish for the settlement and help in the garden.

Lucy noticed Joseph looking at the two young women who smiled coyly at him. She knew he was a fine looking young man and that nature would soon take its course but Aboriginal law still prevailed and Joseph knew he would suffer badly if caught with those women, hence his decision to hide on the yacht.

The next few days were idyllic as they settled back into the routine Mr Kim had long ago established. It surprised Lucy how quickly human nature returned to normal despite upheavals but knew for her, one more trip had to be made. How she missed Lyndon's intimacy and company. 'One more hurdle to overcome!' she thought as she went about her daily tasks.

On the Sunday, Lucy was at the beach settlement selecting two new sites for the houses that were to replace the ones burnt in the 'incident', as it was referred to. She had decided to build on stilts and fit floors into them instead of having dirt or sand floors as in the older buildings, and to have larger verandahs for extra shade during the heat of the day. Missy Pluey's father and brother turned out to be keen workers as did Joseph who appeared to join in the island activities with great enthusiasm. He was now well fed and Lucy assumed, sexually satisfied from the attention he was getting. Even so they decided to keep an eye on Joseph for the time being just in case he started telling locals about the 'sit-down money' his people collected. They did not want dissatisfaction amongst the workers.

Around mid-afternoon she was surprised to see one of her seaplanes doing a slow circle before coming in over their heads and dropping out of sight as it rapidly descended onto the inland lagoon. Lucy smiled. Hans seemed more than keen to once again meet Sheridan, even though she was pregnant with another man's child. However, since leaving her old life, absolutely nothing would surprise

Lucy again. 'Be prepared for the unexpected', she thought.

Finishing up, she told Joseph that it was time to return home. Although the others had the two new vessels they seized as the spoils of war from the 'incident' to return in if they wanted to, they were all keen to remain and camp overnight. They wanted to get the job completed as soon as possible. Over the next few days several other loads of material and furnishings were transported. Lucy shook her head at their attitude. With no red tape and no building restrictions the local people, once in possession of the materials needed to erect a dwelling, simply got on with the job.

Lucy looked forward to soaking in a hot bath after such a big day. On their way back she chatted to Joseph, 'a likeable rogue', she thought. She allowed herself to relax and she felt happy with the way things were going. Hopefully for all their sakes, it would continue. Surely Joseph could do no harm and Nic was under the assumption they had moved to another island. 'Steady as she goes!' she mused.

Hans and Sheridan were already in the large pool and to Lucy's shock, they were both naked! 'What the hell', she thought and took off her clothes and joined them in the warm water. 'Get used to it Lucy', she told herself, 'you're living in a different world now and your previously miserable life is behind you. Unwind and relax.'

"How are you Hans, good flight over?" asked Lucy breaking the silence.

"Always a pleasure flying over the islands as indeed it is flying over North Queensland but my favourite is The

Gulf! It's amazing," said Hans passionately.

"Mum, Hans is a little worried about Joseph. He feels as Mr Kim did, that he could be a little unreliable having been used to government handouts and not the subsistence life of the locals who are just grateful to be cared for and have good housing and food," Sheridan broke in.

"Yes. I must be careful I know but he was good to me coming here so I felt I owed him. Still, let's all be vigilant with our Joseph," Lucy replied nodding.

"Mum, also, I've checked the paperwork associated with Mr Kim's real estate in Darwin and it's all in his name. Unlike in Papua New Guinea where we can change paperwork easily, I suggest we get our Port Moresby legal firm to proceed with the transfers. The letter from Mr Kim will no doubt do the job but Australian law is a little harder. If I have to, I can manufacture documents here to satisfy Port Moresby along with Mr Haan and his contact so I don't really see a problem," said Sheridan.

"Okay. I'll check them out, that's all. I'll be there for a week until Hans picks me back up. Perhaps you can do the Port Moresby run this time. It'll be easier as we now know the drill. I'll get some two-way radios and aerials to set up communication between here and the beach to save time running messages. I think it's safe enough here to do that," Lucy replied.

"Leave that to me if you like Lucy. I can get what you need in Port Moresby and if you like, I can put a discreet tower up on the mountain then we can all keep in contact by radio," suggested Hans.

"That sounds great although Mr Kim dreaded

communication because of the security risk. Here though I can see no problems as long as we keep all conversations natural and don't give any indication of what we are doing illegally," Lucy replied.

"Thanks Lucy, I want to tell you both also that you need not fear me wanting any more than I have now. The plane operation is full-on as you know and all I need is to be able to fly freely. As for money, I have more than I can spend. My wants are few and to be totally honest, Sheridan has given me what all men crave, a relationship. I know it was quick but over here our lives are different and we live every hour to the fullest," said Hans smiling at Sheridan.

"Hans, when we first met I trusted you and nothing has crossed my mind to change it in any way," Lucy replied.

"You are certainly different to Mr Kim," Hans laughed. "He was paranoid to the extreme but all the same Lucy, keep your guard up. I hear Tom is buying his bride on the next trip. I suggest five hundred kina as the bride price and two pigs. I'll buy them on the main island and have them ready."

"Thanks Hans, you're a big help with local customs. The girl was not very pretty I must say, but Tom seems happy," replied Lucy.

"Perhaps a wise move, Mr Kim always tried to keep his troops happy. He would have had something planned but kept putting it off all the time, again because of his deep distrust in letting anyone new in on his paradise. It was strange to me that he even let Nic come here but he obviously had some plan or scheme in mind," said Hans.

"I think it was a last resort escape if all went wrong. He would hide out and go to sea and meet up with Nic if all else failed. I'm sure that in his apartment in Darwin Mum, you'll find money. With that and his rental income he could have lived quietly there if he needed to. I am sure he had no Passport and that's why he entered the way he did, as you will ," Sheridan expressed her views.

"Two velly clebber women!" chuckled Hans.

Lucy got out of the warm water and wrapped herself in a towel then went to her room and packed a few clothes. She had made up her mind to buy more clothing in Darwin during the week and check on her lawyers to see if the divorce proceedings were underway. She also wanted to sell the Troopy. The satellite phone she would leave with Sheridan and they would communicate at six o'clock Darwin time daily. She would buy another sat phone in Darwin and connect it to the same company that was already deducting service fees from her Darwin bank accounts.

Making a last check of her case, Lucy joined the others for dinner. With Hans being so helpful, Lucy felt satisfied and focused on her last hurdle. Once that was accomplished she intended to spend the rest of her life living in paradise, or for as long as 'Lady Luck' would allow.

Daylight saw her and Hans taxiing down to the western end of the lagoon. Hans then turned the plane and gunned the motor. As they sped over the smooth surface of the lagoon, they majestically rose into the sky under Hans's expert guidance. Lucy looked at her paradise disappearing beneath, with the people waving on the jetty looking like ants. She drew a deep breath. It was exhilarating. Looking at Hans smiling, she decided not to tell him that this was her first time in a plane! Another hurdle crossed as she gazed below. She was feeling inspired.

When they landed on the main island, Hans transferred the case to another plane that was waiting and after fuelling he took off once again into the air, making a small circle as he set the course for The Gulf and the Australian mainland. Hans had put headphones on Lucy on take-off and after a couple of hours they started to pick up chatter from other aircraft.

"Must be a funeral at one of the Aboriginal communities, good, that means plenty of activity," said Hans winking.

Lucy looked to her left as Hans flew low and pointed out Groote Eylandt, then Bickerton Island. As they passed over Cape Barrow heading inland he pointed out several airstrips that were near empty and many isolated communities.

"The Walker River strip is only ten kilometres from here," Hans pointed out.

Lucy was amazed at the sheer size of Arnhem Land. Viewing it from the air she could see so much land but no population. All the communities were situated on The Gulf inland but they were empty.

In what seemed no time at all, Hans circled a small airstrip where a vehicle was waiting in the shade of a tree next to a building. Expertly, Hans landed the plane and taxied to the building.

Two men approached with a case. They handed it to

Hans who opened it and checked it before passing three sealed boxes to them. One of the men cut one open with a knife and looking inside, smiled.

"No need to check the others, spot on as usual," he said.

"This is Lucy, Mr Haan's assistant. Can you get the car out for her and start it?" Hans requested, and the younger man immediately ran to the shed. Lucy heard a car start and out backed a Mercedes, dusty but modern.

Parking the car he saluted Lucy and without further conversation they drove off, seemingly anxious to get away from the airstrip.

"Make sure you fill up with fuel on the way back and just follow the track to the main road. Turn right and that will take you to the Stuart Highway. Note the distance from Katherine so you can find the road back in, it can be hard to find as it's an old station road," advised Hans to Lucy. He was keen to get airborne and continue across The Gulf to North Queensland to an island for a rendezvous with another customer.

Lucy watched as Hans turned at the end of the runway, pulled on full power and rose into the air, waving as he flew past. Suddenly she felt lonely and a wave of panic engulfed her. She looked for the track out from the airstrip and luckily dust from the departing men still hung in the air. Already the heat was dancing off the runway as she got into the car which was still running as was thankfully the air-conditioning and she drove off, following the dust.

For over two hours Lucy drove on little better than a bush track, hoping she had a spare in case of a puncture and promising herself to have it checked in Darwin when she got the car washed. Eventually she came to a graded road but it was still corrugated and progress was slow until finally she spotted some traffic! She turned onto the sealed road after setting the instruments to work out the distance from Katherine.

Lucy was amazed how smoothly the luxury vehicle responded when she hit the highway and was surprised when she looked at the speedo to find she was exceeding the speed limit. Glancing in the rear vision mirror in horror, she cursed herself and immediately slowed to the legal limit.

Her heart began to race. 'Would Lyndon be home?' She had phoned to tell him to expect her sometime Monday. Hopefully he would be waiting.

Finally, just on dusk she drove into the familiar driveway. It seemed a lifetime ago since she had left in the Troopy full of expectation and hope venturing into the unknown. She was returning now, a different woman, her life having changed dramatically. She had even killed fellow human beings.

Then she saw him and gasped. He had lost weight and looked gaunt and old. Slamming on the brakes, Lucy jumped out crying and they fell into each other's arms.

Neither spoke. Hand in hand they entered Lyndon's modest home. They sat at the dining table and Lucy saw how he moved awkwardly and with a slight limp.

"Lyndon, you first, tell me what happened, the whole story then I'll tell you my incredible story," she said softly and there was sadness in her voice as she looked lovingly at her one true love.

Lyndon put the jug on and returned to the table. With a deep breath he began, "When I left you which now seems an eternity ago, I realised I truly loved you so proposed. After that I really began to worry about you being on your own and alone and going into wild country. I kept feeling that somehow I had let you down, so basically I phoned the company who had purchased my truck and contract and they agreed to take over upon my return. I then drove day and night to get to you, all the time seeing you looking at me and smiling. It was my own fault but the rest is history, I fell asleep at the wheel. Thank God no one else was hurt and here I am, still recovering. Lucy, I won't blame you if you want out. I am not the man you first met."

Lucy cried and cried. She felt that it was her fault after hearing what Lyndon told her. She had been too busy looking after herself and her greed to return to the man she knew she deeply loved. She hated herself for it and decided to tell him the truth and persuade him to return with her so she could take care of him, forever.

"Lyndon, please, don't blame yourself! It was my fault." Lucy explained, "I'm not the same person you met a few weeks ago and I must ask one thing of you. When I tell you my story, warts and all, you must promise never to tell anyone. I really want you to come with me, to love me and share my new world with me just as I want to love and look after you." Lucy wiped her eyes and waited for his response.

Lyndon had made them a coffee and sat opposite Lucy, listening to the full story of the happenings since they parted all those weeks ago.

When Lucy finished, Lyndon did not hesitate. "Lucy, not to have you or be with you is unthinkable. To remain here in misery on my own is not an option, so the answer is 'yes' but now I need to tell you that I am not the wonderful person you think you know either. I served gaol time for assault years ago and while I don't condone what you do now, I'm not in any position or fit to judge you or anyone else. To be perfectly frank, if I were in your shoes in the position you describe, I would do the same in a blink of an eye," replied Lyndon.

They stood up and held each other tightly. "I promise to look after you and above all else, nurse you back to health. Sheridan and Hans can run the business and we can live the 'quiet life'," sobbed Lucy, with her head against his chest.

When they retired to bed, they made love, not with the wild passion as before, but gently and slowly. They came together several times during the night, desperate to please each other, their bond stronger than ever. Lucy knew she had found her soulmate.

Waking early and laying in the arms of her lover, Lucy felt true contentment. Lyndon woke and smiled at her and she whispered, "Lyndon, it was highly unfair of me to ask you to live my life of crime, so I am offering to give it all up. Sheridan and Hans can have it and we can live here, peacefully."

"Lucy, we would end up fighting and hating each other! I know I'm trying to justify what I'm about to do but the whole bloody world is corrupt, even here in Australia, it's changed. Corruption is rampant, the cost of living for ordinary Australians has skyrocketed and housing is beyond the reach of the working class unless they enslave themselves to the banking system. Seriously, what you now have is a dream and I want to share it with you," said Lyndon pulling her closer to him.

"You've made my day! Honestly. I've been sweating over what your response would be for weeks. I suppose in reality I've been putting it off, but now that it's a deal I need to see the solicitors to check what is going on with my divorce. I also want to inspect the real estate we've acquired and sell the Troopy," said Lucy jubilantly. Now she had Lyndon back in her bed she vowed it would stay that way.

"The Troopy is in the shed where we put it," Lyndon advised.

"Let's leave it there then, we may need it sometime," suggested Lucy bouncing out of bed.

Once again she cleaned up the kitchen and then over breakfast they discussed Lyndon's property. Lucy was surprised when Lyndon suggested they keep it as he suspected the apartment in town could be under surveillance and that Mr Kim might not have been as low key as he had imagined. He also suggested that Sheridan could use it when she was due to give birth. Lucy was impressed.

As they were about to leave to go into town Lyndon's phone rang, it was Roz and Ken wanting to know if Lucy was home and if they would consider selling the Troopy as their vehicle had broken down. Lucy agreed at once, negotiating a good price. They arranged to come out that night and pick it up.

"Gee whiz, some plans do change quickly," Lucy shrugged, 'but we can always buy one again if we need to." The two of them just looked at each other and laughed.

Chapter Fifteen

Their first port of call was to a car wash and Lucy looked proudly at the new car that emerged from under all the dust and grime. They then drove slowly past the property that Mr Kim owned and even Lyndon was impressed. He had certainly chosen well and they decided to check out the apartment on their next trip after it had been transferred. They concluded that with Lucy's bank accounts no one would wonder at her purchases.

Next Lucy paid her lawyers a visit and was informed her 'ex' had accepted her offer and conditions and that the final papers would be completed within the next month. All other instructions had been dealt with. Lucy then went to her bank instructing the teller to draw a bank cheque in the name of Lyndon Savage for one hundred thousand dollars. Lyndon was seated outside when she returned and passing him the cheque she said, "Now, no carrying on, let's pay off your house since we are going to use it, consider it 'ours', the last thing you want to worry about Lyndon, is owing money back here," Lucy told him sternly as he sat shocked and speechless.

"No … Lucy …" he argued "this is not about money! It is only you I want or need, how can I convince you of that?"

"Just go and pay off the bloody house and stop talking about money. We're partners from now on," lectured Lucy.

"Oh God Lucy ….. Kevin the cop wants to see you

....sorry .... I forgot," Lyndon stammered as Kevin, in full uniform, saw them and strolled up.

"Hi Lucy, how are you? Why don't you sit down and tell me what happened?" asked Kevin, "Laurie told me you managed to get on a yacht and were going out to your daughter on an island."

"Yep, one dilapidated, old yacht Kevin. Sheridan was on a small island a little north of the river. We stayed a couple of weeks and then to be frank, the love affair with Nic waned when the reality of her situation sank in after she unfortunately discovered she was pregnant," Lucy responded thinking fast, having been taken off guard.

"Yes, we're in the process of installing a device on the yacht to track it but there's not much we can do if they leave Australian waters. We think they might have a supplier on the Admiralty Islands or thereabouts and if so we'll need to intercept them back in our waters, but I am glad your daughter is out of it," Kevin told her cheerfully.

"Have you informed the New Guinea authorities Kevin? Maybe they can help you out?" asked Lucy.

"Seriously Lucy, it's a waste of time. 'Inept' and 'corrupt' are two reasons that come to mind," answered Kevin.

"Do you blokes know of a Mr Kim, Kevin? Lucy is going to buy some property from him, he has a few units on The Esplanade," broke in Lyndon to Lucy's surprise.

"No, never heard of him. Not surprised though, heaps of Asians have bought over the last few years so we've no way of finding out really if it's dirty money they use or not. I didn't know Lucy had money," Kevin replied enquiringly.

"Quiet one, our Lucy," Lyndon replied, "she sold some property in Tasmania and wants to invest the money. I've even borrowed some from her to pay off my loan."

Lyndon casually showed Kevin the bank cheque and, giving a low whistle he replied, "Bloody hell, you can never pick them! You are a quiet one Lucy, but I suppose there's no need to big time yourself just because you have money."

"Well, money's no good to you without a good partner but now that I have one we'll live at Lyndon's place and travel a fair bit, so guess we'll be seeing you again," said Lucy.

They bade Kevin farewell then Lucy looked at Lyndon, "Cunning bugger, now we know Mr Kim is not known in Darwin. You had me sweating there Lyndon," Lucy felt relieved and glad she had stopped Nic from ever coming back to her island.

"One thing about Kevin, had he known anything, he would have been only too glad to air his knowledge and impart his expertise," laughed Lyndon.

"Honestly you're a bastard, what a corrupt pair we make! I agree, if Mr Kim was a known figure Kevin would certainly have been aware. Let's get some lunch after we pay off your house and then check out the apartment," said Lucy.

While they enjoyed a leisurely lunch, Lucy mused that deep down Lyndon was indeed her soulmate and she was amazed at his cunning but then, thinking about her own transformation in such a short time from downtrodden housewife to drug baron and killer, not much surprised her anymore.

Lucy returned to the vehicle, confident that the key on the key ring was that of Mr Kim's private apartment on the top floor of the luxury complex. They entered the lift and travelled to the top floor and finding the correct number, Lucy tried the key. The door opened. Lucy and Lyndon turned to look at each other in surprise – it had all been so easy.

Stepping inside, they closed the door to find themselves in a most luxurious three-bedroom apartment. Like excited children they ran around inspecting each of the rooms all of which had been furnished in a Chinese theme. Everything was spotless and nothing out of place. Lyndon opened the door of a beautiful, large wardrobe and beckoned Lucy to see that inside it was a small safe.

Sifting through the keys and eventually finding one that fitted the safe, they opened the heavy, metal door and stared in wonder at its contents. It was crammed full of bank notes! Lucy pondered Mr Kim's obsession with storing wealth, yet he and those in his community lived a quiet, simple life. At Lucy's goading, they stuffed their wallets with as much cash as they would hold and returned to the master bedroom, collapsing onto the bed, laughing hysterically.

"Do you really think Lucy, after all this we could ever go back to our old life? You'd be bored in a day and so would I! Never had so much fucken fun in my life!" said Lyndon laughing, "It all sounds so surreal but now knowing that what you say is for real, I cannot wait to see the island."

They turned their heads and looking at each other, hurriedly began to undress. Lucy's arrival and the subsequent events had added a new fire and passion to Lyndon and he rode her like a raging bull, bringing her to an earth-shattering orgasm. They spent the rest of the day and night in bed.

They found the fridge full of food and the cupboards well stocked. Lucy, knowing Mr Kim as she did, expected nothing less. It would be midday the following day when they left the apartment and returned to their vehicle.

Like a man possessed, Lyndon went through his clothes looking for items to take but Lucy suggested they both splurge and buy new clothes. Lyndon was happy with that as most of his clothes were old trucking shorts and shirts nearly all stained with oil. Eagerly they planned a shopping expedition for the next day not only for clothes but also for a new phone.

It was great that evening to meet up with Roz and Ken Baker. They had had some bad luck with their pension and only had a small savings. Unfortunately they had lost a minor court case resulting in them having to sell their home and it appeared the Troopy would be their only possession.

Lucy looked at Lyndon and he knew what she wanted.

"Tell you what we think" Lyndon began, "you can live here rent free if you'd like to and look after the place for us, but we'll pay all the outgoings. Lucy has a unit in town to use when we are home. She tells me too that she wants you to have the Troopy for all your help and friendship."

Roz and Ken were speechless and then Roz burst into tears, releasing her pent-up emotions, not even trying to maintain her dignity. They could finally drop their façades in front of these virtual strangers, now offering them a new life.

The four of them chatted well into the night and, at Lucy and Lyndon's invitation moved in straight away, staggered and delighted at the positive turn of events, vowing to take good care of the property and anything else they may want done during their absence.

Lucy and Lyndon went to bed feeling elated, it was as if everything was falling into place, as if it was meant to be. Aware the property would be in good hands they decided to move into the apartment the following day and to make it their headquarters when in Darwin. Sheridan would also stay there while awaiting the birth of her baby and would now have Roz and Ken as backup. Lucy believed everything was coming together and wished she and Lyndon could return early to the island, knowing the wait would be boring.

The following day they bought their new clothing, mostly shorts and light tops. They also bought a satellite phone and stocked up on enough supplies to last them the final few days in Darwin. Lucy admitted to missing the island immensely and they were both counting down the time to when Hans would pick them up.

Chapter Sixteen

For several days they made love and enjoyed leisurely walks along The Esplanade watching the ships come and go. Their bond grew and grew. Lucy noticed Lyndon's health improving daily, his doctor delighted with his progress and that Lyndon now had a more positive and happy outlook on his future, an excellent pre-requisite for a good recovery from the trauma he had suffered.

One evening after a long walk, they sat on the balcony of the apartment enjoying a glass of wine and Lyndon looked at Lucy smiling, "You know what Lucy? When I left hospital and retuned home I honestly thought I'd never see you again and must confess I became so depressed I even thought about suicide. You see, I'd worked hard all my life but it never really got me that far and for the last two years I'd been treading water so to speak. I was sick of it. Costs had just about made it unrealistic to continue with the business and I'd considered getting an ordinary job but after a life on the road it would have been soul-destroying. Then my Lucy turns up and asks me to go on a big adventure to some island and here we are sitting together, having a wine in a luxury apartment, and you ask me if I want to stay home. Are you kidding? Since you came back I've been on a constant high! Great company, fantastic sex, money I could've only dreamt of and to top it all off, I feel incredibly well!"

Lucy laughed heartily, "I have wondered if in fact there

is someone out there for everyone so when the right one comes along, and for many it is never, perhaps we should throw all caution to the wind and live the dream! Just like Sheridan, shagging Hans and six months pregnant to Nic but neither seems to care."

Since meeting Lyndon she was far more outgoing and particularly after her experience on the island, she had finally emerged from her shell. Lucy was now forthcoming, brimming with confidence and at the stage in her life when any man she met from now on would be on an equal footing.

"Lyndon, you're right," Lucy continued, "money and power changes us all. It's not that good being poor and we must make sure it never happens again. I intend to be like Mr Kim and carefully cover all bases. I honestly believe it'll be far easier with the four of us than it was for Mr Kim being on his own. I admire what he achieved, even if he was shagging seven different women and fathering children to them all!"

On their last night they visited Roz and Ken and were pleasantly surprised to find that the house was sparkling clean and the lawns mown. They were clearly very appreciative of their incredible change of fortune. The four of them had a wonderful evening and as she and Lyndon were leaving Lucy gave Roz and Ken a key to the apartment. They offered to check on it occasionally and to wash and change the sheets ready for their next visit. Lyndon promised to give them plenty of notice so they could stock the cupboards with fresh supplies.

At daylight they left Darwin as the first of the morning

sun streaked across the city. With Lyndon driving Lucy felt more at ease as it was a long, slow drive. They stopped at Katherine for fuel but Lyndon, now enthused, was unable to settle so Lucy took over the driving. She kept a lookout for the turnoff, continually checking the distance, and although it was hard to find she was delighted when she noticed the almost obscure entrance, obviously used only on rare occasions.

Three hours later they pulled up at the deserted airstrip. They placed their luggage on the ground and Lyndon parked and locked the car. Lucy decided it was too risky to leave the keys in the vehicle bearing in mind keys to other real estate and the apartment were on the keying. She failed to understand why Mr Kim had left them in the car despite his meticulous planning but rather thought he would have had a good reason for doing so.

Sitting in the shade of a tree on an old bench seat they heard a car approaching. It was the two men who had met them on their arrival, neither of them that friendly but luckily they recognised Lucy. "Thank God," Lyndon whispered to her, "or we might be dead!" Lucy nodded in agreement, they certainly looked hostile.

Then Lyndon cocked his ears at the same time Lucy heard the approaching plane. Right on cue Hans came in for a smooth landing and, spinning around stopped in front of the shed. The two men approached the plane and passed Hans the case. He unloaded four boxes but this time neither checked the contents. It appears last time had been a 'show' for Lucy, both sides having already done the trade many times before and to cheat or short-change either party was not in either of their best interests. After loading the car the men quickly disappeared.

"Hans, this is Lyndon," introduced Lucy.

"Pleased to meet you Lyndon, we'll talk later. Let's get back in the air, to be on the ground makes us vulnerable. Even though this is isolated, one never knows," replied Hans and, making sure they were both buckled in, helped Lucy into the front passenger seat and then Lyndon into the one in the rear.

With the plane still idling over, he closed the doors, spun it around and applied full power, steadily climbing north over uninhabited country. After some time he turned on the headphones and started chatting.

"Sheridan knew you would bring him back," laughed Hans, "and I for one am glad because when we get back we will talk. I want to abduct your daughter and take her to my island."

Again, Lucy was not surprised and saw no reason why not, all the book work could be done on either island, and she and Lyndon would run the home island, it seemed quite feasible.

"If that is what you both want," Lucy replied, "then that is what will happen. We old folk can keep the home fires burning."

"Literally," laughed Hans and Lyndon, having 'got' the joke, chuckled quietly from the back.

"Hey, not so much of this 'old' stuff young man," laughed Lucy, feeling good to be on her way home to her 'Island Paradise'.

Lucy pointed out all the different landmarks as they

wound their way north. Hans kept low to avoid the only radar he knew of, at Groote Island airport. It hosted large commercial aircraft because of the mines' fly-in fly-out personnel.

Hans informed them he was being a little over cautious but the area had a fair concentration of light aircraft servicing the Aboriginal communities which even owned their own airline, based in Gove. As they talked, one of the planes flew overhead and with that Hans climbed steadily, giving them a magnificent view of The Gulf. Lyndon was intrigued when Hans pointed out Cape Barrow where Lucy's adventure had begun.

"One dedicated mother," he told Lyndon, "and one clebber lady". Lucy explained to Lyndon what 'clebber lady' meant which set them off laughing again. It was such an enjoyable trip.

A few hours later Hans drew their attention to Lucy's island. He told Lyndon that he would return them to the island once they landed and changed planes. He had arranged to stay with Sheridan that night and she was so looking forward to seeing them all. Shortly afterwards, Hans began to descend and lining up the home airstrip he again landed perfectly. They pulled up next to the smaller seaplane and transferred into it so one of his pilots could refuel their plane ready for the following day. Hans had a quick conversation with him and joined them in the smaller seaplane, taking off immediately. Forty minutes later he swooped in low over the main beach and Lucy was surprised to see that both new dwellings had the roofs on and that work was still in progress. It would be dark in half an hour. Hans made another faultless landing and ran up to the jetty where Sheridan and a smiling Joseph waited with several of the women. Everyone was happy to see Missy Lucy home.

Lyndon was the last out and stood quietly on the jetty. "Lucy, you underrated this place. It's unreal! I will die happy here," he said emotionally.

"Hi! You must be the wonderful Lyndon, Mum's true love. I am the awful daughter who caused her so much trouble," beamed Sheridan with outstretched hand.

"My dear girl," Lyndon replied as they hugged, "if I had a daughter who got me into so much trouble, believe me I'd tell her to 'bring it on'!"

Lucy gave all the reception staff a big hug including a smiling Joseph. They loaded up with cases and headed to the main house, everyone talking at once. When they were all inside, Lucy looked at her daughter. She too was glowing with happiness.

"It's lovely to be home and to see everyone so happy, especially Joseph. Why is he so bloody happy?" Lucy asked.

"Mum. He's shagging at least five women! The cheeky bugger is in high demand. We'll have no problems with our Joseph, he is in a state of total bliss with five horny women chasing his services and from what I hear from Moe, he is doing a brilliant job!" answered Sheridan, laughing.

After a light meal of fish, rice and fruit, Lucy guided Lyndon to the pool and slipping out of their clothes, entered the crystal clear water. Later they wrapped themselves in towels and she led him to the bedroom. He just stood still, in shock.

"It's no wonder you wanted to come back here Lucy, you have indeed found paradise and my greatest wish is to spend many happy years here with you," said Lyndon as he sank into the bed, exhausted.

"Now you can see why I was hooked. It is my sanctuary and I do not care if I never go back to Darwin or anywhere else! Sheridan can do those trips while we stay here and live in perfect peace with our islanders," Lucy replied as they entwined themselves in each other's arms. 'Home,' she thought, 'with my Lyndon. My life is now complete.'

As they were drifting off to sleep, Moe crept into the room, naked.

"Ah Moe," Lucy laughed, "you can sleep with Joseph now and tell others to sleep with him too. Missy Lucy has man now, no room!"

Moe looked perplexed but smiled and replied, "Joseph fucky good" as she glided out of the room.

"What the hell was that?" asked Lyndon, he too slightly perplexed but seeing the funny side of things.

"Good question my love. Mr Kim had a different woman every night to 'fucky' and when I arrived they were so regimented they still came to this room on their appointed night, and slept here. I promise nothing ever happened," Lucy giggled.

Lyndon roared with laughter and, curling up to Lucy they both drifted off to sleep.

Chapter Seventeen

Lucy woke rubbing her eyes and noticed Lyndon wasn't beside her. Sitting up she saw him standing at the window, staring at the lagoon and jetty below.

"Come back to bed my love, it's still early," Lucy coaxed.

"Lucy, this really is heaven. Hans is ready to take off and Joseph is out fishing with two of the ladies," Lyndon told her as he walked back to the bed.

Lucy grabbed Lyndon playfully as she heard the plane start and take off. She wanted him badly and set free all of her inhibitions, mounted him, going completely wild! She groaned as she climaxed, falling back onto the bed panting and covered in sweat. In the afterglow of their lovemaking neither spoke. Lucy, knowing she now had time to relax was determined to do just that.

Downstairs, Sheridan sat doing the books. She'd heard the lovemaking upstairs and smiled, 'We both have studs to satisfy our needs and more money than we can ever spend. All because I got horny in Ceduna,' she mused.

Sheridan heard Lucy come downstairs and noticed the sheepish look on her face. Lucy saw Sheridan smiling at her and made sure she got in first, "Sorry Sheridan, I was so happy to be back and with Lyndon that I got a bit carried away this morning."

"Now listen Mum, most women would love to be able to experience what you just enjoyed! Luckily we aren't obliged to live the perceived moral lifestyle bigots expect us to. This is our island and our lives and the outside world can fuck off!" said Sheridan, laughing.

"You're right of course. Take a look at the world! It's in turmoil and I intend to do as I please. Life is so damned short!" replied Lucy passionately.

"In my case, I've worked since leaving school for a shit bunch of conniving solicitors screwing clients for thousands when it wasn't necessary. I'm not trying to justify how we're living our life now, but reality has set in. I spent up to eight hours every business day on a computer to earn an honest living and now, well, Sheridan is getting her rocks off and living the dream! Screw the lot," said Sheridan.

In many ways Lucy agreed with her daughter but in the back of her mind she knew she would never really feel comfortable with her current lifestyle, although until she could think up an alternative she would go with the flow.

Lucy spent the day showing Lyndon around. They inspected the main beach building and were more than happy with the results. Only a few more days and the project would be finished. They met a happy Tom and his new bride as they were transporting the last of the building material to the new houses.

Tom's brother had taken up with Missy Pluey, apparently at the behest of Sheridan! Now everyone on the island was happy and life settled back quickly into a routine. Hans set up radio contact between the beach camp, the main village and his island and Sheridan moved over and joined him a few days later. Lyndon just loved the lifestyle and joined Joseph in his fishing expeditions.

They became good mates.

Lucy didn't leave the island for some months and during that time it was Sheridan who joined Tom on the boat for the trips to Port Moresby. It was only when she went to Darwin for the birth that Lucy again took up the duties and always with Lyndon by her side.

Hans stayed in Darwin for the birth. It was the wet season and some of the airstrip had become unusable so operations were closed down for three months. Sheridan gave birth to a baby girl and they returned to the main island two weeks later. Hans was as proud of the baby as if she were his own. Lyndon was also incredibly proud and regarded the baby as his own grandchild. Sheridan named the baby 'Elise' an old family name, after her great grandmother.

A few weeks later, Lucy took herself off to Port Moresby to see the doctor. She had not been feeling herself for a while but was more surprised than anyone to discover she was pregnant! Lyndon was over the moon and couldn't stop beaming! Lucy was in too much shock to think anything, nearly forty two and pregnant. She thought her pregnancy days were over but when she saw the elation expressed on Lyndon's face, she was more than happy to give him a child of his own.

Not only was Lucy pregnant but several of the island women were too. Sheridan was of the opinion they had all gone sex mad! Lucy was more than happy to see her people happy. Babies made the island more personal and the atmosphere was one of human love and warmth. Lyndon chided Joseph for being such a good bull. He had impregnated two of his women and of course Joseph loved the comments. He was in his element with no talk of being homesick. He had made the island his home.

If it had not been for her pregnancy Lucy and Lyndon might never have left the island. It provided all the necessities of life, simplicity and satisfaction, a lifestyle without the problems that raged in the outside world. They were now cocooned in their own paradise, no one complained and life continued its cycle as it had done on the island for decades.

They often wondered who the original settler had been. They knew he was a German but 'Who was he?' What a difference the island was from the horrors of Europe during the Second World War.

It appeared from what papers were left on the island that the original owner had not kept any documents. It must have been Mr Kim who started the drug empire. Whoever the original builder and settler was he obviously wanted to keep his identity and whereabouts absolutely secret.

On one of his excursions, Hans while trekking the sheer cliff face looking for a suitable place to inconspicuously place a radio mast, came across a mind-blowing discovery. An enormous cache of explosives was stored in an underground bunker and either the original owner or Mr Kim had carried out a large amount of works over the archway that hid and covered the entrance to the lagoon, evidently in readiness to blow it up if ever the need arose. Lucy and the others had often discussed the matter but agreed the explosives were so old and unstable that to try to move them could prove disastrous.

It was with much sadness that Lucy and Lyndon looked back out of the seaplane as they left on the journey to Darwin for the impending birth of their child. Even the thought of spending a few weeks away was disturbing to them as they were so entrenched in their paradise. So used were they to the peace of their new lifestyle they dreaded the traffic and problems of the 'real' world. Although the island had radio neither listened to it, to them the murder and mayhem happening outside their island seemed surreal and so far away. They both wanted to block out old memories of their past lives. Here was where they lived now and they were happy in their perfect isolation.

They arrived in Darwin exhausted after a long flight and then the drive. Having driven long distances all his working life, Lyndon just shook his head at the amount of traffic and noise. Happy to admit he had succumbed to island life and to no cars.

After settling into the apartment Lucy showered while Lyndon cooked a small meal, grateful that Roz and Ken had stocked the place with some food. For the next few weeks they only left the apartment for grocery shopping and to visit Ken and Roz who had moved into Lyndon's place. Appreciative of not having to pay rent, the pair had painted most of the house inside and replaced all the curtains. Lyndon was delighted at how they had changed the place, it looked immaculate!

Lucy gave birth to a son. When the infant was only one week old they returned to their island home and almost wept when they landed. This was far more than a mere home. Standing on the jetty gazing at the mountain backdrop and lagoon, Lucy looked up at Lyndon, "I've made up my mind what to call our son, if you agree," she announced quietly.

"I'm so happy to have a child of my own Lucy, you can call him what you like," Lyndon replied holding his son close to him.

"Liam," she said, "my 'Liam' died so young and so far from home, doing what he thought was right, now his namesake can live on in paradise."

Lyndon smiled, "Good choice Lucy, what a remarkable thought. I totally agree, how about 'Liam Walsh Savage' in memory also of his parents, your benefactors?" Lucy smiled back thinking 'Lyndon was every woman's dream - kind, honest and caring.'

Several people ran from the house and village, all chatting and waving their arms with excitement! They had missed Lucy, she was their guiding light. Her presence meant stability and the continuance of a system long developed that worked well. When she was absent the islanders felt vulnerable. Even Lucy knew that if she were to ever leave the system would disintegrate.

Lyndon completely recovered. His healthy living and eating, combined with an active lifestyle, had worked wonders. Contentment and happiness with his family and surrounds had allowed his body to rebuild itself to its former glory, far beyond what traditional medicine could have offered. Moe helped Lucy with baby Liam as she went about her daily routine and the child grew into a happy, well-balanced toddler playing with his fellow island children along with his Aunty Elise, an olive-skinned beauty, who like Liam had never had modern-day toys or phones but simply played on the beach, in the gardens and fed the animals. Lucy often had a dread that one day, for some reason, their perfect existence would end abruptly and so kept everyone on alert for any impending danger.

Lucy visited the front beach weekly, checking on members of the island community who took turns in having a break from the home routine. Although they now had radio contact with the main village Lucy intended to always check in person wanting those living on the beach camp to remain alert by never being quite sure when she would suddenly pay them a visit. Joseph loved the break because he did not have to do much work and apart from the constant visiting yachts now sailing the area, all stayed quiet and calm.

Four years passed. The only small changes were that of Mr Lynch retiring and his daughter taking over, cutting ties with Nic and finding another customer from The Gulf. Buyers continued to pick up at the same airstrip as before.

Hans bought another plane, a much more powerful one capable of carrying a bigger load with more safety instruments and offered a longer range. Port Moresby became more violent and law and order collapsed. Lucy and Lyndon were in no doubt this was in their favour as there was little chance of any interference from local authorities – as long as they 'greased the right hands'.

Chapter Eighteen

It had become a regular event for Hans and Sheridan to arrive at least once a week to enjoy a meal and discuss business. Of late though Lucy had begun to lose interest and was far more focused on pottering around with Lyndon and their son, revelling in the tranquil lifestyle.

After lunch, as they sat on the deck enjoying the light breeze and watching the dark clouds build up to the west as a storm rolled in, Sheridan turned to her mother, "Mum, Hans and I have some news and I think now is the time to discuss something with you both."

Lucy looked alarmed, "Nothing wrong I hope?" she queried.

"No Lucy," Hans replied, "great news actually. We're going to have a baby, but there is something else I would like to talk over with you," he added.

Lucy and Lyndon were thrilled with the news and hugging her daughter Lucy said, "That is good news Hans but what is it you want to discuss?"

"Lucy, what we have here or rather what you have here is the idyllic lifestyle but we must never forget the trade we are involved in. Do we really want our children to grow up and become drug dealers and outlaws? For me I am stateless, although I do now hold a German Passport with Sheridan's help and by having greased the hands of the authorities. I would like our children to grow up normally. While we ourselves enjoy our lives, should we impose it on the young members of our family? Nothing lasts forever. We've been so lucky but the world is now different from when this island was set up. We've checked and there is no record of any ownership existing for this place. If the Government of New Guinea ever realise the true status of this island we would lose it immediately," Hans warned.

Lucy and Lyndon looked at each other. Never ever dreaming of leaving their paradise Lucy burst into tears, "What do you suggest Hans? We are so happy here."

"Mum, it's an illusion, an unsustainable dream which potentially could turn into a nightmare at any time! We don't plan to just pack up and leave. We must also think about the islanders when considering our own future. What we've planned, if you agree, would take us at least two years or more to put in place. We're simply making a 'Plan B'," explained Sheridan.

"Lucy and Lyndon, my status has changed. I came to this part of the world on an adventure and like you I fell for the illusion of this lifestyle. I always wanted to fly and dreamt of my own airline, especially in this part of the world. Mr Kim made my dreams come true but now I want to marry Sheridan and raise my family as a normal person. Every day I risk my life flying into airstrips meeting in many cases the scum of the earth. Over the years they too have even changed and we now deal with unsavoury characters only one of whom seems to be a decent human being. The rest as you are fully aware, would kill us in a minute if it suited them," Hans replied.

Lucy gulped and reality gripped her, "Oh my God, I am

so sorry Hans I never realised. I suppose I didn't want to admit it but deep down I've had a feeling that one day all this would go. I have bad dreams of fire rising again on the island and of the killings, but try to ignore them."

"Mum, listen to what I say. It can be done but it'll take some time. Hans suggests we buy a large but isolated cattle station in Australia, hopefully on the coast with our own river and airstrip. We would quit the present trade and live a normal life, mainly for the sake of our children. We would sell all the contents of the cave, empty all the safe deposit boxes in the banks in Port Moresby and somehow legitimise the money then form a company with all four of us having a twenty-five percent holding in the shares," Sheridan told them.

"I suppose it really hasn't much to do with me, but listening to all this Lucy they are absolutely correct and we definitely have to take care of the people here who rely on us all," said Lyndon sombrely.

"Lyndon, I'm sure Lucy agrees that we are all part of this now. To sell the gold will take time if we don't want to arouse suspicion but the Port Moresby Chinese will gladly help for a commission. Even the art can be sold underground but it must be done slowly and methodically and the bank safety deposit boxes need to be emptied over time so as not to alert the bankers," advised Hans. "What about you Hans? How can we make you an Australian Citizen?" asked Lucy.

"Mum, we're going to get married in Port Moresby then Hans, when we form the company and buy property, will apply under the Business Migration Scheme to become an Australian! We can sell the airline as a legitimate enterprise and borrow money overseas ourselves to fund the station. I must emphasise that careful planning is vital so as not to cause any suspicion. Even though you have a few million, which will help Mum, we will not use that or the real estate in Darwin. Look how long it took to transfer the Title Deeds! We are dealing with Australian red tape on this one," said Sheridan.

"You're right," said Lucy, "I'm so sorry for not thinking of that myself, it was selfish of me."

"No! We're all in this together Mum! Hans is getting older and the long hours of flying are taking their toll. Also, on reflection, I most definitely do not want my children to be drug barons. As things stand we would be committing them to a life of crime! Times change Mum and even now I still hear the screams of those killed or injured when we blew up the buildings on the beach. I simply don't want that for my kids," said Sheridan.

"You had a bit of luck back then Lucy but it may not turn out that way again. I feel that out there one of our clients is looking into us at this very moment and that our luck might not last for much longer." said Hans, adding, "My life has changed too. Now I have Sheridan and soon, two kids to think of."

"Okay, it seems we can continue for some time at least but let's start Plan B now!" said Lucy.

"Great! We'll form a company in Port Moresby to begin with and commence funding it with an Australian Dollar bank account. When we have sufficient funding in whatever Australian Bank we decide to use, we can form a company in Darwin and transfer funds from the parent company to fund our new purchase. Hans suggests that like here, we set up our own little piece of paradise on the Australian mainland. You and Lyndon can still live here and we think Mr Lynch's daughter, Amanda, will buy our manufacturing base and contacts then move to another island in The Gulf somewhere," said Sheridan.

"It would be risky going into Australian territory," suggested Lyndon.

"Lyndon, do we really care? We will be out of the business with another place to set up. If you want to stay here that's fine but you and Mum will always have a quiet place to come to if something goes wrong," responded Sheridan.

That evening laying in bed and hearing the laughter of Moe and Liam downstairs, Lucy felt shattered. Just the thought of ever leaving here had never crossed her mind. What of the islanders? She could never abandon them. Many had never lived in the harsh world of reality like those on other islands and mainland New Guinea.

Sheridan gave birth to a son some months later and she and Hans married. They made an ideal couple, both free spirits. Hans called his son 'Wolfgang' much to Sheridan's surprise. Like his father, he had blonde hair and blue eyes. Watching Hans look down at his son she knew he had been right all those months ago, to involve innocent children in a world of drug running would be irresponsible.

Over the next year nothing much changed apart from the cave gradually being emptied as the contents were removed and sold, many for a lot less than their real value, disappointing Lucy. Her spirits however were raised when Sheridan pointed out that art now appeared via many channels and was exposed globally, thereby creating a lot of interest. One item they had was worth five million dollars but sold at auction in London for twenty million. The gold was melted and sold on the world market to Chinese buyers who were only too glad to pay cash for the much sought after metal. Even so, it would take two long years to empty the cave of what remained and the bank deposit boxes. As the fortune grew, the company accounts were meticulously looked after by Sheridan who researched all the lawful ways to fund the new company. They all agreed to keep a large amount of paper money in one of the major banks along with the bank investments already held.

The company formed an offshoot in Australia exactly two and a half years after the original decision. It was well-funded, with the intention of purchasing large tracts of rural land. Hans became an Australian Citizen six months later, around the same time Lucy and Lyndon finally married at a registry office in Darwin, watched by their son who was now six years old and ready to start school.

The company bought two initial holdings, one of which was in the Pilbara consisting of one and a half million acres within which there were sixty kilometres of coast and a large river system. It was here they decided they would build, under Lucy's direction, several cottages with modern facilities in case one day they had to abandon the island. Hans sold the airline to Amanda Lynch together with the cooking equipment plus all contacts for supplies and sales, but kept the new plane.

The other property was on the coast north of Cairns. It was a small cattle station with a large airstrip and popular tourist venture. Ken and Roz Baker jumped at the chance to run this property which allowed Lyndon to sell his property south of Darwin. Hans and Sheridan flew the plane to the Pilbara property and settled in, supervising the new buildings and upgrading the property to a show piece.

Lucy, Lyndon and Liam returned to the island. Amanda had promised to fly them to the mainland whenever they wished but now with no seaplane they would have to revert to the old method and go by boat to the main island and the airstrip.

Island life settled down and they found it much easier without the kitchen being operated as a drug manufacturing room. Lyndon and Lucy did their best to educate their son and the island children but knew that one day it would be necessary for them to arrange a proper formal education for Liam.

Chapter Nineteen

Lucy checked her phone for messages. Nothing important, except for one to call Sheridan as Hans wanted to pass on some information. Frowning, Lucy called the station and Sheridan answered, "Hi Mum, how are you, Lyndon and Liam? We're busy and Hans is finding it very frustrating dealing with the bureaucracy after a lifetime of just getting on with it,"

"We're all fine, living the quiet life, usual routine," Lucy replied.

"Mum, Hans reminded me that the car is still at the Katherine airstrip. In all the excitement we forgot about it. I think it should be collected," said Sheridan.

"Yes, agreed! What does he suggest?" Lucy replied, angry with herself as she knew the vehicle was registered now in her name.

"Hans suggests that you pick it up. If you can, hitch a ride down with Henry, one of his old pilots, then take it to Darwin and sell it. I'll pick you up in Port Hedland if you can fly down and Hans will fly you home. Sorry to be a pain but it has to be done," replied Sheridan, "and you may need another battery, it hasn't been driven for six months."

"Fine no worries, I want to see the station anyway. By the sound of it, all's going to plan," said Lucy.

"Yes it is! You'll be surprised. We've spent a fortune but first income is due this week – sold cattle – three trucks left yesterday," announced a thrilled Sheridan.

"Alright, I'll phone from Darwin," Lucy replied and ended the call.

Lucy returned to the main house. Lyndon, Moe and Liam were out in the boat fishing so she walked to the jetty and waited. Although she hated leaving her sanctuary, Lucy knew having left the vehicle at the bush airstrip was a serious oversight, an important detail she had completely forgotten about.

That afternoon she discussed the trip with Lyndon and suggested he and Liam stay on the island. She would carry out the mission in the shortest possible time and return.

Lucy phoned the main island. Henry in fact was flying down on the Tuesday for a drop and Lucy was welcome to join him. She already knew she would have to ferry her boat to the main island as the old seaplane was no longer in service, something she found very annoying. He sounded a little strange on the phone and it made her feel apprehensive about her forthcoming excursion but she was fully aware that to abandon the vehicle could cause major problems.

Lucy hardly slept over the next two days. She knew that age, contentment with her idyllic life and shunning the outside world had mellowed her. 'If only we could live and die peacefully here', she thought to herself wistfully. She was being silly. She knew Hans was right. It was an illusion, a wonderful dream. One day all this would be a memory but in the meantime she planned to enjoy every day here amongst the people who relied on her as they had done in the past on Mr Kim and his German benefactor.

When it was time to say goodbye to Lyndon and Liam, Lucy became terribly upset. It had been months since they had parted and then only for a few days while she went to Port Moresby to close the business. Unfortunately, since the large amounts of money had stopped, their reception had been unfriendly so they just loaded up with supplies and left immediately, travelling home by night. It was decided then to return only when absolutely necessary.

As she stepped onto the jetty, Henry was waiting for her. He told Lucy that there had been a major 'indiscretion' in Darwin and he had fled Australia. Hans had met him in Port Moresby when he came looking for work. He'd been a pilot in Australia but with a Licence having long since expired, he had no choice but to keep flying for the new owner, Amanda Lynch.

Henry helped Lucy load the battery onto the plane and taxied down the runway. Taking off, as he had done hundreds of times before, Lucy noticed he seemed a bit nervous.

"How've you been Henry?" Lucy asked adjusting the headphones, "You seem a little nervous."

"Look Lucy, since you and Hans left the business, although things prospered initially, Amanda has got too bloody greedy. She expanded the business so fast that things have gone haywire! She's even got Nic running stuff again and I suggest when you get to the airstrip, you get out quickly and get going! Three lots now pick up from there and trouble is brewing," warned Henry.

"Really, so what are you going to do?" asked Lucy concerned. Henry had always been steady and reliable.

"To be honest, all the planes are way overdue for service and some are actually unsafe, but I keep this one in reasonable order. When it all goes belly up as it will, can I fly it to your Queensland property and think of something to do from there?" enquired Henry.

Lucy knew Hans had told Henry about the Queensland property, in case of problems disposing of the gold and art, when they were storing it in the hangar ready for transport to Port Moresby and sale by the Chinese agents.

"By all means Henry, but is it really that bad?" asked Lucy, shuddering and breaking out in a cold sweat.

"Worse. I can feel the whole thing blowing up. Be warned Lucy, Nic is in with some really bad arses and he'll try and take over your island with the help of his mates, middle-eastern blokes to whom killing means nothing, they're ruthless," Henry replied seriously.

"Thanks Henry, I'll get rid of the vehicle and pay a quick visit to Hans and Sheridan, then Hans will fly me back. He wants to see you too, perhaps he has something in mind for you," said a worried Lucy.

"Old Hans, despite his drug running, isn't a bad chap. I think he only did it in the early days to keep his dream of flying alive. He always found it a bit distasteful as I did, having to mix with types you don't want to be associated with," Henry replied coming in low over The Gulf, listening to the radio chatter.

"As soon as we land, can you help me change the battery and get going?" asked Lucy.

"No worries, I told the contacts I'd be late in to help you out, so hopefully no one will be at the strip," he replied.

"Thanks Henry, do you have to wait for money?" Lucy asked.

"Yep, as usual, but the boys that are cooking now had a few bad batches and the pricks blame me, so it's a bit hairy to say the least," answered Henry as they skimmed over empty, wild country below.

Henry, as he had done many times before, circled the airstrip. It looked lifeless and empty so he landed. Immediately they went to the vehicle and as soon as Lucy tried it, to her great relief it started. She transferred her case and the spare battery, gave Henry a hug and headed off across the strip, but as she did she noticed a plume of dust rising on the exit track and without even thinking turned onto the strip and raced to the top end, parking under a large tree out of sight.

Shutting the motor, Lucy peered down the strip into the heat haze now dancing off the strip. She recognised two men who were old customers get out of a vehicle and pass Henry a case which she knew would be money. They then loaded the vehicle with boxes but suddenly Lucy looked right and froze as two carloads of men raced onto the strip. Henry, who had not shut off the engine, hit full throttle and tried desperately to get to the end of the strip. He pulled on the power and took off using about a third or less of the usual take-off length.

Lucy almost stopped breathing as shots rang out. Luckily it was from the two pickup men, at the intruders. Eyes wide open, Lucy watched as Henry clipped the top of trees at the end of the runway but miraculously continued to climb into the clear blue sky as automatic gunfire erupted in front of her.

As Lucy continued to watch in horror, old memories returned. The two couriers died in a hail of gunfire so thick that their vehicle was virtually cut to pieces. Then everything went quiet and Lucy heard her heart pounding. Her clothes were wet with sweat and even her head pounded as she watched the scene, her whole body trembling. Casually, the visitors drove up to the bodies, kicking them to make sure they were dead. They loaded the drugs and nonchalantly drove off leaving Lucy listening to the crows calling as they circled in the dead calm. It all happened so quickly, but now it was over!

Lucy sipped on some water, still shaking and disorientated, unsure of what to do next. Although she had once before been involved in a blood thirsty confrontation it had taken place a long time ago when she was much younger. Now she was used to leading a quiet and tranquil life, choosing to not even watch TV, yet before her lay two dead bodies with noisy kites and crows already starting to circle greedily.

'Why did they want to kill Henry?' Lucy wondered. Then it dawned on her, 'Of course! They wanted to take over the business completely, manufacture and all.' If in fact it was Nic who was working with them they could in time make their way to her island, although Nic was under the impression that she had moved to another island.

Lucy skirted the landing strip even though she knew the attackers had left. She decided to wait until dark before exiting the track onto the Stuart Highway in case they returned or stopped on the way out. She also decided not to make a call on her satellite phone. She had been told many times before that calls from this location could now be tracked so she was definitely not going to take any chances.

Coming up behind the old car shed, Lucy was relieved to see that they had not been aware a car was stored there. Looking at the bullet-riddled bodies, Lucy decided to leave them as they were. It would one day turn into a crime scene and any disturbance would leave evidence that someone had witnessed the killing. Very slowly she made her way over to the bodies and using a stick, lifted their pockets open. A notebook was in one of the pockets and as she glanced at it she saw that it contained phone numbers and some names. Her name was not there but Hans was listed at the main island airport. Lucy took possession of the blood-stained notebook wondering why they had become so careless but then, they had been carrying out the same routine for over two decades and obviously had become blasé about it all. Now sadly they had paid the ultimate price for working in the dark trade of which she was a part, she had to confess.

Lucy waited all afternoon. She was too afraid to leave. Then at dusk, when she was certain her dust trail would not be visible, she headed off on the five-hour drive to Darwin. Although having done the trip many times, a wave of uneasiness embraced her as she set off on this, her final trip.

Sweat saturated her and a pounding headache made her even more miserable as she drove through the night. She was so relieved to see the headlights of other vehicles on the highway ahead, flashing in the night sky. Glancing at her watch it was eleven o'clock. If all went well, she'd be in Darwin by one.

Pulling onto the highway she felt a little easier as she recognised NSW number plates on many of the cars. Lucy wondered if the eight men who had arrived at the airstrip were part of the middle-eastern gangs now spreading their tentacles all over Australia. They were ruthless and had no regard to their host country or its people, a far different breed of criminal than the older crime families who had been more discreet. The thought crossed her mind that there must be a reason why they didn't fly themselves or hire cars, but then returning a hired car with the odd bullet hole in it would obviously create suspicion and their credit cards would also leave a monetary trail.

With Roz and Ken having left the Northern Territory no one would have stocked the apartment with food. Lucy was hungry and still had a headache. She spotted a late-night shopping centre and pulled into the carpark. It was good to stretch her legs and grabbing a shopping trolley she strolled amongst the aisles picking out some long-forgotten treats. She stopped immediately, recognising Nic and an Aboriginal woman on the other side of the aisle. They had two young children with them but Nic hadn't noticed her as yet.

Lucy thought quickly. This was her big chance to confront Nic and make sure he had not told his new friends of her old island location.

Walking up behind him she said casually, "Hi Nic, can we have a quick chat?"

A look of utter loathing came over his face and he paled as if he had seen a ghost. "Sure Lucy, sure," he replied, and talking in his language to the woman and children, they scampered off. Lucy noticed the supermarket was almost empty, so this was an ideal opportunity.

"Now listen Nic, don't bullshit me. I know you're in with some rather loathsome types these days and if by chance they ever come to our old island, we'll know that it was you who guided them there or told them about it. Mr Kim will have you killed within a day of that happening. Do you understand?" Lucy was tired and angry but looked him squarely in the face.

"I'd .. never do .. nothing like that," stammered Nic.

"For your sake I hope so Nic because if you do, I promise the next time I see you, you'll be dead," Lucy spat in her most toxic voice.

"Promise, Lucy! Those blokes no good. I'm trying to get away from them," Nic replied shaking.

"You are out of your depth Nic. Get away from them or they'll destroy you. You mean nothing to them apart from information and they'll kill you as soon as they have no more use for you. Go back to Numbulwar and live comfortably on your government money Nic, as soon as possible," replied Lucy, actually feeling sorry for him. He was visibly trembling and sweating profusely. Nic was really rattled.

"I'll go now Lucy, this big problem for sure. I leave tonight," Nic replied shuffling off, appearing defeated and frightened.

Lucy paid for her items and as she was leaving noticed

Nic loading one of his women and kids into a Landcruiser. As he sped off hastily she heard him yelling at the woman who was remonstrating with him, 'no doubt about the sudden decision to leave Darwin', thought Lucy.

Locking the vehicle Lucy went to her apartment but after placing the food in the fridge and cupboards decided she only wanted a glass of water. She fell into bed and was asleep as soon as her head hit the pillow.

She awoke at ten o'clock the next morning, shocked at having slept so late. While making herself some breakfast she phoned the travel agent and was livid with herself for not booking earlier. Due to the mining boom there were no seats available for six days. Hanging up, she considered her situation.

It was vital that she discussed the events of the last few days with Hans. She also had never seen the station and as it would possibly be her new home sooner rather than later, she would have to drive down. Then out of the blue she had a thought.

Phoning Hans she relayed some but not all of the news, telling him it was necessary that they meet up. Without hesitation he told her he would leave within the hour and fly to Darwin. If needed, he would then return her home. No mention was made of the island or anything else.

Lucy then called Lyndon and avoided telling him what had actually taken place. She said all was fine and that there was a possibility she would be home early. Without trying to alarm him, she suggested he keep his guard up as a lot of air and boat traffic had been seen moving in and out of The Gulf.

Lucy showered and changed, then returned to lay on the bed. Having lived so long in isolation, she found the traffic and crowds of people draining. She had become a virtual hermit at home along with her small group of islanders and family.

To her surprise it was dark when she woke to gentle tapping on the door. Switching on the light she saw that it was midnight. Hans and Sheridan were at the door and they looked worried. The three sat at a table and Lucy passed Hans the notebook, telling him what had taken place since leaving the island.

"Lucy, I always suspected that someday this would happen. Amanda Lynch was a bad choice but at the time her father was the one we dealt with. She's spoiled and unreliable. God only knows who she's told and my guess is that the Australian authorities possibly know more than we give them credit for. With this turf war now underway, anything can happen," Hans told them gravely.

"What do you suggest?" asked Lucy, frowning.

"To always expect the unexpected. I thought we'd cleaned up behind us rather well but this notebook indicates that might not be the case," replied Hans deep in thought.

"Mum, all our Australian business enterprises are legitimate and beyond scrutiny by any authority. We just have to ensure we left no tracks in New Guinea," said Sheridan.

"We can assume that all the clients thought Mr Kim was still running the business. All accounts have been closed in Port Moresby apart from one at an Australian based bank and that would appear legitimate now. Our companies are above board and pay taxes, so there's not much more we can do," said Hans. Lucy could almost see his thoughts churning over in his head, searching for any mistakes they had made over their two year transition into a fully legal enterprise.

"What about my home on the island?" Lucy asked with pleading eyes.

"Lucy, unfortunately you have no legal right to it. When it was built by the original squatter it was a far different planet to the one we now live on, but perhaps in some ways it's as safe as here," he answered.

"What do you mean?" Lucy shot back.

"We live in a country of politically-correct apologists and they've had it too good for too long. Half the population considers it a right not to work but to be a bunch of whingers and loud-mouthed experts who consider that the small percentage of those who do work and run a business, owe them a living! It's unsustainable and the end must come. Combine this with a militant and corrupt union movement, whose demands make us uncompetitive in the free trade world market, with businesses closing down daily, you can see the future doesn't look too rosy," continued Hans. "Then combine all of that with the Aboriginal population who own twenty-one percent of the nation and demand that the government keeps them in housing and every other service, believe me, it cannot continue on what is now, borrowed money.

"Sorry Mum, Hans has found it a bit frustrating watching the news here, after living so close to Australia where the island people get nothing from the government. It is all a little overwhelming," interrupted Sheridan.

"But Sheridan, the people of Indonesia get nothing from their government either, yet your government gives them thousands of millions of dollars and ships and planes to threaten and bully you with! We are soft and not living in reality but one day soon you'll have to wake up. That's enough from me," argued Hans sighing.

"Hans is absolutely right! I was one of those who sponged off welfare for years simply because I could. The world can be a violent place and we are too complacent. Many people would love to live in a fantasy world and that's why the island would be so hard to give up, it's my sanctuary and the locals are so innocent and beautiful," said Lucy in a whimsical tone.

"I know, I agree, we are becoming a bit paranoid. I don't think Nic'll pass much on now. Let's not panic. Thank goodness Lucy got hold of the notebook! I suggest we go home and show her the station so at least she can be happy knowing she has another option, if needed. After that, I'll fly her back. At least the car is gone but I am sorry for putting you through that Lucy, it was just that we had become so tied up in the station," said Hans.

"No problem. It's good though that you didn't land there with Sheridan to pick up the vehicle! Heaven knows how long they'd been waiting," said Lucy.

Hans jumped to his feet, "Right! Let's sleep here till daylight and we'll fly south for a couple of days. You have to let Lyndon know and warn him to be vigilant and get Tom to keep the boat fuelled, it'll be big enough to get everyone off, if we need to."

Lucy still had a headache so she took a couple of painkillers and went back to bed. The apartment went quiet.

Chapter Twenty

Lucy awoke at daylight. Her mouth was dry and she felt unwell. The harrowing experience of the last few days was taking its toll and all she wanted to do was go home but she knew that she should inspect the station as she and Lyndon were both shareholders.

Hans and Sheridan waited patiently for her while she had breakfast. Lucy decided to lock and leave the vehicle in the space allotted to her in the underground carpark. Hans had a hire vehicle from the airport to transport them back.

Pulling up at the private plane section of the airport, Sheridan handed over the hire car keys and carried out the usual formalities while Hans prepared a flight plan, something he found extremely irritating after years of flying freely without all the formalities. An hour later they walked over to several parked planes sitting on the tarmac. Lucy got a big surprise when they stopped at a new state-of-the-art Piper aircraft. Six seater, low wing! 'Wow,' thought Lucy, 'a great deal more expensive compared to the old, high wing Cessna she was used to!'

"Hans needed a faster, long range plane especially since we have our Queensland property to check on," Sheridan remarked, as they loaded their bags ready for departure.

Lucy did not give the incident much more thought but did wonder about the Queensland bit. As far as she knew, no such visit had taken place, perhaps it was a plan for the future.

Once airborne they climbed to an altitude Lucy had never been before and then they settled into the flight. Looking out of the window, her eyes wandered over the vast distance she had travelled so many years before. It now felt like a dream. If it were not for Sheridan she would still be living a mundane, unhappy and unfulfilled life in Tasmania.

Lucy tried to relax and closed her eyes, hoping that sleep would not elude her as it had been doing since she'd left the island. Her most recent traumatic incident had left her drained but she knew that it was all 'part of the territory' and lifestyle.

When they finally came in for a landing, Lucy stared at the large number of buildings surrounding an enormous homestead. Two helicopters sat in a new hangar, the runway was sealed and in perfect condition, with lighting lining each side for night landing.

Alighting from the plane Sheridan said, "We'll take you to the main house Mum and let you rest. In the morning I'll show you around. We've upgraded the property hoping to earn a bigger income from the tourist infrastructure which is nearly completed."

Lucy happily agreed. She was very tired and her legs shaky after the long flight. As they approached the main homestead Lucy gasped! It was a mansion, far bigger than her island home, and it sat on the banks high above the river below.

They entered the huge hallway, the walls of which were all adorned with superb pieces of art! Lucy stared at the pieces and recognised them from the cave but she was so tired she decided it was not worth commenting on. 'They must have decided to keep a few pieces,' she thought.

When she was shown her room, she went straight to bed and was sound asleep when Sheridan and the children brought up her evening meal. They quietly placed it on the bedside table and tiptoed out, turning off the lights as they left.

Lucy woke up during the night and made her way to the luxurious ensuite. Seated on the toilet, she tried to make sense of the last few days. 'What's really happening? Does my take on the reality of life need a bit of a shakeup?' she thought. Although large, her island home seemed to have a different ambience. This was opulence for opulence sake. 'Why would they build this if they wanted to blend into Australian society?' she pondered. Even though they were isolated here, word of such grandness would spread, and if the press ever got wind of it they would soon pay a visit. Lucy went back to bed.

In the morning having showered and dressed she felt a bit better and was most inquisitive to learn what she and Lyndon were part owners of.

Lucy met Sheridan and the two children downstairs and she was surprised to see how big Elise had grown, but then remembered her own son was nearly seven! The last few years had flown by.

"Have some breakfast Mum and I'll show you around. What do you think of the house?" Sheridan asked.

"It's certainly far bigger than I visualized! Why so big?" enquired Lucy in response.

"Come on Mum. We agreed to build another community remember? It's for you, Lyndon and Liam also. We want you to be happy if you ever need to come back to the mainland," Sheridan explained.

Lucy smiled, "Sorry, it's just way more opulent than I ever imagined."

"The nanny will look after the children. I think today they're horse riding. We'll look over the place together, Hans went to work some time ago," said Sheridan.

"Nanny, where did she come from?" asked Lucy shrilly.

"This one is from France, a backpacker. Unfortunately we don't have Moe here," laughed Sheridan lightly.

Lucy smiled. Things are certainly contrary to the norm here, and they are supposed to be building a new empire. I'd better get used to it as I did with life on the island in the early days. Better not judge too harshly, after all it is only a very different lifestyle.

Lucy sat, looking in wonder and admiration. Two rows of villas had been built surrounded by a tropical-style garden. Water misted over the manicured lawns, which she later learned were maintained by backpackers. Down by the river, several tourists waited to be loaded into boats to go fishing. Further from the main area, large new cattle yards and facilities had been erected. The place was a hive of activity. It was a beautiful and luxurious resort with large barbecue areas dotted around the villas. There was a large swimming pool in the middle together with showers and a smaller, sheltered entertainment area. As the tourists were admiring the pool, one of the helicopters took off.

"We offer helicopter flights up the coast and to quiet picnic and fishing spots. We're aiming for the top end of the tourist trade Mum, a real outback station experience but an upmarket one. Hans has loads of other ideas and so its development is ongoing," Sheridan proudly told her mother.

That evening Hans and Sheridan hosted a barbecue for their guests. They both looked resplendent in their rural clothing but for some reason Lucy felt completely out of place and uncomfortable. She sat alone watching the hosts mingle. 'This is not my domain at all,' she thought. She missed her son and Lyndon desperately, along with all the island people she had grown to love.

Seated amongst the guests, who were all trying to outdo each other, boasting about wealth while moaning about the entire government, Lucy thought of all the poor island people living a day-to-day, hand-to-mouth existence without complaint, always smiling and happy.

A part-Aboriginal then appeared and gave a lecture on indigenous people in the area and berated the government for lack of money and everything else. Lucy doubted they had any idea just how lucky they were when only a short distance from their shores, other indigenous people in Indonesia and New Guinea lived without any government subsidies at all! She recalled Hans's words about how "we have built expectations above what as a country, we can maintain".

Quietly leaving the gathering she retired to bed, feeling homesick and lonely. She missed the smiles and happiness of the island people along with Lyndon and Liam. It was at that precise moment Lucy decided to remain on the island until they absolutely had to leave.

Sheridan woke her the following morning. Hans wanted to leave early as he intended to put in a flight plan to their Queensland property then go from there to the main island where he would drop Lucy off and return the following day. Lucy had breakfast with Sheridan while Hans was fuelling the plane. The two children had already left with their nanny, not even bothering to say goodbye to their grandmother. Lucy was disappointed about the whole trip. There had been no mention of business or books but then she had given the job to Sheridan long ago, when they had taken over from Mr Kim.

Lucy said goodbye to her daughter but there was now a distance between them – they had grown apart since she had left the island but Lucy shrugged it off, blaming their hard work in setting up a new life for them all on the station. As the plane rose into the air, Lucy looked back. She was hugely proud of all the work they had done and all that was still underway. It looked a real showpiece of planning from the air, but she did wonder at the cost. Lucy knew they had a fortune when they left New Guinea. 'Still,' she thought, 'I have my inheritance and enough money in Port Moresby to run the island for another decade at least.'

On the trip east, Hans fuelled at Mount Isa and decided to cut inland over The Gulf direct to the main island to drop Lucy off. It was late in the afternoon when they eventually landed. Henry met them with the disturbing news that Amanda Lynch had been murdered and the long established drug trade had halted, but had heard nothing else since the news the previous night. He was so relieved to see that Lucy was alright, having seen her hiding in the bush as he took off that fateful afternoon.

Hans instructed Henry to pack the best plane with anything of value and to follow him to Cape York and down to the North Queensland property. Henry told them he had already burned all files and documents and that the other pilot had left that morning for Port Moresby, terrified of what might happen next.

Tom arrived as they were still talking and at Hans's suggestion Lucy agreed from now on to head straight to Port Moresby for supplies. There would then be no reason to visit the main island again and she could keep a low profile. Hopefully all would quieten down in time.

Lucy watched as the two planes were fuelled with the last of the fuel and packed with any valuable items remaining. She then boarded the boat for the return journey, pleased that Lyndon had decided not come along with Liam, obviously concerned for the child's safety.

They had just lost sight of the main island when both planes flew overhead, Henry dipping his wings in farewell.

Lucy's relief was almost palpable when Tom skilfully entered the lagoon and she stepped onto the wharf, falling into the arms of her loved ones.

That night she called all on the island to a meeting. A decision was made to abandon the village on the main beach and instead build and man a watchtower back in the jungle with a good view of the beach. The local men would change shifts every eight hours while maintaining radio contact on the hour. They decided to pull the houses down and clean up the area as if no one had ever lived there and to use the timber to construct the lookout tower. The islanders were understandably nervous but Lucy was upfront with them, believing they deserved to know the truth. Lyndon and Lucy also believed that it would make them more vigilant, watching for any sign of trouble. Joseph was the most upset as he was now a family man and had no wish to leave the island, surprising them all by declaring he would work non-stop until the work was complete.

The next day two heavily armed boats made the trip to the other side of the island and every member including the younger children worked silently, which was incongruous for such happy, carefree people.

Camping on the beach with two keeping guard, they finished the arduous task in five days. Lyndon and Lucy joined in, stopping only for food and drinks, until total darkness overcame them.

Lucy was the last one to step off the beach and onto the second boat that was leaving. She looked back, satisfied that there were no visible signs of anyone having ever inhabited the island. The watchtower was placed on a rise in the jungle some way back and camouflaged behind a massive tree, yet still allowing the guard to be in a position with binoculars to look out to sea and to the horizon. They had stacked all the iron deep in the jungle, along with furniture and other materials. Too cautious to make a large fire, they knew the ants would eventually dispose of the timber or that it would just rot away.

Joseph proudly volunteered for the first shift! A bed had been placed in the tower for the night staff and Lucy knew that one of Joseph's wives would stay with him to feed him and attend to his needs! She smiled to herself.

The following day a roster was posted on the noticeboard in the main village, which included everyone. Lyndon and Lucy would take their turns accordingly. It was Lyndon who, looking at the radio mast amongst the palms high above the hidden entrance to the lagoon, suggested a tower be manned there also during daylight hours. Lucy agreed. With their drug trade days now over they had a surplus of eager workers but 'were they being paranoid' she wondered. 'With the spate of recent shocking events however, including the murder of Amanda, perhaps it was best that they err on the side of caution?' Lyndon and some of the men built the lookout. It wasn't a big task as it sat on the ground amongst the foliage. Tom and Lyndon then went out to sea in one of the boats and came back satisfied, the lookout was superbly hidden. Now, with two lookouts and radio contact, they all experienced a real sense of security.

Lucy was surprised at the amount of traffic that sailed past the island. They were mainly 'yachties' from a more affluent society. Many retired couples invested in a yacht and wiled away their free time exploring the islands in relative safety. Some disembarked and wandered along the beach and others even camped overnight, nothing abnormal happened and life continued.

Sheridan had left Lucy a message asking her if Henry could move back to the island as he wasn't settling into mainland life. He was a bit of a hermit and had found it hard going since leaving a lifetime of island living.

Since Henry had been a long-serving and loyal pilot, Lucy agreed that he could. Hans dropped him off and no one could have been any happier than Henry when he stepped onto the jetty at the main village.

"Bloody hell Lucy, no wonder you and Lyndon want to stay here! I promise to pull my weight and cause you no grief," said Henry humbly, beaming with happiness as he looked around.

True to his word Henry blended in, becoming a full-time observer. He loved nothing more than to sit looking out to sea on his own, but in time one of the older women moved in with him and they could be seen sitting together peacefully on the lookout.

Lucy and Lyndon decided to keep Liam on the island with them and, along with the other children he 'went to school' several hours a day. They were taught by Lucy from lessons Sheridan sent to Port Moresby, made available to her by the School of the Air. Lucy then downloaded and printed copies for the students.

Life continued peacefully. The trips to Port Moresby became less frequent as the island was now nearly self-sufficient and no one seemed to want to leave. Port Moresby was a lawless and corrupt city and Lucy knew her influence had waned making each trip more worrying as the wretched gang who had supplied security for the boat while it loaded was becoming more demanding and the Chinese were gouging more money for supplies and services. Lucy had begun to store more and more with each trip, just in case it became too difficult. She considered other methods of supply, even going to Darwin and made enquiries about the requirements to undertake such a supply trip so she could determine its feasibility. On their last trip to the bank she'd emptied her safety deposit box and now held all the cash in her safe in their bedroom. The trip back to the boat had been hair-raising. If anyone had known of the large supply of cash in the large suitcase their lives would have been in terrible danger.

Chapter Twenty-One

Lucy and Lyndon sat on the deck of their home enjoying the sunset disappearing over the rim of the mountain range hiding the tranquil lagoon below. Henry had finished his duties up on the lookout and was making his way across the lagoon. He was so content to sit there all day on his own or with his woman that Lucy did sometimes wonder about his past. She respected his privacy however and knew that if he wanted her to know, he would tell her.

They watched as Liam and two island boys helped tie up the runabout and assist Henry and one of the older women from the boat. After a day's work, they would sit and talk about anything and everything.

"I wonder if we've done the right thing by our son Lucy. Perhaps we should think of introducing him to the outside world. Sheridan believes he should go to private school in Perth with her kids," said Lyndon casually.

"Strange you should say that! Last time I was in Port Moresby I looked at buying a satellite dish and TV so the children could learn about the outside world," answered Lucy.

"Good idea! Let's do it! I absolutely agree," Lyndon replied.

"I'm also wondering if we're being paranoid. It's been four years since Amanda was murdered and nothing has happened. Do you think we should ease up on the security a bit?" asked Lucy.

"Look, I have thought about that but it gives us all something to do and keeps the routine. A lack of direction causes discontent and everyone seems happy at the moment to take their turn, so I think we should continue as we are," said Lyndon.

"True," said Lucy nodding, "Mr Kim kept a tight ship and it always worked, it's important to make people feel wanted and useful."

Lucy turned on the satellite phone. It was something she and Sheridan did every night at the same time. Although calls were becoming more infrequent she wanted to keep this routine as they now seemed to be living in different worlds.

The phone rang, it was Sheridan. She gaily announced that she and Hans had sold the Darwin properties as no one used them and so they considered they were not required. They exchanged a few pleasantries and Sheridan hung up.

Lucy turned to Lyndon with a look of shock on her face. "Hans and Sheridan have sold the Darwin properties," she told him.

"What?" cried Lyndon angrily, "and they never consulted you?"

"No, but I suppose it's my fault. I really didn't enquire much about our company's finances," responded Lucy quietly.

"Lucy. It's always been my intention to never interfere but our names are on the company documents as Directors and fifty percent shareholders! To be frank, Hans has no business background and he only ever worked on a percentage for Mr Kim after going broke when his airline venture failed years ago," said Lyndon, who was now gravely concerned.

"Lyndon my love, I have no business background either and would feel useless if I attempt to intervene," said Lucy.

"If it goes belly up, we're responsible for the debt! Honest! I've a few hundred thousand from the sale of my property but you risk millions," said Lyndon.

"That's so strange because luck has been on my side for so long and yet only last week I had a premonition to get my money out of the bank and to hide it," said Lucy.

"Shit old girl, so should I, let's do it," Lyndon replied eagerly.

"No, let's think about this, it would take forever to get it out in cash. Let's go to Port Moresby and talk to some solicitors and to the accountant I was told about. Obviously we can't use the same ones Sheridan and Hans did. I thought of forming an entity of some kind that can't be traced to where we are and to then buy a parcel of land somewhere," suggested Lucy.

Lyndon was not only exasperated but frustrated too, "You know Lucy, one day we might need to leave here and as it stands, we now have nowhere to go if it does all blow up with Hans and Sheridan!" Lucy could see how worried he was.

Lucy went to see Tom and Henry and told them they had to go to Port Moresby the following morning and to prepare the boat. She then packed her bank cards and statements into her handbag. Luckily the same bank she used in Darwin had an office in Port Moresby, as did the one holding Lyndon's savings.

Over dinner that evening, Lyndon looked at Lucy and said seriously, "You know in hindsight, perhaps we should have been more pro-active in the company business.

"Lyndon, I never was a business woman and that is why I was always happy to let Sheridan attend to legal matters for me. At least she had a legal background and some experience having worked in a firm of Solicitors," said Lucy.

"Thinking back, I'm sure Hans saw a wonderful opportunity to become a major player in the whole operation through Sheridan. I'm also sure that business-wise, he's rather naive. When he was with Mr Kim he was only running the planes. Mr Kim was the one who handled all the bookwork and he was absolutely meticulous," continued Lyndon, frowning.

"To be honest, money has never meant a great deal to me and these figures mean nothing to me either. All I really ever wanted was to live here in peace with you and Liam. Do you think we've let him down? He is such a child of innocence living here, completely oblivious to the outside, and often cruel, world?" questioned Lucy.

"Have you noticed how he's starting to take an interest in girls? He hangs around with one of Mr Kim's younger daughters all the time," said Lyndon.

"God Lyndon, he's only sixteen!" cried Lucy, her eyes widening.

"Yep Lucy, not far off the age you had Sheridan," Lyndon reminded her sheepishly.

"You're right of course and there's not much we can do about it I suppose but let nature take its course," agreed

Lucy.

Lucy dreaded the forthcoming trip over to Port Moresby. Having been isolated for so long, she was more than content to live out her days in peace on their island. Old Henry too hated leaving even though he knew that at times it was necessary, if only for short periods.

As they had done many times before, Tom skilfully negotiated the exit from their hidden paradise and opened up the engines for the direct trip to Port Moresby. Even though the vessel was ageing, it had done little work and Lyndon and the other men took great pride in maintaining it in pristine condition.

Arriving at the jetty in Port Moresby, Lucy and Lyndon hailed a taxi. It was a constant worry when travelling in lawless cities such as this with cars and taxis vulnerable to being pulled over and the occupants robbed. Lucy carried her revolver in the bottom of her bag as usual and hoped she would not need to use it.

Keeping their pre-arranged meeting with the bank manager, Lucy and Lyndon entered the office and were seated by a somewhat nervous-looking manager.

"We would like to withdraw as much money as possible from both our accounts," Lucy told him, wanting to get straight down to business so they could return to the island overnight.

"Mr and Mrs Savage, surely as principals of your company you are aware that all your funds were withdrawn and used some time ago," the manager informed them.

"But," Lucy stammered, "those monies were our private

funds."

"Really Mrs Savage," the manager replied, "you must have known when you both signed as guarantors for company loans against your bank deposits, that when the company defaulted the bank had every right to take those funds."

Lyndon, looking in horror at Lucy replied, "But we never signed any such documents."

"Mr Savage, as major company shareholders and directors you are obliged by law to attend company meetings regularly and I find it hard to believe that you are unaware of your company's collapse last month, owing one hundred and twenty million with no assets, apart from one plane which we are at this moment arranging to seize." The manager, unrecognisable now, gone was the grovelling helpful individual with whom she had met so often in the past.

Lyndon got up and pulled Lucy to her feet making ready to leave, "There seems to be nothing more we can do here," he told the 'smiling assassin' sitting behind the desk.

Back in a taxi, Lucy and Lyndon were silent, shocked and gutted. How had this happened? Lucy's body started to shake. Her brow was clammy and sweaty. Surely it was some kind of nightmare! But then she thought, 'why had she had trouble getting in touch with Sheridan over the last few weeks?'

"Lucy, have we any money left in other banks here?" asked Lyndon, snapping her out of her shocked state.

"Yes but not much. I left about fifty thousand in Mr

Haan's bank. Let's go and get that if we can," Lucy replied, shaking uncontrollably as she sorted through her handbag.

Arriving at the bank she was told she could withdraw ten thousand kina at that time but if she wanted more the teller would need to arrange further cash. Lucy withdrew the ten thousand kina and they returned to the boat, paying for the fuel and the gang who had protected the boat. They hurried on board telling Tom and Henry to get underway as soon as possible.

Lucy and Lyndon sat in the galley, their heads pounding. They decided not to tell anyone on the island of the unfortunate state of events. They both knew, with the pool of cash on the island, they now had about one hundred thousand dollars left of a fortune so large neither had ever really known the full extent of its worth. Going forward they must be incredibly careful with what they had left and try to maintain the island and its people for as long as possible, but they knew they would need to come up with a way of making some more money.

Arriving back at the island about three o'clock in the morning, Tom anchored offshore and waited until daylight to enter the narrow entrance. Lucy and Lyndon dozed fitfully, finding it hard to comprehend how they had lost such a huge fortune in less than a decade! They realised the Queensland station was gone also and were angry they had never even been informed of the impending disaster. Sheridan and Hans must have been signing documents on their behalf. Deep down Lucy and Lyndon knew they had been complacent, living their 'peaceful life', trying to avoid any stress at all and that now, reality set in. Their slackness and unwillingness to confront Sheridan or Hans had created a huge mess with possible legal repercussions for them both.

She was nearly sixty but Lucy felt a great deal older and worn out thinking, 'once again we're on the run from the law committing serious offences, simply because we trusted others.'

Lucy sat on the deck watching the sun rise. Her decision so long ago to keep the island paradise she had taken over from Mr Kim had been a costly one. 'In hindsight,' she reflected, 'if only I had taken Sheridan and returned to Lyndon in Darwin, we could have lived happily on his little block and my inheritance would have got us a nice little business, but then,' she considered, 'one can never change yesterday and to live in the past is a complete waste of time! I made decisions based on greed and on my own needs and wants, so will now pay the penalty.'

Lyndon walked over to join her and for the first time she recognised how tired and very old he was looking. 'It's my fault,' she thought, 'all caused by my selfishness.' "Lyndon my love, I am so sorry to have caused you such pain. What have I done to you?" she sobbed, burying her head in her hands.

"Lucy, never ever let me hear you say that again! I've had the best years of my life with you and Liam and honestly, I'd do it all again in a flash old girl! Come on, cheer up! We'll just have to be a bit more self-sufficient," said Lyndon putting his arm around her tightly. The vessel then got underway and they made their way into the hidden entrance as they had done dozens of times before.

Alighting onto the jetty, Lucy felt revived! It was so good to be home in her paradise. Here she felt safe and protected and it was here she knew that she would live and die, hidden from the world.

'Money doesn't bring happiness,' she mused, reflecting on her childhood, 'her parents, dirt-poor farmers, worked hard but they loved each other and she had had a happy childhood.' The thought gave her comfort and she decided to phone Sheridan to tell her she was forgiven and that if they wished, they could come back to the island and join the family.

Switching on the satellite phone Lucy noticed she had a 'message'. It was from Sheridan. "Mum, please forgive us for what we have done. I will explain all. Am on the way by plane and will fly over to let you know when to send Tom to pick us up at old airstrip. Love you."

Lucy smiled. She still loved her daughter and grandchildren, and despite all that had happened they were to be a family again.

Lucy and Lyndon walked hand in hand back to the house. They knew they had to face reality and accept that Hans, Sheridan and the two children were returning to the fold. Liam came out to meet them, skipping along with his girlfriend ready to go fishing.

"Hi Mum and Dad, how was your trip?" he asked cheerfully.

Lucy hugged him, "Fine, now you go and catch us some fish! We are expecting visitors so I don't want to see you both until you have a really good catch!"

Lucy and Lyndon watched them hop into the boat and row out to the reef in the lagoon. They then looked at each other and smiled, each knowing the other's thoughts, 'two children, innocent and in love.' They were both determined to keep it that way.

Lucy began making coffee while Lyndon turned on ABC News 24 but she never finished making it because Lyndon screamed out, "Lucy! Come quickly! God help us, this is unbelievable!"

The news was constant. A German business man and his wife and two children had gone missing in The Gulf of Carpentaria, possibly running out of fuel and ditching into The Gulf. It was believed all four had perished when the plane shattered on impact. Several Aboriginals had witnessed the shocking accident.

Lucy and Lyndon stared at each other. 'So, on top of the devastating trip, now this, I am being punished for all the bad things I have done. I am now paying the ultimate penalty,' thought Lucy, frozen to the spot.

Chapter Twenty-Two

For several days they moped lethargically about the house. No bodies had been found even after an exhaustive search by the authorities. Lucy sensed that all was lost. Then the rumours started about the company crash and that they might have been fleeing to avoid prosecution. Some experts believed they may have had insufficient fuel for the journey they had planned. Then there was news of two other company representatives who had mysteriously disappeared weeks before! Interpol had been alerted as hundreds of millions had been involved.

Lyndon turned off the television, trying to convince Lucy that it was all over and that to watch the speculation and media hysteria would not be in their best interests. "We just have to keep moving forward Lucy,' he kept saying, but they were certainly now trapped on their island home forever.

From that fateful day, Lucy was never the same. She simply went along with the daily routine, as did Lyndon. They chose not to let the others hear about the deaths but instead said they had changed their minds about coming. Only Lucy and Lyndon knew the truth. To tell the others would have been upsetting for them all and maintaining the status quo was more important. The satellite phone was disconnected and fuel was conserved for the boat and to safeguard the life of the engine. Life at the settlement was now the polar opposite to when Mr Kim had been in charge. Simplicity and a subsistence lifestyle, now their way with even the television service being cancelled.

Lucy dared not leave her island again. Interpol now had their names and were on the warpath. Taking a trip to the bank in Port Moresby might even risk them being monitored.

One evening while Lucy was sitting on the jetty, old Henry approached and sat down next to her. For some time they just looked out across the lagoon then Henry began to talk, "Lucy, I want to thank you for letting me return here and live the balance of my life in peace. I don't know what happened to you or Lyndon but something dramatic did, some time ago. I've not said much to you but I wish to tell you that whatever happens in the future, I'll not be leaving here. If you and the others ever leave, I'll detonate the explosives above and die here, on our beautiful, unspoilt island."

"Oh Henry, I'm sorry I never told you what happened but at the time we felt it was the right thing to do but really, you of all people have the right to know," said Lucy. She never turned to look at him but kept her face forward, too ashamed to meet his eyes. Then quietly she relayed all that had taken place since she had come to the island.

Old Henry sat quietly listening, then turned to Lucy and in a solemn voice said, "All of us who came here had some dark secrets to hide, including me. One night, long ago in Sydney, I killed a man in a drunken fight. So you see Lucy, none of us are exactly innocent. Things often happen in life and we act on impulse which impacts on our whole life. Like you, I'm stateless and that's why I want to die here. I've never been so happy and I really wanted you to know. He slowly got up and as he walked past, patted her head gently. Lucy knew then they were both tied by circumstance forever.

Lucy had long ago given up educating the children. She'd lost her will and spirit and often reminisced on her life. Her early days after marriage had been miserable and wasted, except for the birth of Sheridan. She now had a man who genuinely loved her. Thinking about the violence she had endured to keep her lifestyle on the island, Lucy knew deep within her heart that given the very circumstances again, she would have made the same decision. No doubt Sheridan would have too. Their lives since coming to The Gulf had been thrilling and intoxicating and, although she had experienced very highs and lows, the overall rewards far outweighed anything she had envisioned on that momentous day she set out from her home town into the unknown, on a quest to find her daughter.

That night laying in bed, she recounted to Lyndon her talk with Henry. He was not surprised as he had always known Henry 'had a past' and like most in the region was hiding from it. Lyndon thought it unusual though for Henry to have killed a fellow human being, he was the last person he'd consider capable of murder.

Life continued for three more quiet years until one morning, for some odd reason, Lucy woke early. She looked across at Lyndon curled up as usual and knew immediately that he was not breathing . Her tears fell onto his face as she drew herself to him and held him close, his skin still warm. He was her great love! The wonderful man who had helped a younger and far more innocent traveller on a lonely road, what seemed an eternity ago, was now dead. Lyndon Savage, the man who had given up everything to follow her into the unknown, was gone. He'd stuck by her as she followed her crazy dream and had lost everything but cheerfully stayed with her and the son he loved so much, turning his back on society and even becoming a wanted man. He'd committed himself to her for life, without question or hesitation.

Lucy was shattered, as was the rest of the island population. Lyndon was buried that very day in the small cemetery on the rise above the settlement. It was as he was being lowered into the ground and Lucy was staring at the mountain above that a thought came to her, 'Did Sheridan and Hans know about the cave higher up, where all that time ago she and Lyndon had moved much of the gold and treasure to from the main cave? Does it really matter?'

The 'wind beneath her wings' was being covered with earth and her life would never be the same again, her greatest confidante and friend, gone forever. If it wasn't for Liam, her life too would be over.

For several weeks Lucy grieved every day until one night, unable to sleep, she got out of bed and went to the kitchen. As she was fossicking in the cupboard amongst the dwindling supplies for a snack and a drink, Liam entered the room. "You must be like me Mum, a midnight snacker!" he laughed, hugging his mother.

"Yes love, finding it hard to sleep," she replied.

"Listen Mum, I miss Dad too but remember how he always used to say 'life must go on'? Missy is pregnant, so you're going to be a grandmother again!" Liam proudly told her.

Lucy stared at her son. Yes, he was right. Life must go on. She must persevere and make the most of what life she had left. This was yet another turning point in her life! She gave him a hug and then they sat and chatted into the early hours. By the time Lucy went back to bed she had a plan for the next day. She would climb to the cave and see if her thoughts had actually been correct. She tried to remember but nothing came to her. 'Had she imagined telling Sheridan about the cave?' she wondered, 'Why did she think of that at the exact moment Lyndon was being lowered into his grave? Was he trying to tell her something?'

Lucy woke up early, feeling strangely strong and positive. She dressed and quietly slipped away from the village, making her way up the overgrown path. She passed the main cave, home to the treasure which had been moved by Sheridan and Hans to Port Moresby and then disposed of to the Chinese. She found the going really difficult and at times lost the track, struggling to find a way forward. Over the years it had grown over completely in parts and was only visible from the graveyard because of its high position.

Hours later and exhausted, she broke through. Finally she faced the cave entrance all covered with vines and pulling them aside stepped into the cool interior. She was absolutely gobsmacked. Stacked before her were a pile of gold bars and several other items all made of gold! Lucy, knowing from the first sale how the gold prices had gone from a few hundred dollars an ounce to close to two thousand an ounce, fell to her knees, her mind racing. She gingerly picked up a bar and made her way back down the track, more visible now because of her breaking vines and branches on the way up. Her heart was pumping heavily just like in the old days, but careful planning would be needed to sell off this last chance at wealth for her family and the island community.

Chapter Twenty-Three

On her way down Lucy's mind was a whirl of questions for which she had no answers, 'Did Sheridan know, at the time they moved the first lot of gold, of the other and as a precaution left it behind for her mother but withheld the information from Hans?' 'Maybe Sheridan had been concerned about leaving her mother destitute!'

Back at the village Lucy placed the gold bar in her shoulder bag and, after a quick soak in the pool felt revived and went off to find Tom and Henry. She asked them to prepare the boat as she wished to visit Port Moresby and wanted to leave as soon after daybreak as possible. She wondered if Mr Haan was still alive. It had been a few years since she had last met him at the bank. This discovery had rejuvenated her old fighting spirit and she decided she would take Liam with her. He now needed to be made aware of what was happening and to be prepared to take over should anything happen to her. She returned to her room for a quick nap and soon fell asleep.

The next day Lucy and Liam arrived by taxi at the Golden Dragon, the restaurant adjacent to Mr Haan's luxury home and compound. Lucy pressed the buzzer on the gate and asked, "Missy Lucy could speak to Mr Haan?" There was silence and Lucy thought the worst, 'Mr Haan was possibly dead'.

Lucy was about to turn and leave when she spied an old Chinese man being assisted by two young men shuffling towards the gate. He was staring at her and she could see he was pleased, yelling something in Mandarin. Suddenly the gate opened and Mr Haan, with tears in his eyes bowed, "Velly welcome old friend Missy Lucy, so pleased to see you," he said.

"Thank you Mr Haan. This is my son Liam. May we talk in private?" Lucy asked.

"Missy Lucy, always welcome, velly clebber lady! It has been velly long time," said Mr Haan. One of his helpers paid the taxi driver and waved him off as Mr Haan beckoned them into the palatial mansion. With his two assistants they followed him into the meeting room where Lucy had often sat before and after offering them seats, Mr Hann clapped his hands and the helpers disappeared. Only then did he speak.

"Missy Lucy old friend, can I help very much please?" Mr Haan asked. Lucy looked at him. He was an old man now, shrunken and wrinkled but the fire still burnt bright in his twinkling eyes.

"Mr Haan, I have a large amount of gold. Can you help me sell it please?" Lucy came straight to the point, lifting the bar from her bag.

Mr Haan looked wide-eyed and grinned, "Please wait. Number one son will come and we make deal like old times," he replied, clapping his hands again. A young man appeared and he spoke to him in Mandarin quickly. The young man turned and left the room.

During the twenty-minute wait Lucy and Liam sipped tea and enjoyed some light delicacies, bringing back memories to Lucy of past times. Mr Haan exchanged pleasantries avoiding any mention of gold or money.

Finally, a well-dressed, middle-aged man entered the room and bowing, sat down next to his father.

"I am Mr Haan Junior," he said, introducing himself in perfect English, "how can we help you?" he asked.

"Mr Haan, we have two problems. One is, we have gold bars, like the one your father holds, that we need to sell and the second issue is, that we need a legitimate bank account, but unfortunately I am not able to have one in my name," Lucy told him.

"Ah yes Mrs Savage, I heard of your earlier problems some time ago and understand, but in fact your current problems are easily solved," Mr Haan Jnr replied smiling.

"Please explain how you can help," Lucy responded, frowning.

"I am led to believe, and you can correct me if I am wrong, that your son Liam was born in Darwin making him an Australian Citizen by way of birth. Am I right?" Mr Haan Jnr asked.

"Yes, that's right, I'd forgotten that," answered Lucy.

"Then, with your permission, I can open an account in his name with our bank. If you agree, we will buy all your gold at one thousand dollars an ounce, no questions asked. We can even melt down any gold items still in your possession," he explained.

"That is excellent, but the next problem is getting it to you," Lucy replied enthusiastically.

"Ah Missy Lucy, that is not a problem. The gold is going to China anyhow and we can pick it up from your island in my yacht. I passed there some time ago and it seemed abandoned but now I realise the jungle holds

233

secrets," Mr Haan Jnr smiled.

"Okay, can we arrange a pickup in say, ten days' time if that suits? I know I can trust my old friend Mr Haan and, as his son, you too," said Lucy gratefully.

"Ah, you are so right Missy Lucy, we want no problems. Please come to the bank with me and we will open an account for the funds. I take it the account will be in Australian dollars! It can be opened with the proceeds of the bar you have and you can be assured, we will keep to our terms and conditions. We will weigh all gold on delivery so there are no mistakes," said Mr Hann Jnr as he got up from his chair, indicating for them to follow.

"Thank you," said Lucy rising with Liam, both following him to a large vehicle with dark windows. They were then whisked away to the bank Lucy had visited many times before.

In no time at all the account was opened in Liam's name but Mr Haan Jnr recommended Liam allow his mother to be a signatory also and able to operate the account. Liam, although confused and unused to banking practices, readily agreed.

Mr Haan Jnr also recommended that Lucy use her maiden name 'Lucy Jones' to avoid any scrutiny by Australian authorities when and if they needed to transfer money to the Australian mainland.

Lucy was impressed with his knowledge and the matter was dealt with quickly and efficiently. Mr Haan Jnr shook hands when the business came to an end and ordered his driver to return them to the boat. Before they left he asked, "Is this bar all your, let's say 'gold assets' Missy Lucy?"

Lucy thought fast. If he thinks we have further stocks, may be there's less chance of being cheated, so she replied, "No, to be honest, I wish to keep some for a rainy day so we will be doing business again in the future."

Mr Haan Jnr raised an eyebrow and ordered the driver to leave, waving goodbye to his 'valued clients'. Lucy felt good. 'What a difference money makes' she thought! 'Money equals power and I've known both sides of the equation'.

Tom and Henry welcomed them back with open arms as they stepped on board the boat, the engines churning up the water as they got underway. Lucy felt better than she had in a long time and watched Port Moresby disappear behind them. It had been a far better outcome than she'd anticipated. Like his father, Mr Haan Jnr was a polished operator and she knew that like most Chinese, he was honest and efficient when it came to business.

The next day Lucy gathered everyone on the island and arranged for them to load the two boats confiscated after the violent altercation on the main beach.

Lucy organised the retrieval of the gold hidden deep in the jungle, posting enough lookouts on the tower to cover until the Thursday when Mr Haan Jnr was to collect it. She also loaded six bars on the boat as a precaution. Everyone worked diligently but it was an exhausting operation.

Come Thursday morning Lucy, along with Liam, Henry and three of the island men took the inland route via the lagoon to the main beach. They were all pretty nervous when a plane circled high above them and then made several sweeps well out to sea. They had just reached the main beach when Lucy noticed a large yacht anchored offshore and a boat being lowered ready to come ashore.

Watching closely, Lucy felt at ease when she recognised Mr Haan Jnr amongst those on their way to the beach. They stepped ashore with military precision and then a table and two chairs were set up. Lucy and her people walked up to Mr Haan Jnr who was waving and smiling at her.

"I apologise Missy Lucy for perhaps causing you some concern but the plane is mine. I did not wish to have any surprises while we conduct our business," he explained, beckoning her to sit down in a chair next to him.

"Thank you. Yes, it was a bit disconcerting watching the plane circle so close to the island," Lucy replied.

"Let's get the business underway shall we," he suggested to Lucy.

"Of course, Liam will show your men to the gold and they can help carry it from our hiding place," suggested Lucy. As Liam led them away, she noticed a young man setting up scales beside a notebook and pens at the table, ready to record the weight of the gold.

"My father always spoke kindly of you Missy Lucy and if you do not mind, we would like to inform you of some intelligence we have that might concern you," remarked Mr Haan Jnr as the weighing and loading began.

"Is there something I should be aware of Mr Haan?" asked Lucy, frowning.

"I don't wish to alarm you but 'forewarned is forearmed' as we say. Perhaps you are not aware that the original settler here after the war was a high-ranking Nazi. Not a military man, but a banker who fled before the war ended and settled here. In fact on the reef in your tranquil lagoon are the remains of several dead men. He was so determined to keep his secret that all the original crew who assisted him in hiding his fortune here were killed after he had finished with them. A coldblooded killer, he recruited two to assist him in the murders and to hide the trail by bribing them with untold wealth, then when they had carried out the atrocity he killed them too and replaced them with local people and of course, as you are aware, with Mr Kim" he explained, then continued,

"Times have changed Missy Lucy. Now with 'Google Earth' you are no longer hidden from the world, and old rumours do persist. Apparently the main instigator of that shocking day has his son now reining over a far more sophisticated and vicious element, a gang of bikies! In fact, it was at his behest that Amanda Lynch was killed and now I am led to believe that he knows that it wasn't Amanda but a supplier on one of these islands."

"Really," Lucy went cold, "how do you know all this?"

"We Chinese Missy Lucy make our money dealing with people not drugs, or any other illicit trade, but the rewards of such trades are so high that it is in our best interests to stay fully informed of what is going on," Mr Haan Jnr replied, smiling.

"What do you suggest I do now?" Lucy asked, feeling quite shaky.

"I have here for you two Visa Cards, one in your name and the other in your son's name. Visa is a great way to obtain money anywhere and it is almost impossible to keep track of the transactions. These will give you access to what you now have, and that is a small fortune. Perhaps not as great as you once had but enough to keep you both comfortable for the rest of your lives," he replied as he passed her the cards.

"With what you have told us and the information you have, is it safe for us to stay here?" Lucy enquired.

"Not now, certainly and definitely not in the future. My father, a very wise man, suggests you purchase an old estate on the main island for your people, where they can live comfortably in those of the dwellings still remaining that are in good condition, and that you and your son go via The Gulf to the mainland and slip into Australia under your maiden name, as on the Visas and bank accounts," he replied.

"We would need to buy a house but where, and what about my son's wife and child, he would never leave them here?" Lucy replied, frowning.

"No problem. Bring her to Port Moresby so we can get a passport photo of her and the child. For a small fee, we can arrange to have her issued with a Passport and papers so you can apply for Australian Visas for them and then later, citizenship," Mr Haan Jnr explained.

"Goodness, how can I ever thank you? Why do you help me so much, what have I done to deserve this?" asked Lucy.

"That's a very good question Missy Lucy. You see, my father has invested heavily in several large projects in Australia and it was his intention to ask you to, shall we say 'go under cover' and advise him if what he is being told is indeed factual. Nothing too risky or strenuous, and a non-Chinese would raise no suspicion," he answered as he smiled his usual smile.

"So, we'll have to move to Australia, might that not be risky?" Lucy asked.

"My father believes that if you move back to your home state under your old name and live a quiet life, you will be far safer than you are here at this present time. My sister lives in Hobart and we can assist in buying a home in your son's name without attracting the authorities," he replied.

"Once again, it seems your father has thought of everything," remarked a perplexed Lucy.

"My father trusts very few people Missy Lucy but you are one exception. You will be paid handsomely and it will provide both you and your son with an interesting post-island living. Your son is unused to the realities of the real world so this will help both our families. Shall we say, 'a mutual benefit'," he replied as the last of the gold was loaded and the table folded and placed in the boat.

Mr Haan Jnr passed Lucy the final figure for her records and wished her all the best. He suggested she visit Port Moresby at her earliest convenience, but advised in the meantime that she 'stay alert'.

Chapter Twenty-Four

On the way back to the community Lucy decided to confide in Henry. She trusted him explicitly and after hearing all she had to say, he looked at her and laughed.

"Lucy! Did you never wake up to the fact that the Haans and their associates supplied you with the updated recipes for the tablets together with the chemicals needed to make them?' Henry asked, 'Take my word for it, they still supply several other outlets including the bikies, but you can be assured of their discretion. Had they wished, we would have been gone long ago and believe me, we need to take seriously all that he has passed onto you," he added.

"That may be so but for the love of me I cannot fathom what they wish me to do for them," responded Lucy.

"Ah dear Lucy, to thrive in the business of money and power one must have a good information service! Who would suspect an ageing woman and her son and daughter-in-law of spying? The legal profession and the accountants are the least trustworthy. Mr Haan is smart, so is his son, and for whatever reason he has placed you in his stable of confidantes. Do not take the privilege lightly, he is one powerful man" warned Henry.

"Why didn't you tell me all this years ago Henry?" Lucy demanded, rather curtly.

"Lucy, if I told you all I know, you would be even more shocked and surprised! I have flown and lived in the north most of my life and worked out very early on that often silence is the best form of defence and safety," Henry explained.

"Sorry Henry, you're right. That's why I trust you above everyone," Lucy replied.

"Then Lucy, let me confide what I plan as my last deed for you! The day you leave the island I intend to blow out the entrance to our hideaway and burn it to the ground, so no-one will ever own it again," Henry informed her and Lucy knew that he meant every word.

"If I have to leave by all means do so, but first we must move the people. Mr Haan Jnr is buying an old plantation for them on the main island and after what you've told me, we'll move them as soon as possible," said Lucy, recognising her life was about to undergo another dramatic transformation.

"One last thing Lucy, thank your lucky stars that the Haans like you and respect you or we would not have had the warning, so take heed of it. I believe they will let you know if something is about to happen, so we probably have some time. This is the modern world now and even I am aware how exposed we are in it. With all the new technology, nothing is hidden, the old world has gone," said Henry reflecting as they pulled into the jetty.

Lucy knew her son and pretty little daughter-in-law had education enough to read and write, perhaps better than most in proper schools, but they had absolutely no skills to survive in the jungle of the real world. Mr Haan Jnr was astute, and knowing this had offered her a way to keep them occupied and slowly adapt to living in the reality of the modern world. Lucy knew too that over the years she had earned the respect of the Chinese community in Port Moresby and that neither party had ever had any issues with each other, having always honoured every deal they had ever made.

Laying in her bed that night, Lucy thought about her life and the new road she was about to take, another turning point, yet another direction. She loved it here but deep in her heart she understood the time had come to move on and to begin again.

Suddenly she sat up in bed. A thought hit her like a ton of bricks! Liam's wife Missy, as far as she knew had never had a real name, she'd always been known on the island as 'Missy'. She was stunning and loved by everyone but she should have her own name. She would see to that tomorrow!

It also struck her just how fortunate she was having been classed as a confidante and friend of old Mr Haan. She felt a chill as she wondered what her fate would have been if they had thought badly of her! They could have passed on information about the gold to others! She wondered too what her exact duties would be once she was back in Australia? She knew the Chinese believed that you should treat others as you would have them treat you, so of course whatever it was would be covert and certainly not confrontational. 'Okay, relax Lucy!' she told herself, and rolled over and went back to sleep.

The following morning over breakfast they chose a name for 'Missy' and 'Kylie Lucy Savage' evolved! Missy loved it. She now had a full title and Liam was delighted that his wife would have 'proper' documents. They planned to leave for Port Moresby the next day to finalise matters. Liam told his mother to keep his Visa Card in her shoulder bag, money not equating to anything for him due to his upbringing. All paperwork had been done for him and he regarded it as unnecessary compared to the day-to-day goings on in his and his family's life. Lucy smiled rather sadly. 'How are they going to adjust to the outside world?' she thought.

As they left for Port Moresby as planned, Lucy looked back and saw Henry's outline against the sky, he was waving. He'd decided, because of the intelligence they'd received, to remain on the island and man the lookout. Her heart ached because she knew that when the time actually came for them to leave, he would remain. His long-time partner had chosen to spend her remaining days with him, even living in a cave he had prepared, if it became necessary. Henry had tried to re-enter society but failed. Although Lucy understood and respected his decision, at the same time she felt sad, but she knew it's what he wanted. He had been such a loyal and steadfast friend, she would miss him dearly.

Mr Haan had arranged for them to be picked up, so after paying the rascals who guarded the boat she left Tom on board and in charge. Lucy, Liam and Kylie were escorted to the Haan's family compound where frail Mr Haan greeted them warmly. He had an affinity with Lucy and always made her feel especially welcome.

As soon as they were seated tea arrived. While enjoying their tea, Kylie had her photo taken for her Passport. Mr

Haan Jnr then arrived with other documents.

"Missy Lucy, I have taken the liberty of having my sister purchase you a house overlooking the water in Sandy Bay, Hobart. I hope it will feel at least a little like home, with the water view. Now when you arrive, everything will be settled and the Deed will be in your son's name. The key can be collected from my sister, her address is included in the paper work," said Mr Haan Jnr, passing her a file also containing bank statements upon which she noticed was marked the agreed price of the gold, down to the very cent.

"Thank you," said Lucy, "the Chinese make every transaction seem so damn smooth and uncomplicated?"

"Missy Lucy," old Mr Haan then explained, "you will need to travel back via The Gulf so as not to use your Passport. As you did not leave on it last time, I suggest that you do not try to enter on it this time. Your son was born there and so as an Australian citizen he will have no problems. Once you make your way to Hobart he can start getting paperwork in order to obtain a Driver's Licence. Missy Kylie can apply for an Entry Visa later as his wife, then she will need to come back and re-enter. From then on, I foresee no problems."

"Thank you Mr Haan for everything. I hope there is some way I can repay your kindness" Lucy replied.

"Ah Missy Lucy, this will be our last meeting. Long time ago, Mr Kim tell me, 'Missy Lucy one clebber lady' and over the years that has proven to be true. Please do not underestimate yourself Missy Lucy. To survive as you have done for so long, Mr Kim was right. I know you will always tell me the truth and in you, I place my trust. My daughter will provide a list of things you can do for me and my son will give you another Visa Card to be used for costs associated with your work for me. When I pass away I ask that your friendship and loyalty be passed on to my son. May you have a long and healthy life," Mr Haan then bowed politely to Lucy as he left the room.

Lucy sat with a tear in her eye as she watched old Mr Haan being helped by two young men. As he shuffled out of the room she felt a strong surge of emotion. She truly appreciated his genuine affection and respect, so welcome in this volatile and often violent land.

"Missy Lucy, we now take you back to the boat," he said, "I have many things to do. Missy Kylie's paperwork will be ready in a few weeks and one of my pilots will drop it off to you. He will circle the lagoon before he makes the drop so you can pick it up as soon as possible," he added as he escorted them to the door and to a waiting car.

Lucy had such mixed feelings when she looked back at Port Moresby as they made their way towards the harbour for what she knew was the last time, a trip that had become part of her life. Suddenly she felt old again, the past few weeks had been tiring. She now wished only for it to be all over and to be settled into the home in Tasmania. She had come full circle. She missed Lyndon.

On the way back she told Tom, that when the time came, he could keep the boat after he had dropped them off in The Gulf. Lucy told him too of the possible impending trouble and that if there was a next time the visitors would not be so easily overcome. He looked confused and worried. She knew he remembered that fateful night of horror years ago but knew also that he accepted his fate just like the other islanders. It was part of their make-up, they simply accepted whatever happened in life and got on with it. Lucy had arranged for Mr Haan Jnr to keep an eye on the old plantation and soon learned that the island airstrip was back in operation, ironically by a young German who she suspected worked for Mr Haan. 'History repeating itself,' she thought.

They decided to spend the night on the boat as they had arrived back too late to chance the narrow entrance. At daybreak they moved slowly through, and as they neared the jetty Lucy felt a wave of sad emotion engulf her. Coming home had always been a happy time but for some reason her heart was not in it, and she was confused by her feelings. Dark clouds had gathered over the mountain, ominous and threatening. 'Why did they look so foreboding?' she pondered.

The next few days were sad days for Lucy and the islanders. Joseph wanted to go home so when his time came he would die in his own country and he with Henry and his island wife, Liam, Kylie and the baby, left the island. It was heart-wrenching to say goodbye to all those she had shared so much with. Henry's wife wept uncontrollably and had to be helped onto the boat, begging to go with Missy Lucy 'wherever she was going'. The two women, both now sobbing, held each other tightly. At one point Lucy felt like calling it all off but then reality struck. Death could easily follow if they remained, so they had no choice but to leave.

After the boat left and Tom had promised to come back to take them to The Gulf, Lucy went to her room and curled up in bed in the foetal position. She was shattered, crying inconsolably, thinking her heart would break, how could she leave Lyndon? Knowing he had loved the place as much as she did, through her heartache she consoled herself by deciding to have her remains returned and buried here with his. 'This is my greatest wish and I will make sure it happens,' she thought determinedly.

Henry turned the last of the goats and pigs out of the pens, telling Lucy that if he wanted meat he could shoot something later. Most had gone on the boat and only a few remained but they were old stock and of not much value. Henry intended anyway to mainly eat fish and had already with Liam's help transferred the large amount of food still held in store, to the hidden cave.

Lucy packed her personal belongings as did Liam and Kylie. It felt wrong to remove anything else from the island, almost disrespectful, yet Lucy did not want to leave any trace of their existence behind. Her dream of wealth and eternal life in this idyllic place would now vanish but she had been blessed to have been a part of an incredible lifestyle and in any event all they had experienced and learned would go with them.

How quiet the village was. No children's laughter or the sound of the adults working happily in the gardens, away from all the trials and tribulations of the modern world. 'How would her people settle into a life where they had to make their own decisions?' Lucy thought. She worried that they would be manipulated by others without the guidance and protection they had lived with their entire lives. It enveloped her like a dark cloud and Lucy went about her final days on the island in a trance. Her head ached trying to think of an alternative but even she feared the impending disaster. Henry had no need to remind her that Mr Haan Jnr was an intelligent man and he would not have told them that a plan was under way to invade and take control of her island unless it were true.

Chapter Twenty-Five

Lucy woke early the next morning and knowing she had to wait for Kylie's paperwork, hatched a plan to do something that she and Lyndon had discussed many times. After a hearty breakfast she packed some lunch into her shoulder bag and made her way down to the jetty where she found Joseph fishing, his favourite pastime nowadays.

"Joseph, would you like to come for a walk and see if we can find a way through to the main beach? Ever since I first arrived I was told it would be impossible but before we leave I would very much like to see if that's true or not," she asked him.

"No problems Missus," Joseph replied in his casual way and the two set off.

Passing the once beautiful gardens, Lucy knew that everything in life had a time frame and all things must end. 'One day' she thought 'all this will return to the jungle and if Henry closes the entrance, it will be lost forever. That is of course, if no other avenue exists from the main beach!'

Progress was slow as they followed the lagoon as far as possible, then went inland but were blocked by the sheer cliff face. Backtracking, a determined Lucy made her way on the old track to the second cave where she had originally hidden some of the gold. It was now empty and only twenty metres along they hit another vertical cliff face. She turned and looking up, to her surprise noticed a barely visible overgrown path. It was steep but could be climbed. Cautiously the pair wound their way up, clawing through the heavy undergrowth until they noticed that there actually was a track chipped out of the stone face of the cliff. Somebody had gone to a great deal of trouble to make the path, now hidden by thick vegetation and vines. Clinging to the vines they slowly navigated their way, not daring to look down at the vertical drop.

They had to stop every now and then to catch their breath. Sweat dripped from their faces but by this stage Joseph was now so intrigued and keen to find where the track ended he was happy to push on. They eventually reached the summit and cool air rushed in from the sea, crashing against the rock face. Lucy noticed a narrow track which led to a large rock and knew they were at the highest peak of the mountain range on the western side of the island. There was an entrance to a small cave on the side of the rock and as they approached it they were flabbergasted to see a seat at the entrance! As she edged closer Lucy was thrilled to see that from this vantage point the entire island was visible. The main beach, even the tower she had constructed, could be seen clearly and to the west, the lagoon and the village.

Joseph sat down, exhausted but Lucy entered the cave. It was dark inside and it took her eyes some time to adjust. Then she saw them, several carved, rock shelves containing old leather-bound books and photos along with some Nazi medals and other items. Picking up a photo, she went to the entrance and found herself looking at a young man and woman standing next to a smiling Adolf Hitler, of this she was sure. This had all obviously been stored here by the original owner years ago, her heart skipped a beat and where she now stood had most assuredly been used as a lookout in the early days to keep an eye on any approaching boats!

Returning the photo, Lucy had a look through all the other items but there was nothing really of any value. Although one item did capture her interest, an early map of the island with even the entrance marked on it. It was carefully wrapped in a leather pouch and she dropped it into her shoulder bag. Joseph was anxious to begin the descent as it was already past midday and from here the village seemed a long way away. Lucy agreed and, as she was leaving the cave quietly promised to leave the life and times of the person who built the island and had placed the items here, in peace. Whatever his motives, they were now history. Glancing back, her eyes now adjusted to the dim interior, she saw what she thought was a leather bag jammed in a crevice and walking back inside dragged it out from its hiding place. As she did, the rusty catch opened revealing several smaller leather pouches. She opened one and then them all, experiencing a sharp intake of breath. Inside were a myriad of diamonds, still sparkling and glittering even after such a long time.

Joseph was irritated and disinterested in the find so, after cramming the pouches into her bag, they turned to retrace their steps down the long, onerous descent.

It was late in the evening when they finally broke out onto the lagoon beach. The trip had taken its toll on both of them and Lucy immediately went to her room.

Placing the contents of her bag on the bed, she could not believe the small fortune in front of her. She rewrapped the diamonds tightly and placed them back into her carry bag, along with the gold bars she had taken from the boat before Tom left to go to the main island. She then put her revolver on top and hid the bag under her mattress.

Her leg and arm muscles began to cramp so she ran a hot bath and enjoyed a long soak before bed. Her mind was racing. She was sure there were no other hiding places on the island but had a feeling Mr Haan Jnr, probably from information supplied by his father, suspected more treasure had been hidden, either here or on another island by the Nazi banker.

Soaking in the bath, Lucy wondered about the pretty girl in the photo and what had become of her. 'Did she ever make it to the island her husband or lover had discovered?' Before Tom arrived and she left, Lucy would check the graveyard where Lyndon was buried and where she will join him in time. 'Who knows, the 'pretty girl in the photo' may be buried there!

After a restless night Lucy walked to the graveyard, surprised to be joined by Henry. "What are you doing here Henry?" she asked, "Never thought I'd find you here."

"Ah, when my time comes, I hope to lay here with all the others. Can't think of a better place to finish up," Henry replied.

Lucy then told him of her find the day before and pointed up to what now seemed an impenetrable mountain.

"No surprise to me Lucy but keep the diamond find to yourself. The thought of so much money can make people do strange things," he warned.

"I also found a photo of the original builder of the village," she told him, "and he had a girl with him in the photo, plus Hitler himself."

"Come with me Lucy and I'll show you what 'true love' is all about. I'm sure even Hitler would have been impressed," responded Henry, grinning.

Under the canopy of overgrown jungle Henry uncovered two headstones. One was of the man, the other of the woman and on the top of hers was a 'Star of David'. Lucy gazed in awe at what this meant. The 'pretty girl in the photo' was a Jew! It was all now so clear. As the war progressed and to protect his one true love, he had meticulously planned their escape to 'Paradise'. A tear streamed down Lucy's face. This was indeed true love and, despite the horror of war and being so far from home, they now lay together in perfect peace.

Henry turned to her, covering the headstones reverently with the vines.

"Lucy, some things are better left alone. Old Lyndon rests with two remarkable people, well, three really. Mr Kim's remains are here too and he kept the island going all those years until you arrived," Henry uttered solemnly.

"I'm coming back here to be buried next to Lyndon, Henry. It was my last promise to him and my wish is to finally be with Lyndon and with you," Lucy replied, looking down at Lyndon's grave. All her questions had now been answered. It seemed like a fairy-tale but she agreed wholeheartedly with Henry, 'some things are better left alone'.

They returned to the village and spent a quiet afternoon on the lagoon fishing. Lucy knew Henry would never leave here but she knew too that she had to, her time was up. As soon as Tom returned, she and Joseph together with Liam and his family would depart, leaving only Henry and his wife. They would remain until the end. The end of an era, gone forever!

For eight days Lucy waited for the plane to arrive from Port Moresby to make the parcel drop into the lagoon and watched as the pilot then dipped the plane's wings and climbed steadily away. Retrieving the parcel she found Kylie's Passport and other documents, together with a note to say that a large force was leaving Cairns and that Lucy had two days at the most, to leave!

Lucy paced the jetty. 'Why hadn't Tom returned?' she thought, 'he'd always been so reliable! Something must have happened.' Little did she know that the boat had been confiscated by the Island Police, now being bribed by the 'soon-to-be new owners' who had been planning the move over several months, covering all bases by first corrupting the local authorities. They actually had them believe Lucy had long gone and that the islanders had abandoned the island.

Lucy made an immediate decision, to 'escape and now'! Nothing would be gained if they were 'dead', as she knew they would be if it came to a fight, they didn't stand a chance. They began packing everything onto the two boats confiscated years ago but still in reasonable condition. Lucy had ensured the motors were regularly serviced and was now relieved to have done that. They loaded all the fuel they possibly could, plus sleeping equipment, and Lucy told Joseph that they would leave the next morning early. She never slept a wink that night.

With Joseph's help she headed to Groote Eylandt in The Gulf where they would catch a commercial flight to Cairns, then onto Tasmania. Lucy was hoping that with the mine in operation on Groote, they would be inconspicuous and blend in with the fly-in and fly-out miners and locals. Joseph's plan was to then make the five-hour trip from there to his homeland in Numbulwar and face the consequences of his past indiscretions.

As they prepared to finally leave the next morning, Henry was missing. Lucy was so upset and could not understand why after all the years of their friendship, neither he nor his partner came to say goodbye.

Joseph, who knew the way, went in the first boat which housed all the fuel and provisions while Liam and his family with Lucy followed in the second. Winding their way out through the exit Lucy was relieved that the sea looked reasonably calm and as she looked back at the island for one last look, she could not believe her eyes when she saw Henry and his companion against the skyline, waving! Tearfully she stood up and waved back frantically, just as a roar filled her ears and she watched in horror as the side of the mountain exploded, the shock waves hitting the two boats! They watched in disbelief as the cave entrance collapsed in a thunderous crash of rock and tons of soil but what was even more shocking to Lucy was that Henry and his long-time partner had planned to perish in the inferno. They died, waving goodbye to the last of the island occupants . Now Lucy understood why Henry had been at the graveside that day, he was saying his goodbyes! She stood in shock, speechless and numb as she noticed a plume of smoke rising from behind the mountain range. Henry had also set the village alight. Her heart was pounding heavily and she struggled to breathe as the plumes of smoke and dust settled. It was gone. All of it was gone, forever. Henry had closed the final chapter in the history of their paradise, hidden for decades from the outside world. The 'new owners' had been left nothing.

Liam took control of the boat as Lucy, still trembling, settled against the pile of bedding. Deep grief and a heaviness of some kind washed over her as they continued to follow Joseph on the long and tiresome trip ahead. Lucy's heart ached as if a large part of her had died but she still planned to return to be buried with her darling Lyndon and all the ghosts of the island's past. It had been the best part of her life.

She now had to set her son and family up for life in a strange new world, the 'real' world.

Chapter Twenty-Six

The first day went without drama and they reached D'Entrecasteaux Island mid-afternoon. As soon as they disembarked, they organised a makeshift camp. Lucy noticed how everyone appeared quiet, all traumatised by the destruction they had witnessed. Lucy wondered why Henry had been so determined to destroy everything that had been such a big part of her life. Then reality hit her, 'he actually wanted it all gone forever.'

They dragged the boats and equipment into the tree-lined fringes to avoid being seen. Sitting around the campfire Lucy noticed how calm it was and with the gentle lapping of the waves, how peaceful. Once they had fitted a tarpaulin and made their beds no one needed an excuse to sleep, each were emotionally drained and physical shattered.

At midnight Lucy woke to heavy rain and wind. Knowing it was the cyclone season she woke the others, directing them to lash the boats together, anchoring them to palm trees on the highest rise inland from their present position. Even though they were all soaked they managed to construct some sort of a shelter between the two boats and placing their bedding beneath they lay listening to the rising crescendo! Daylight was quiet, the 'eye of the storm'. The beach was littered with rubbish and the trees although not very tall, were broken and bent by the deluge and high winds.

The eye had passed over but Lucy knew that the storm would hit again. She hugged her grandchild close to her as they all partook of some food and then bunkered down between the two boats. Joseph commented that they were lucky it had been a low-grade cyclone but it wasn't long before the wind picked up and howled for many hours.

Everyone huddled beneath the tarpaulin as the storm vented its rage around and above them. It eased by the afternoon but they decided to stay the night and continue the following morning, having fortunately stored plenty of food and water on board. In the evening they all went for a walk along the beach, surprised at the amount of rubbish the storm had deposited on the sand.

At daylight they dragged the two boats down to the shoreline and deciding to lighten the load abandoned some of the bedding and supplies. Joseph said if they had a good run they should arrive at Groote Eylandt later that evening under the cover of darkness and they could catch a plane the following day. Lucy this time went with Joseph to even up the loads and set off, leading the way.

Keeping well out to sea they rounded the Cape mid-morning and encountered a large rolling swell in the wake of the storm. By now Joseph was a good way ahead and as Lucy watched, the second boat rose above a massive wave and to her horror rolled over dislodging Liam, Kylie and her grandchild! Immediately Joseph turned and battled against the mounting waves making his way back to the last sighting of the hapless trio.

Lucy was in a state of hysteria! This could not be happening! First her daughter and family and now her son and his family, both taken from her by The Gulf! She felt cursed. Joseph fought the storming waters for over an hour but the boat had disappeared below the waves. There was not even any visible debris! Eventually, as Lucy lay sobbing on the bottom of the tossing boat, Joseph reluctantly headed off aware his own fuel supply was being used for what was now a hopeless situation.

Lucy allowed the boat to continue tossing her around its floor. 'Had her life been so bad that this was her karma? What did I do wrong?' she asked herself, 'Perhaps we should have stayed and died together in our little piece of paradise.' From here on in she was on her own. All those she loved had gone, forever. 'Maybe I should join them too?' she thought. In the following hours she felt like standing up and throwing herself overboard to join her loved ones in The Gulf. 'Why is it such a beautiful place, yet so unforgiving?' she puzzled, then she saw the brave Joseph seated at the motor, covered in salt spray battling on and remembered that it was his wish to die in his homeland. 'Have I done all of this only to die here and now?' she questioned herself. 'No, I must survive and eventually return to the only place I found happiness, to be with the one man who really loved me just as our son is with the family he loved' she thought in answer to her own question, adding, 'my dream is over but I must, and will, live to join Lyndon, Henry and Mr Kim as I promised.'

Lucy was shaken into reality by Joseph. The waves had subsided a little and he wanted to fill the fuel tank from the last of their fuel cans so she took the controls and watched Joseph empty the cans into the tank and causally throw them overboard, too shaken to even remonstrate at his polluting the water. She moved as if she were a robot, too tired and too heartsore to do anything but go through the motions.

Returning to her position, Lucy succumbed to fatigue. Her head throbbed and she vomited several times. She had lost control of her life. How carefully she had always planned events, particularly since arriving on her island so long ago but everything changed after receiving Mr Haan Jnr's note. Her decisions cost her dearly and she blamed herself for the loss of her family. It was her choice to abandon the island and although she knew Henry's intentions she did not intervene and had therefore allowed it all to happen.

The time seemed to drag by for Lucy. Darkness eventually came and she was pleased Joseph knew The Gulf even in the dark, having navigated these waters as a young man. Then at long last, in the distance she saw twinkling lights of what she guessed was Groote Eylandt. Joseph pulled into a small beach area and then helped Lucy from the boat. She slung her bag over her left shoulder and waited while Joseph tied the boat to a log embedded in the beach.

Joseph carried her small suitcase and they made their way up a small track to a few isolated houses. Dogs barked and Lucy saw a few Aboriginals sitting by a fire. Joseph approached them and after a short conversation beckoned her to come on in to the fire.

"Lucy, my cousin will take you to the airport in the

morning, you can sleep here till then," Joseph told her as he turned and walked away. She felt a pang of guilt as here was her old friend who had no doubt saved her life, walking out of her life without even a farewell. Lucy felt like running after him and hugging him, but before she knew it he was gone into the darkness and out of her life forever.

One of the women came out and escorted her into a room where several others lay. Lucy was guided to a mattress on the floor which she fell onto and was asleep in a matter of minutes.

When Lucy woke the next day, it took her a few minutes to get her head around everything. Remembering the previous day, it was as if someone had kicked her in the guts. Her only consolation was to think that Liam might never have assimilated into the modern world and that now he and his family were at peace. The serene life that he had led was no more. The modern world would have destroyed him and his family. Lucy needed to convince herself of this or go mad with grief!

As she lay in the room with Aboriginal women who did not know her but had so generously welcomed her into their modest sleeping area, Lucy tried to think clearly about what to do next. She needed to go to Tasmania, as she and Mr Haan Jnr had planned, and once there could make other plans.

Lucy changed into clean shorts and a shirt and left her old clothes laying on the floor with heaps of other discarded clothing. She washed outside in a sink and drank a cup of sweet tea provided by an old white-haired lady with no teeth.

One of the Aboriginal men escorted her to an old Landcruiser and she placed her suitcase on the back seat with three happy children all piling in for the drive to the airport. Once at the terminal she got out and grabbed her case as the vehicle was driven off without comment, leaving Lucy standing alone.

Making her way to the counter she was told a plane was leaving for Cairns in one hour and 'yes' it had some spare seats. Lucy handed over the credit card but the clerk looked at Lucy and said, "It's been declined, insufficient funds." Lucy was speechless. Mr Haan Jnr had told her the card had plenty of money and so she began rummaging in her shoulder bag for her purse which thankfully was full of cash. After she paid for the ticket, Lucy sat down, her mind racing. She looked at the paperwork Mr Haan Jnr had given her and suddenly felt suspicious, something was not right.

Lucy found a phone and dialled the number in Hobart of his sister. A young lady answered in English and Lucy asked for Celia Haan. She was told that no one of that name at that number existed. She then asked for the address and to her absolute surprise was given the number and street of the house she was supposed to own! She dropped the phone and collapsed in a nearby chair. The whole thing had been a hoax. Mr Haan Jnr had played her for a fool. He had the island and her money and knew that she, now being broke, would not be able to return or cause him any further problems.

Getting her breath back, Lucy sat thinking. He was

wrong on both counts. She had the diamonds and he had no island. Henry may have known or perhaps suspected this and that is why he had to take the final step and destroy everything. Lucy knew there were two options, to walk away or seek revenge. Her choice was immediate. She had lost her son and his family because of the actions she had taken as a result of her association with the Haan family. A smouldering hatred rose within her. She would seek revenge. They might be laughing now but when they next saw her she would wipe the smile from their faces, even if she died carrying out her plan.

Boarding the plane, she placed the diamonds under her feet and settled down for the trip. She was not really sure what her next step would be but she had sufficient cash to stay in Cairns long enough to source a buyer for the diamonds and to work out a plan to destroy the Haan dynasty in Port Moresby.

It was her hatred that kept her from sinking into absolute despair. It boiled within her. Lucy was furious with herself for her naivety as it had resulted in the loss of her son and the last of her family. Lucy, now a ticking time bomb, was cold, calculating and dangerous.

Checking into a hotel in Cairns, 'Lucy Jones' showered and changed her clothes. She poured herself a glass of whiskey, her first drink in decades. She then searched the phone book and made the first of many calls.

Chapter Twenty-Seven

Lucy Jones looked at herself in the mirror. She had spent the morning shopping and nodded in satisfaction at her reflection. She was sixty-five years old, tanned, fit and healthy after years of good, natural food and daily exercise. Her blonde hair had been styled for the first time ever by a young and enthusiastic hairdresser and her new, tight-fitting dress hung just above the knee. To an observer, Lucy looked years younger than her real age.

Now on a mission, she picked up her mobile off the bed and made an appointment with a diamond buyer she knew had recently flown in from Sydney. She chose a small number of what she considered the best diamonds and placed them in her new handbag, the rest she placed in the hotel safe as she was leaving. She hailed a taxi.

The driver pulled into the seafront precinct at the nominated café and upon entering Lucy spotted her man immediately, he was immaculately groomed. As soon as he saw her coming, he rose from the table to greet her.

"Mrs Foster I presume? So glad to meet you! I am more than interested to know how you came by my name," said Mr Horan the Jewish buyer as he pulled out a chair for her to be seated.

"An old acquaintance recommended you Mr Horan," Lucy charmingly replied, smiling her best smile. Mr Lynch had supplied her with the name 'Foster' and they were to catch up that evening in her hotel room.

"Now Mrs Foster, have you any diamonds on you? I am anxious to conclude any business and return to Sydney if possible this evening," Mr Horan asked impatiently.

"Certainly, here is a small sample for you to inspect and, like yourself, I too have other appointments Mr Horan," Lucy replied curtly.

Lucy watched guardedly as he looked at the diamonds she had laid on a serviette. She did notice an ever so subtle change in his face when he looked at the largest diamond through his eyeglass. Lucy knew she had him hooked.

"Mrs Foster, may I ask where you obtained these diamonds?" he asked.

"They have been in my family for generations Mr Horan but changed circumstances force me to seek a buyer," Lucy replied offhandedly. Mr Horan cleared his throat and continued, "I'm afraid this diamond has been missing for nearly eighty years or more, if my memory and information is correct. It is part of a large number that went missing from a bank vault in Germany during the war. I could be wrong but the collection was worth a fortune then and is now. To be honest it is far above my buying ability," Mr Horan replied, looking dejected.

"I am sorry to hear that, perhaps you know a buyer who 'has the ability'?" Lucy replied sweetly.

"That is what I was going to suggest. 'Yes', there are those who can buy the collection. May I act as agent?" Mr Horan replied, now sweating on the fortune he envisaged. "How can I contact you apart from your mobile? Are you staying in Cairns?" he asked.

"Mr Horan, my only contact is the mobile number and

I do not stay in Cairns. Where I stay is my business. One other thing, this deal, if and when it goes down, shall be in cash, in Australian dollars. I will only meet with you and always alone. If you try to cheat me or try any other tricks, be assured my man, who is watching this even now, has orders to shoot you and make no mistake, he never misses," said Lucy looking casually at him with a cold stare.

Mr Horan got up from his chair, his forehead wet and clammy. He was in no doubt that Mrs Foster was not joking. He had seen that 'coldblooded killer' look before. He was fully aware she knew the true value of the collection. This was a legend in the diamond trade and just to see the few he had inspected gave him cold shivers down his spine. The one alone was worth tens of millions. If it had not been for greed, the downfall of most humans, he would have left the café and returned to Sydney that night, but as a middle man, he stood to pocket immensely from this deal. If he could pull it off, it would be the most he had ever made in the decades he had been in the diamond trade.

Lucy picked up her handbag and glanced around her. Everything appeared normal. She gave Mr Horan a cheeky wave and exiting the café hailed a taxi back to her hotel. Lucy felt rather satisfied with the outcome and laughing to herself, mused 'this was not the Lucy of old.' She now trusted nobody, was careful, calculating and, like a snake, ready to strike at any time.

That evening she ordered two meals to be delivered to her room at seven o'clock. Mr Lynch arrived right on time and when Lucy greeted him she inwardly disguised her shock at seeing him as now an old man in his eighties. She sat him down and they exchanged pleasantries over their meals.

Lucy gleaned that he had been destroyed by the loss of his daughter. He informed her that the trade had become vicious and there were killings taking place all the time over territorial claims involving huge amounts of money. There were large crime families, middle-eastern gangs and bikies all slugging it out for control. He had retired years ago, sick of the fear of being killed at any time and had moved to a small gated-village some years before his wife had passed away. Like Lucy, he was on his own.

Lucy relayed everything that had taken place since they had last met and how his daughter had taken over the entire business. When she told him of the Haan's betrayal he sat bolt upright, his old eyes blazing, "Lucy, the same thing happened to my daughter and it cost her her life," Mr Lynch declared, confessing, "I've wanted to pay them back for years but it would've taken a huge sum of money, something I didn't possess."

"That's not so now!" responded Lucy, "I have resources that could help. What do you think it would cost to get our revenge?" she asked.

"Look Lucy, they're all powerful and cunning but perhaps too cocky in some ways. We would need a large, fast boat and at least three million dollars to pay some people I know who would join us in such a mission," he replied, deep in thought.

"Done, I will finance it. Do you know where we can

pick up a boat?" Lucy enquired.

"In Sydney, we dare not buy it here. There are too many 'eyes and ears' in Cairns! We'd do best to meet it at sea. I suggest you wear sunglasses and keep a low profile Lucy, as for me, they wrote me off years ago. My past showed no guts for violence but that has changed. By killing my daughter they crossed the line," Mr Lynch replied quietly, but angrily.

"Will you be coming with me then, at your age?" Lucy asked, surprised.

"My dear Lucy, if I get killed it would be far better than dying here slobbering in a chair. I already feel a new lease of life flowing through my old veins! Let's together show the bastards!" responded Mr Lynch, now chuckling.

"How many can you get that we can rely on?" Lucy asked.

"We've got a lot of middle-eastern types here strutting the streets trying to get some type of crime business going but they mostly rely on government support. The bikies keep them curtailed but I don't trust the buggers. I know though, for one hundred thousand each, I can get at least ten men with whom I have 'sort of' made friends, some young guns who found out about my past and look to me to give them advice," Mr Lynch explained.

"How about weapons, mine were all destroyed when we left the island?" Lucy queried, her mind racing ahead.

"Lucy, anything is available for money! We'll rent a shed in the industrial area north of here to store them and any other items we need. I'll start all this in the morning. When can we have the money?" Mr Lynch enquired.

"I'll need at least a week or two to arrange that much but, in the meantime can you get me a revolver, just in case?" Lucy responded.

"Easy, I'll bring it over tomorrow night if you like and we can talk further," Mr Lynch said, yawning as he got up to leave.

Lucy knew she was at a watershed in her life. Unless she had a carefully planned strategy and was prepared to carry it out without a moment's hesitation, she was doomed. As she lay in bed she committed to seek revenge for what had been done to her and her family and would prove beyond doubt that she really was a 'velly clebber lady'. Never again would anyone treat her like an imbecile and play with her mind. From here on in she would be in charge of her own destiny.

The following morning, while she was watching the news on TV, her phone rang. It was Mr Lynch. He'd arranged an inspection of a shed out on the industrial estate and would pick her up in half an hour. Faced with a long, boring day Lucy was glad of the inspection and pleased that like her, Mr Lynch had an agenda and was anxious to get the show on the road.

Arriving at the industrial estate they found the shed was perfect. It was in a busy precinct with lots of traffic and any movement in and out of it would create no interest. Mr Lynch paid for a twelve-month lease on the spot and later Lucy would pay him back. He also suggested to Lucy that now they had the time, he would arrange a meeting with the young men to gauge their response to the planned takeover of her old island from the Haan family and the bikie enforcers.

The meeting was arranged to take place in a carpark in one of the major shopping centres. Two men, Mohammed and Abdul seemed more than interested in what Mr Lynch told them and after Lucy had been introduced she wasted no time in confirming their intentions. "As Mr Lynch told you, we require at least ten men and are willing to pay one hundred thousand dollars to each of them for about three weeks' of dangerous work. We'll be up against heavily armed and dangerous men but they'll have no idea we are coming and so we'll benefit from the element of surprise. If you are prepared to help us we will also help you take over from the bikies here, and I offer to supply you with, shall we say, 'products' to sell in Sydney. I've no doubt you have good contacts there," Lucy told them calmly.

Abdul grinned, his eyes glinting, "We are both Syrian ex-Army fighters Mrs Jones, used to extreme violence. Be assured we will keep our part of the bargain. Two of our brothers infiltrated the bikies here to learn their ways. They treat us like dogs but I am sure they have underestimated us and our inside information will help us in this coming battle."

Lucy looked at them both thinking, 'Would not trust these people for one minute, but any ship in a storm' and said, "Then let's call it a deal. We'll contact you when we are ready to leave and let's hope this is beneficial to both sides. Might I suggest your brothers remain in the bikies gang and keep us informed! It will come in handy later to be aware of their movements and to know exactly how many we are dealing with," Lucy remarked.

"With the government now cracking down on bikie gangs, it's hard to say how many there are at any given moment as they come and go. They're unable to form large gatherings with the police hounding them constantly, but in Cairns there are normally about fifty or more members," Mohamed replied, surprising Lucy by how well-educated he appeared.

"Okay then, please do nothing to attract attention until we call you. I might need a few of you for company within the next couple of days when I go to collect the money to pay you guys. As there's so much at stake, I'll also get you to check out the place before we go, just in case anything goes wrong," said Lucy.

"Please, call me day or night," Abdul told her, "but give us at least two hours' notice. We won't be seen but don't worry, we'll be watching to see if anyone turns up early and likely to cause a problem."

On leaving Mr Lynch looked at Lucy, telling her, "You've certainly changed Lucy, from the woman I met years ago."

"Sadly yes, but my heart has been wrenched from me so many times and I've endured so many highs and lows that if I reflect on the past I'll go mad. Now I try to blank out my mind and just do what I must. The Haans and the bikies will pay big time for what they have done, even if it costs me my life, they've already destroyed it," Lucy replied.

"We were dealing in a sick and sad trade and I did wonder if some higher being was paying us back. You would know the old saying that 'we reap what we sow', declared Mr Lynch.

"Actually, I never thought of it that way but, if I am condemned to hell I intend taking a few with me," Lucy replied, grinning.

Over the next few days they packed five SKS rifles with several hundred rounds of ammunition and four Win Mag 300 bolt action rifles and two hundred rounds, in the rented store. The site was secured and a guard patrolled it at night. On one occasion Lucy went alone to the store and in the office set above stairs on the first floor she removed some panelling from one of the walls and hid the diamonds. Standing back and surveying the wall she was confident they were now safely hidden. Mr Lynch had given her a revolver together with a pack of twenty bullets and after loading the weapon she placed it snugly inside a hidden compartment of her shoulder bag. She felt good.

Mr Horan phoned telling Lucy he had a buyer and that his representative would arrive the following day. He said that even though she had specifically told him to come alone, they would both like to attend since there was so much money involved.

Lucy agreed and suggested the carpark in the busy shopping centre where she had met with her army of fighters. She immediately called Abdul and told him of the meeting. He was thrilled that something was happening and assured her again that he and his brothers-in-arms would be waiting and watching several hours before the arranged meeting.

Lucy took one small bag of the diamonds and waited for

Mr Lynch to pick her up. He dropped her at the arranged meeting place, carefully parking his vehicle so as to keep her in full sight. Lucy looked around but saw no sign of her security cover. 'Either they haven't turned up or they're rather good at keeping out of sight,' she thought, but it wasn't long before a hire car pulled up and instead of the two men as arranged, three got out of the car.

"Hello Mrs Foster," Mr Horan greeted her, "apologies but because of the large sum of money involved we thought it prudent to bring along another person for security."

Lucy smiled as she watched a black van pull out from the rear of the carpark and slowly come towards her.

"Can you show us the diamonds please?" one of the three men asked.

"Can you show me the money please?" Lucy asked in reply.

One of the men beckoned her towards the car and opened the boot. There was a large case packed with money.

"There's not much money there," Lucy remarked.

"Mrs Foster, be fair, we have three million in cash. If the diamonds are what I think they are, then we will need to pay in bank cheques spread over a period of time. The amount you want is far beyond what cash we can gather here without raising suspicion. This amount was hard enough," Mr Horan replied glancing about.

'So, they intended to rob her of the diamonds and pay her only three million for diamonds worth tens of millions,' Lucy deduced. She reached into her handbag and knowing the two men were armed, smiled as they closed in on her, then pulled out the small pouch of diamonds and passed them to Mr Horan.

"Thank you Mrs Foster or whatever your name is," he said curtly, "now let's have the rest please, and quickly. Three million will keep you in luxury for some time for simply giving us something your family obviously stole."

Lucy wasn't sure what happened next but the black van screeched to a stop next to her and five men with balaclavas jumped out. Out of the corner of her eye she saw one of the men had collapsed, with his throat cut. Lucy grabbed the case of money and the diamonds from Mr Horan who was frozen to the spot. He was petrified as he witnessed the carnage going on around him. Mr Lynch pulled up alongside Lucy and she jumped in hurriedly, throwing the large case onto the backseat as he drove off.

Looking in the rear vision mirror she saw three dead bodies next to the hire car and noticed that the van had disappeared. The operation by her enforcers had been coldblooded but professional and was all over in seconds. Driving straight to the warehouse they used the automatic roller door, drove in and closed it behind them immediately.

"Wow," Mr Lynch sighed, "That was just like the old days! I hope those boys keep up that type of response, it was awesome. I spotted them coming towards you and had my fingers crossed they knew what they were doing. Quick and competent, they've had army training all right."

Over the next few hours they counted the money. Mr Horan was right. Three million neatly bundled in one hundred dollar notes. They counted out fifty thousand and decided to pay the five men ten thousand dollars each as a bonus and the balance on completion of the main job.

Mr Lynch dropped Lucy off at her hotel to clean up and arranged to meet Abdul to pay him the money.

Over dinner in her room later in the evening after Mr Lynch had paid the men their cash he told Lucy how they were now 'hooked' and that at least she had some loyal followers. They both watched the news coverage of the three bodies found in the carpark with their throats cut, neither surprised that the 'Police believed it was a drug deal 'gone wrong' and that the abandoned black van had been stolen earlier in the day by the assailants, thought to be bikies.'

Mr Lynch had done some research and come across a large ocean-going vessel with twin diesel motors, which was exactly what they wanted. It was moored in Brisbane and the owner had agreed to deliver it to Cairns. He was delighted to be paid in cash as he was a retired engineer who had lost his money in an investment scheme and the boat was his last asset. A price of four hundred thousand was agreed, payable on delivery.

A few days later, Lucy sat in the wheelhouse of a hardly-used sixty-five foot vessel and watched as Abdul and his nine accomplices loaded supplies, including the weapons they had acquired. Mr Lynch too had obtained a box of hand grenades, direct from an army store.

Lucy left her diamonds hidden in the warehouse along with the balance of the money, after having paid for the vessel. She kept one million dollars in the case on board for her helpers, after the job was finished, together with a good amount for any further expenses. Lucy knew that, once they had control she had to lure Mr Haan Jnr to the island. Her 'brothers' on board told her that only four gang members at a time lived on the island and that they changed over on a monthly basis. The last changeover had taken place only two days ago. It occurred to her as she sat watching the last of the stores being loaded, that she had intimated to Mr Haan Jnr she had other gold still on the island.

'Now that,' she reasoned, 'would be the bait to get him to come to me but first I must take control,' and with every faith in her brothers-in-arms, she knew that was achievable.

Mr Lynch arrived at last in a taxi and waved at Lucy as he boarded. She knew he had dreamed of this moment for a long time and like her, knew they were facing either success or death. They shared a grim determination to win the battle or die trying.

Now fully loaded and with drums of spare fuel strapped to the deck, the sleek vessel churned up the water as they got underway. Lucy felt the familiar rush of adrenaline. She was on the way to her island with a fierce determination to win it back. No matter how, she would rebuild and bring her people back. It would be like old times.

The vessel had sophisticated equipment and Lucy set a course direct for her island. The instruments showed speed and expected duration of the sailing, thirty seven hours at their current cruising speed. How she wished Tom was aboard as she always had faith in his ability. She felt bad at having abandoned him and the others and often wondered how he was coping.

Leaving Mr Lynch in the wheelhouse along with one

of the other men, Lucy retired to her cabin. Locking the door she lay on the bed, drifting off to sleep, calmed by the throbbing of the engines and the slight sway of the boat.

Chapter Twenty-Eight

Lucy had no idea how long she'd been asleep but was awoken by the popping of gunfire. The men were testing out the weapons in readiness for the coming conflict as she had told them to do when they were well out to sea. She had a quick shower and looked at the time. It would be dark soon and they would pass Cape York during the night, leaving Australian territorial waters at midday and arrive at her island around midnight, if all went as planned.

Lucy made her way to the galley to find most of the men seated around the table eating and talking loudly, each trying to show more bravado than the other. She smiled and made herself a chicken sandwich, deliberately avoiding pork and ham out of respect for her guests. Then making her way to the wheelhouse she found Mr Lynch still on duty, and on his own.

"I gave the others time off, it seems they had prayers or something, can you take over?" he asked. "Not much to do. The course has been plotted, it's pretty much automatic. We've met a few boats but mainly yachts, the larger vessels carting coal have a course further out on the reef," Mr Lynch explained. He looked tired.

"By all means, I'm sorry I didn't think of it sooner!" Lucy remarked.

"Better if one of us is on deck all the time. As we get closer, these guys are becoming more blood-thirsty, and a cool mind might come in handy if something unforeseen happens," suggested Mr Lynch as he vacated the large chair he was seated in.

Lucy watched the large screen, picking out other vessels and often the twinkle of lights on some of the islands and anchored vessels. Not many travelled at night it seemed, but she felt safe. This was a state-of-the art vessel and only a few years old, although it had never been out to sea but simply used for entertaining clients around Brisbane and the islands.

Lucy sat staring intently into the darkness, glad that the vessel had self-plotting technology and radar to warn of other vessels or objects. 'Still,' she thought, 'nothing is failsafe' and was determined to remain alert. Several of the men came and went but she didn't enter into conversation with them as she knew, in their culture, women were of a much lower order, that they should be covered for the sake of modesty and walk behind the men. She wondered what they really thought of her!

As the first rays of sunshine materialised over the sparkling waters, Mr Lynch appeared, refreshed and relaxed. Lucy was glad of his friendship and that she could count on his advice. 'Although,' she reminded herself, 'she thought she'd had Mr Haan's friendship and would never forgive herself for being so trusting.'

They had decided once they were clear of the Cape, to plot a course to come in on the western side of the island and there wait until midnight to lower the boats and make a landing on the southern end of the main beach. Following the data displayed on the screen, they dropped anchor at ten o'clock after slowly inching as close to the main beach as they dared. Lucy looked at the bearded swarthy-looking group of men as they were standing, ready to launch the two boats she had on board. One was only a twelve footer which she had loaded on impulse before they left and the other one, lowered by the winch, was sixteen. This went over first and nine of the men climbed into it then the smaller boat was lowered for Abdul, Lucy and Mr Lynch. Starting the motors, they idled slowly around the point and then as silently as possible landed on the main beach. Lucy saw lights at the old campsite and beaching the boats, they wound their way along the palm tree lined shore. Lucy felt she was home!

Padding along she could almost feel the breath of the men following her. She looked back, noticing that Mr Lynch was falling behind but still she kept up the pace. As her eyes adjusted to the light she saw a fire in between two tents to the left, fifty metres away on the sand. Slightly back into the jungle and not far from her old watchtower, she saw a light and fire with what looked like two figures working over cooking equipment. Of course, it had only been six weeks since she had fled the island and the new owners would not have had much time to build any structures. Melting further into the fringes they inched their way closer to the two figures. Lucy gasped! One of the men was Tom and the other, his younger brother.

Indicating for her men to stay, she moved forward. The men were totally absorbed in their jobs and hadn't noticed her as she glided up next to them. Tom saw her first and beamed. She held up her forefinger to her mouth indicating for him to keep quiet. He knew what she meant and held up four fingers and pointed to the tents. Lucy turned and repeated the signal to the waiting force. She watched as they slithered up to the tents, one reaching for a can of fuel left outside and poured it around the perimeter of both tents. Another threw a burning branch from the fire into the fuel-soaked tents and what happened next was vicious but quick. The tents erupted in a loud roar and as each man ran out, the bark of a Win 300 sounded and all four died instantly.

Tom and Leo ran to Lucy, all hugging each other. Tom told her how after they arrived on the main island the policeman took their boat and that the new owner of the plantation was the Island Chief. He and the others had been used as slaves on the plantation and the women had to cook and clean for his two wives. Some only allowed a few hours' sleep a night were beaten and starved, the same as the others back on the main island.

Lucy told Tom how sorry she was and that she would rescue his people and bring them back. His eyes lit up and he fell to her feet, sobbing.

Mr Lynch finally arrived and smiled at Lucy, "I told you these boys were just waiting for a chance to kill some infidels."

"Better take a couple back and bring the boats around. At daylight we'll bring the big boat around and clean up, then erect a couple of new tents to make it look normal. Tom informs me our old boat was taken to the main island today and will not be back for a week at least," said Lucy.

Lucy questioned Tom as to the whereabouts of the radio

and was told it was up behind the tower she had built.

Glancing through the wallets of the four dead men Lucy noted the names of two. She ordered that the bodies be disposed of and the site cleaned up. By morning everything was back to normal.

Lucy wasn't worried that Mr Haan Jnr would fly over the island at this time. He'd be no doubt concerned that the bikies would find out he was trying to remove gold from the island without sharing the spoils and he'd most likely still have the buyers with him.

Lucy went up to the tower and finding a bed, wrapped herself in some of the old blankets and dozed. She was satisfied the first part of her plan had gone without a hitch. She was back in charge of the island and determined to remain so.

In the morning she found Mr Lynch and told him of her plan. When he got hold of the radio phone he dialled Mr Haan Jnr's number. Lucy had kept it amongst the papers she still carried, along with the Visa Cards. In a disguised voice he introduced himself as one of the bikies, using one of the names Lucy had noted. He didn't hesitate in getting his message across. He and a colleague he said, by the name of the other bikie Lucy had given him, had located a large stockpile of gold bars, in fact hundreds, and they wanted to sell them. He made it quite clear that he and his accomplice did not intend sharing with the other two men and had in fact killed them. Mr Haan Jnr took the bait without question. He'd always suspected, from his father's information, that there was a much larger amount of gold involved than what Lucy and her daughter had sold.

He arranged to collect a large amount of cash and meet on the main beach in three days. Mr Haan Jnr suggested that they not contact Cairns. Instead he would tell them he had just visited the island and all was in order. A consignment of tablets had just been delivered to the airport, giving them time to load the gold and the two, now wealthy men, could leave the island and rejoice in their newly enriched lives. Mr Haan Jnr knew that greed, if handled correctly, could be a wonderful tool. He would then advise the Cairns contacts that he had learned the men on the island had disappeared, or some other story. They would never suspect him, because why would he cut his own throat? He mused at his success. He supplied the raw material, laundered the money and now owned the two planes on the main island making the deliveries, all for a handsome sum. Hardly able to contain his excitement, he thought of the money he had already made from Missy Lucy's gold. He found it hard to believe she was so gullible but then, his father had told him so, and he was always right.

Three days later as arranged, Mr Haan Jnr dropped anchor in his luxury yacht, licking his lips at his incredibly good fortune. From the front of the boat, he noticed two tents and two men seated by a fire. Behind them were two locals, cooking the tablets. He could see several boxes that had been used to deliver the chemicals in, all stacked neatly at the side of the tents. He presumed the boxes were now filled with gold bars. 'Ah, it was a glorious day' he thought as he strolled ashore, feeling not unlike

Captain Cook, followed by men carrying two chairs and a table. Two of his crew stayed on board together with his personal butler.

Indicating to his staff to place the table and two chairs beneath an umbrella, he sat looking out to sea, smiling confidently. Life was good. At home he had a young wife and was banging two younger women smuggled in from China to housekeep for him and his father. Yes, this was a great period in his life and even he was amazed at his planning and cunning.

His daydreaming ended abruptly with the sound of two loud blasts behind him. The brains of his two helpers splattered him as he fell forward onto the table. He jumped up and saw Lucy smiling at him. She was surrounded by the most savage human beings he had ever seen, their eyes were flashing and they gripped their weapons menacingly. Looking back out to sea, he saw the men on his yacht and watched helplessly as their throats were slashed, and their bodies thrown overboard.

Lucy sat down under the shade of the umbrella.

"Now, you listen to me carefully" Lucy told Mr Haan Jnr, "or join your companions in the afterlife. My comrades will not hesitate to cut more throats, and yours in particular they know would please me immensely."

He slumped in the seat, blubbering uncontrollably. The remaining members of his party stood in absolute terror glancing at each other. None of them were armed and no doubt suspected that death was just a breath away. Total fear racked their bodies.

"Missy Lucy, please, you misunderstand my intentions,"

babbled Mr Haan Jnr, his polished voice breaking up.

Lucy looked at him and smiled, "Mr Haan, I understand perfectly and if you fucken bullshit me once more, that seat shall be your execution platform and my smiling face will be the absolute last vision you see on earth! Do you understand? If not, I will say again, to stay alive you must listen to me ever so carefully and do exactly what I tell you. Now, do you understand me?" questioned Lucy.

"Exactly, please I beg you, whatever you want is yours," Mr Haan Jnr mumbled and Lucy saw that he had even pissed his pants.

"That's great Mr Haan," she said, "but if you try anything from here on in or refuse any request I make then," pulling out her pistol, "see this, I will personally blow your fucking brains out as I did your clerk's. Now let's try that again, do you understand?" Lucy queried.

"Yes," he whispered, his body shaking so much he coughed up some bile which dribbled down his front.

Lucy despatched some of the men to bring her boat around and anchor near the yacht. She told Mr Lynch to take over as she had one more job to complete before she left for Port Moresby. Mr Haan Jnr was shackled to a tree and one of the swarthy men sat in a chair next to him. Lucy pointed out to him that if he moved or even pissed his pants again, the man, who gave him a toothy grin, would firstly castrate him and then cut his throat. Lucy knew she had instilled so much fear in him that he would follow her instructions without question.

Tom and Leo got the four terrified Chinese crew to pick up the smaller boat and follow them. Mr Lynch was more than happy to stay and oversee the proceedings on the beach. He could not believe that the man he held responsible for his daughter's death was now cowering before him. He was elated.

Following Tom, who was clearing a path through the jungle, the Chinese men carried the boat while Leo carried the outboard motor. Lucy too followed with the revolver on her belt. She was on a high but still concerned as to what she would find at her old settlement. 'Was Henry alive? Had he survived the blast or would she only find ashes?' she pondered.

When they reached the lagoon they launched the overloaded boat. As they made their way around the headland, Lucy's heart skipped a beat. It was as she had left it, all intact. Then she understood why the second plume of smoke had risen after the initial blast. She saw that this exit had been detonated as was the one sea side. Both entrances were now well and truly obstructed but yet even with the tide rising, Lucy noticed the water was still somehow finding its way through the rocks blocking the entrance.

Then to her complete surprise and joy, she saw Henry and his wife sitting in a little dinghy, fishing. He looked up and when he realised who it was, waved madly! Lucy couldn't help but notice that they were both heavily covered in bandages.

As they drew near he shouted, "Bloody hell. What are you doing back here? Nearly killed us both when she went up and we're still deaf, so you'll have to shout!"

Landing on the jetty Lucy thought everything was

much the same as if she'd never left, but then could see that even in such a short time it had gone a little wild in places.

Lucy walked to the main house and wept tears of joy and relief. She was home again and this time she was going to stay strong enough to remain here. It certainly would take a lot of cleaning up but she was determined to somehow supply the island with whatever necessities were needed. If they had a new tractor and trailer perhaps they could build a new jetty on the side they had just left, via the old way they had come so they could unload on the main beach.

Lucy left the Chinese with Henry who was already instructing them to follow his orders to clean up the place. They were grateful and told Lucy they were from mainland China and had been and forced into service far from home by Mr Haan. She promised them that when things quietened down they could return to their homeland. They bowed and touched her hand as she left on the return journey.

Once back on the main beach, Lucy immediately set sail for Port Moresby with Mr Haan Jnr aboard his yacht with Tom and Leo as crew. She took a further four of her men, leaving the balance on board her boat, under the watchful eye of Mr Lynch.

On the way Lucy allowed Mr Haan Jnr to clean himself up. He had become fully cooperative and she intended to keep him that way. Reaching Port Moresby they entered the exclusive marina under his guidance and tied up at his private jetty. The place was guarded and gated so Lucy only left Tom and Leo on board.

Lucy instructed Mr Haan Jnr to request two vehicles with darkened windows, as she knew he had used those in the past when picking her up. Lucy and he sat in the back of one while one of her men sat in the front with the driver. The other three men followed in the second vehicle.

Arriving at the compound housing the luxury home of Mr Haan, the gate opened automatically and they drove up to the front of the palatial residence. Lucy reckoned the old man would still be in bed. She then remembered the security cameras and the room off the main entrance where a member of the house monitored them twenty-four hours a day. As they entered the hallway, she with one of her men went straight to that room but it was empty and unattended. Lucy turned just as a young male came into the room carrying a cup of tea and some food. He was immediately grabbed and tied up.

Lucy calmly dismissed the unsuspecting drivers of the two cars, letting them out via the main gate to catch a taxi home. They didn't hesitate, it was late and the call out had been unwelcome.

Lucy then had Mr Haan Jnr tied up and with two men, went from room to room rounding up his wife and mother-in-law plus two frightened female staff members. Lastly they found the master bedroom and roughly shook Mr Haan. He awoke to find Lucy looking down at him smiling. She was holding a gun to his face and behind her stood a man, holding a very large weapon .

A look of complete terror and then resignation came

over the old man's face. Lucy spoke, "Velly clebber lady has come back Mr Haan. Now if you want to live, do exactly as Missy Lucy tells you."

He nodded, clutching the sheet to his chin and Lucy hoped he would not have a heart attack as he looked distinctly unwell. He clambered out of bed and Lucy led him back to the main room where the other hostages were glancing nervously at each other.

"Now Mr Haan," said Lucy to Mr Haan Jnr, "the rest of your family will be going to your yacht under guard. If anything goes wrong, all will be killed. Please tell them to cooperate fully if they wish to see another sunrise."

Mr Haan Jnr spoke in Chinese to them and they all nodded thinking 'at least this was better than death' having imagined they were going to be killed. Loading them into the vehicles, Lucy sent all her men, two in each car, to transport the prisoners. Out of earshot, she instructed her men to place the others below deck in the main cabin and to give them food and water and await her instructions. After they left, she returned to the house where only Mr Haan Jnr remained, still tied up. He looked sheepish and frightened.

"Now today we have a busy day. Your family will be taken out to sea. If anything happens to me, they will be killed immediately. I can understand enough Chinese, Mr Haan to know if you are translating anything more than I tell you to, so please understand you will live only as long as you follow instructions, is that clear?" Lucy told her captive.

Mr Haan Jnr nodded, his mind working overtime. He

knew Lucy had the upper hand and that he had no choice. He could only hope that if he played his cards right, she would make a mistake. But his first priority was his family.

"Mr Haan, I need a Passport and a Driver's Licence in the name of 'Lucy Jones' and I need them now, so make your phone calls," Lucy told him passing him the phone.

"This may take time, photos have to be taken and offices open," Mr Haan Jnr replied.

"Let them know that money means nothing, I want the papers waiting in your bank when we arrive at opening time. I reiterate, if there is any deviation from my instructions, I will shoot you," she warned.

An hour later Lucy posed for photos but watched Mr Haan Jnr intently, never taking her eyes off him. She then got him to open the safe containing the Deeds to the house and the Certificate of Registration for the boat. All these she placed into her shoulder bag along with a few items of jade and some diamonds.

"You will get these back Mr Haan, at the end of the day if you follow orders, do you understand? You murdered my family and that of Mr Lynch so we have nothing left to lose. You may yet still save yours by doing exactly as I tell you. Right, how much have you in ready cash in the bank?" Lucy asked menacingly.

"About twenty-seven million in cash, plus bonds worth thirty million and gold hidden on an island not far from your island," he replied.

"Fine, I would like to remind you that if I find you supplying me with false information you are 'dead' and so is your family. I want a map of the island marking the exact location of the gold. Remember, before you're released, I will check if this is fact," she said.

Mr Haan Jnr passed her a small leather-bound book he had in his pocket. Inside, written in Chinese were the island's location and all the bank details. She knew they would correspond with his information.

When the bank opened they stepped from a taxi and upon the manager recognising Mr Haan Jnr, he ushered them into his office. After Lucy was introduced to Mr Qwon they sat down.

"I am here to make Miss Lucy Jones my representative with Power of Attorney to sign and operate accounts on my behalf. Certain matters have arisen which require me to be absent for some time," Mr Haan Jnr informed the concerned bank manager.

"Miss Lucy Jones, ah yes, there are some documents here for her. Mr Haan, perhaps your father could act for you? It is highly irregular for a virtual stranger to act on a family's behalf," said Mr Qwon, frowning.

"Mr Qwon, Miss Jones is a long and trusted family friend. My father will be going to China for treatment soon and as I have urgent family business to attend to I will be absent for long periods. Our time is precious so please prepare the paperwork now for us to sign."

"I apologise Mr Haan, please stay seated while I arrange the necessary documentation," said Mr Qwon, getting up and shouting orders to his secretary.

An hour later they left the bank. Lucy had her Passport, Driver's Licence and the Power of Attorney authorising her to operate Mr Haan Jnr's bank accounts. She had already checked with her old firm of lawyers by phone in Cairns that with the Power of Attorney she could also transfer ownership of the yacht and the house.

Lucy ordered the taxi to take them back to the marina and Mr Haan Jnr appeared surprised to see his yacht still tied to the jetty. He was helped on board and placed under guard in a separate cabin. Lucy gave a sigh of relief as they left Port Moresby and headed to the main island.

Chapter Twenty-Nine

Once at sea, Lucy had Mr Haan Jnr brought to the wheelhouse and held her gun to his head as she gave him instructions. She ordered him to phone his bikie mates in Cairns and to speak only in English.

In clear English he told them Lucy had returned with eight men and that they killed the four Chinese men stationed on the island. He then gave instructions to gather as many men as they could muster and fly them to the main island where he would have a boat ready to transport them to the island to retake it. A large force would be necessary, he told them and that weapons had been placed on the boat for their use. He made it clear that the matter was urgent. Lucy was satisfied.

As they tied up next to her old boat, Lucy reckoned they had about a day or even less to prepare. While Tom ran to the old plantation to get his people, Lucy and her men booby-trapped the vessel by planting all the hand grenades on the floor and rigging them with wire. When the propeller wound the wire tightly enough it would pull the pins from at least five grenades and it was hoped the others would explode as well. They estimated that five would sink the boat but to be sure, they loaded drums of fuel directly above the grenades making it look as if the fuel had been left for emergencies. The Win Mag 300 rifles and ammo were loaded in the state room.

If their plans failed she intended ramming the vessel with

her larger and faster boat and die fighting if she had to!

By the time they'd finished Tom had returned with the islanders, all ecstatic. Moe especially was overjoyed to see Lucy and wept and clapped her hands in delight.

Lucy hoped that the 'missing' islanders would not cause too much concern too early on. She wanted her people to be safe and out of harm's way and was pleased to have found out that the two pilots were off making deliveries. With the airstrip some distance away she knew they would be unaware of their arrival and departure.

Once back on the water, Lucy was faced with a shocking task, one that made her feel sick but that she knew was necessary. She had the Haan clan brought up onto the deck. The island people were eating down in the large galley. Looking directly at Mr Haan, Lucy spoke, her voice wavering, "Mr Haan, you and your son broke your word and cost Mr Lynch and me our beloved families. We trusted you both yet you betrayed us. If we let you go we know you will betray us again. Forgive us, but you have each sealed your own fate."

With that she nodded to the two men holding the captives. She watched as each victim had his throat cut and body tossed overboard. Her revenge was almost complete. She now had to deal with the bikies, probably in Cairns preparing to make their way over to kill them all.

Anchoring the yacht next to her boat, Lucy and her crew transferred to the bigger, more powerful vessel. Tom and the others rowed ashore, all laughing happily on their way back to the main village and to their old homes.

Lucy, not wanting the bikies to see the Haan's yacht

or her boat near the island as they flew overhead, chose to sail them back out to sea and head to the main island from where she would observe if the plan they'd hatched had worked.

Mid-morning the following day, they watched through binoculars as several planes ferried passengers to the airport. Lucy and Mr Lynch reckoned that with the large number of bikies coming, a raiding party would most likely be grouping on the island. Lucy left one of the men guarding the yacht and prepared her crew on the much bigger and faster boat, ready for a chase and attack, if necessary.

Observing guardedly, she saw men walking the gangplank onto the boat. The deck was filled with men and she watched with baited breath. One cast off and a puff of smoke indicated they had started the engines. Lucy swore. They began to reverse! 'Would it work?' Then thankfully the boat began to move forward from the jetty. Suddenly an enormous ball of flame shot skyward and debris rained down in a wide ranging ark around the vessel.

Hurriedly they motored to the jetty. Burnt bodies floated out to sea and the old vessel she had used for years had completely disappeared.

Disembarking, Lucy had one more job to do before returning to her island, to give her peace of mind for at least some time in the foreseeable future. It was strange that the explosion had created no attention, with the main village only three kilometres away. Taking two men with her in one of the old vehicles parked nearby, they drove to the police station to find the same fat Sergeant sitting behind the desk, dozing. When Lucy walked in he woke with a shock.

"Sergeant, I'm back and from now on you'll deal only with me. Here's one thousand kina as usual. Now tell me, who would actually run the island if the Island Chief was not here?" Lucy asked the smiling lawmaker, as he counted his money.

"Me number one man then," he grinned.

"Then from today, you are in charge. The head man is coming with me to stay indefinitely," advised Lucy and the heavy Sergeant, now empowered, stood to attention and saluted.

They drove to the airport where Lucy advised the two young Australian pilots that she had just taken over the business again after a few years break. She told them that money and conditions would remain the same and that she was considering buying a sea plane. They would be notified when to pick it up. Shaking hands and smiling, she turned and left the two rather bemused young men. She yelled back that they would be receiving a pay increase! Upon reaching the main house of the head man, Lucy walked to the front verandah where two overweight women sat discussing the no-show of the house staff. Lucy asked to speak to the head man. He surfaced from the house, huffing and puffing.

Lucy explained that she wanted to discuss 'big business' with him and asked if he would 'like to come to Port Moresby to collect a new car and lots of money.' She told him she was again taking over both the airstrip and the business with immediate effect. He just smiled from ear to ear and followed her.

"Please bring wives also, we buy pretty clothes," Lucy giggled to herself as the two women jumped at the prospect of a trip away from the island and, of course, new clothes!

When they returned from the village it was as if nothing had happened. There were just a few pieces of debris floating about and a scorch mark or two visible on the jetty but it was in such bad order that no one would notice. 'He who dares wins,' thought Lucy, now far more confident in her abilities.

With everyone back on board they headed towards the island. The head man approached Lucy, pointing north towards Port Moresby. She nodded at two men standing beside her and they suddenly heaved the head man overboard. His wives looked on in horror as one of the men decided to have a little target practice with the body in the water!

"Both of you take off your clothes now!" Lucy pointed her revolver at them. They stripped off their clothes and handed them to Lucy who threw them over the side of the boat. "From now on, you will wait upon and serve your 'old servants' and by chance, if any of the men want you, you will oblige willingly."

This was her final vengeful act. She was now in total charge and needed to remain strong. The old Lucy was gone.

Dropping anchor at the main beach Lucy sent for all the men who had helped her and passed each the money promised, plus a bonus. Lucy spoke to them, "The contract we had is now finished. I am sure any elements of your opposition in Cairns can easily be cleaned up. Thank you for your help. We will take you back in the morning."

Mohamed stood up, declaring, "We would like to still work for you or if that's not possible, we'd like you to work with us and supply us with products? Rest assured though that even if you don't, we will always be very grateful to you and to Mr Lynch."

Lucy looked at Mr Lynch who shrugged and then spoke. "To be honest, I want to stay here and if Lucy agrees I will run that side of the business and work with you."

Lucy added, "Fine with me, you and Mr Lynch work out the details," then, with the two naked ladies, returned to the village.

Settling back into a more tranquil state, Lucy's anger gradually disappeared.

Mr Lynch arranged with Tom to take their hired guns back to Cairns and arriving back noticed a more normal routine had returned. Even the Chinese wanted to remain with them and Lucy happily agreed. The little community again became a hive of activity as everyone set about starting their new lives. They rounded up and trapped the pigs and goats and their vegie gardens sprang into life.

However, night after night Lucy lay awake, thinking of a long-term plan to protect her island from any future threats and violence. She had to protect these people who had lived their entire lives here but were always under threat, and eventually came up with an idea.

One morning she called the Chinese men to a meeting. She discovered that two of them had formal training in bookkeeping and that one, Yoti, spoke fluent English. They were all from poor farming families and had been transported there illegally to work for Mr Haan. Having been promised a better life and pay, they sadly found themselves trapped with no documentation, in a strange and hostile land.

Lucy carefully explained her plan to them. She said she knew that with money it was possible to obtain Passports and make them legal citizens of New Guinea but that would take time and careful preparation. She then went on to say that she planned to open up the island, register its citizens to vote and become a small democracy. They already knew of the gold as they had helped bury it, and she told them it would later be transferred and sold in China.

Their response was enthusiastic and they were happy to remain on the island and assist in getting a legal trade in fish and fruit going with Port Moresby and Cairns. She explained she would have to go to Port Moresby to form a trust in which all the island people would hold a share and that the Chinese would be in charge of keeping the books. Their excitement was contagious and although many times Lucy found herself wondering if it were all a crazy dream she knew they could not 'go back', they had to move forward. All she wanted was to live the rest of her life on the island and in peace.

Lucy advised Mr Lynch and Henry of her plans and they both agreed that the time had come to open up and enter the real world. Mr Lynch offered to transfer the cooking equipment south to another island and arrange with the now, up and coming middle-eastern gang to take over the drug trade. It was a foul trade bringing only death and destruction, and all present wanted no more killing.

Mr Lynch confided to Lucy that when he'd gone back to Cairns he found that the men who'd assisted them had burnt the bikie headquarters to the ground. The local police praised themselves on the successful breakdown of the gangs and put it down to their constant pressure. Even the Premier commented on the outcome, referring to his unrelenting campaign to crush the bikie gangs.

A week later Lucy travelled to Cairns, meeting up with Abdul and Mohamed. The two men greeted her, resplendent in gold chains, like a hero, aware she had been the source of their success. Lucy smiled to herself knowing it was only a matter of time before revenge was sought by fellow members of the largest organised crime gang in Australia. These boys would boast but she knew her name would not be mentioned as their religion would prevent them acknowledging that a woman had played a pivotal role in the scheme of things.

Lucy explained how she was going to bring the island into the modern era and that the 'Law' would help and protect them. She would give them the cooking equipment and even teach them how to use it. They would need to move to another island well south, towards the Cape. From there they could collect a boat that she would help finance as her parting gift. She was going to keep the planes and had ordered a new floatplane for dropping chemicals to the chosen island. All payments would be in cash.

The meeting ended with both men thanking Lucy and slapping her on the back like old friends. As they left, Mr Lynch asked Lucy why she still kept them involved by selling chemicals to them and Lucy turned and said quietly, "So we can keep an eye on the bastards, that's why."

Going to the warehouse, Lucy collected her diamonds. She asked the caretaker to let the owners know, when the lease expired at the end of the year, they would no longer require the shed. The keys they left with him.

Chapter Thirty

Lucy looked out the plane window at Port Moresby below. It appeared quite picturesque and serene from the air but she knew, just as in all major cities, violence and crime were forever present, hidden beneath the surface like a cancer.

When they landed, Lucy alighted from the aircraft, together with Yoti and Yuan. She informed the pilot she would make contact with him when they wanted to be picked up, depending on when they got through the long list of things to be done.

A car belonging to Mr Haan was waiting as arranged and they were driven to the now empty compound. Yoti opened the gate with the code and asked the driver to wait. They only had one appointment for the day but would perhaps call at one of the Australian-owned construction companies with a base in Port Moresby, servicing the mining industry.

Yoti made a call to an employment agency and arranged for two house staff to be interviewed that evening when they returned. He checked the house and set up rooms for each member of the team then Lucy ordered the car to take them to the bank where the manager was waiting for them outside. 'So far so good,' Lucy thought. He seemed more assured by the presence of Mr Haan Jnr's clerks.

"How is Mr Haan Senior, has his health improved?" he asked.

"Tremendously, thank you for asking. The last time I saw him he was sleeping peacefully," answered Lucy.

Seated in the opulent offices Lucy took the bull by the horns, her plan dependent on the next few minutes.

"Mr Qwon, without any further ado, Mr Haan Jnr has had to return to China on a rather delicate matter. It appears the Chinese authorities, shall we say, detained him indefinitely and therefore we have been instructed to form a Trust for the island people who were beneficial in helping him and his family reach the high level of wealth they enjoy today. All his monies and assets are to be placed in such a Trust. 'Mr' Yoti here has a full list of those Mr Haan Jnr wishes to be members of the Trust," explained Lucy. Mr Qwon sat in silence for a moment then grim-faced said, "Yes, unfortunately it comes as no surprise. When one plays with fire, one runs the risk of being burnt. I only hope that such an account will remain with this bank," said Mr Qwon.

"Of course, we wouldn't want it any other way! Now, perhaps to start, 'Mr' Yoti and 'Mr' Yuan, and myself of course, will be signatories to the Trust cheques and all documents. I assume the bank's solicitors can set up the Trust as discussed and transfer all monies and assets to it when established. I happen to have the house and boat documents here," Lucy replied passing them over.

"Certainly," Mr Qwon beamed, "May I suggest a trading account for day-to-day expenses?"

"Excellent Mr Qwon, thank you for your understanding and assistance in these most trying of times. We intend to stay until all this is finalised. Do you think it is at all possible for you to complete everything by the end of the week?" asked Lucy glancing at her smiling accomplices.

"Normally a month is required but for such an important matter I will do my best. Just one last item, what do you intend to name the trust?" asked Mr Qwon.

"Sheridan's Island Trust," Lucy replied as she got up to leave.

Mr Qwon escorted them to the waiting car and Lucy directed the driver to take them to the Australian engineering company's headquarters.

The three of them looked extremely business-like as they confidently strode into the reception area and requested to see one of the managers.

After a short wait a man came from a nearby office. "Ken Hanson" he said, "and how may I help you good people?" he asked.

"I am Lucy Jones and these are my associates 'Mr' Yoti and 'Mr' Yuan. We have a rather large project we would like you to quote on please," Lucy replied in her most professional voice.

"Certainly, come into the office please," Mr Hanson gestured, and as they sat them down enquired, "Tea or coffee anyone? Coffee was the order of the day so Mr Hanson pressed the intercom instructing his assistant and then asked, smiling, "Right, now what is this project?"

Lucy placed a map of the island on the table in front of him.

"We require a large wharf built here on the main beach and to maintain deep water, it must be at least five hundred metres long. Then from here," she pointed directly into the jungle, "we need a road three kilometres long to this hidden lagoon, a small jetty for loading boats and finally storage sheds on the main beach and at the wharf area."

Ken Hanson looked and listened intently. This was just what his company needed, a major contract.

"Off hand, it will cost quite a few million, especially since the main wharf would need to be made cyclone-proof in this area. It is a major undertaking and we will need evidence of proper financing before we even commence to inspect the site and quote," he replied seriously.

"Mr Hanson, our Trust already has money ready to pay for this new infrastructure. We would like a projected time frame and to know that your engineering credentials suit undertaking such works. Please feel free to contact Mr Qwon at our bank if you have any doubts as to our ability to pay. Your ability to deliver the proverbial goods is what we will need to consider carefully," Lucy replied curtly." His demeanour changed quickly and Lucy noticed he had gone a pale shade of grey.

"My sincere apologies to you all but one has to be careful. Perhaps we can arrange an inspection later this week?" Hanson replied apologetically.

"This week is not feasible. Let's make it next Wednesday. One of our planes will pick you up at the airport and take you as far as the main island. From there we'll pick you up by boat," Lucy responded, then, "One last question, have you someone who can advise on the feasibility of building a small, light plane landing strip at the same time?" she asked.

"We've just finished building a landing strip inland

on a high mountain range so anything after that will be easy," replied Mr Hanson.

"Great, thank you Mr Hanson. I eagerly await your inspection," said Lucy, getting up and shaking his hand. Back to the car they went.

Their next call was to a chemical supply company. They spoke briefly with the manager informing him of the changed circumstances. He was not surprised at the news and shook hands with them saying that as long as all payments were in cash, it was no business of his. Returning to the vehicle they found a truck and tractor dealership where they invested in a medium-sized tractor and truck and arranged for a local barge company to deliver them the following week.

Back at the house Lucy was surprised and relieved at how easy it had all gone. After all those years of hiding, Lucy now wondered why she had not been more forthright in the past. On reflection however, she knew that without having undertaken her violent killing spree, it would not have been possible. 'Dead men tell no tales.'

That afternoon they had photos taken and arranged for Passports and Drivers' Licences for both Yoti and Yuan. Lucy knew she could always trust and rely on them. They confessed to her that they had girlfriends back home and she agreed happily to assist them in bringing them out. Lucy said too that she would help in sending money to their families back home as the Chinese boom had not yet impacted the rural people.

Because of Yoti's personal experience with Mr Haan, he knew just how to bring Chinese people out from China to Papua New Guinea and he happily began the process of arranging for two girlfriends to join them on what was now the island called, 'Sheridan's Island'.

Over the next few days they attended to many tasks including registering the entire island population on the Electoral Roll and with other government departments. The Trust's operating account was even registered to pay tax and surprisingly, ten days after they left, 'Sheridan's Island' was a legal entity.

They had to postpone a meeting with Ken Hanson but on the rearranged day he arrived with a small team to inspect the island. He suggested that even their small airstrip could possibly house some hangars and two weeks later Lucy received the documents and costings. She accepted and three days later two large barges arrived from Port Moresby with enough men and equipment to begin the work.

The tractor and truck also arrived by barge, along with the fuel they had ordered, and was parked temporarily on the beach while their new store shed was being assembled.

For five months the island was buzzing! Yoti and Yuan married their girlfriends in a simple ceremony on the beach and three more young women arrived, seeking 'a new life.' Two were given jobs in the Port Moresby house and within weeks the other married one of the Chinese men.

On the road to the lagoon, now used to cart freight from the main wharf, the Chinese built houses and set up huge market gardens. Lucy, Yoti and any others who from time to time wanted to visit and stay in the house in Port Moresby, now flew by plane. The boat Lucy and

Mr Lynch bought in Cairns was used to cart supplies and the luxury yacht which the Trust now owned had a berth at the wharf, jutting out from the main beach.

In addition to selling fruit and vegetables in the Port Moresby markets, the island also had a small but growing trade supplying fresh food to passing yachts, whose numbers grew yearly.

Lucy transferred the gold back to the original cave and the whole island community, who now participated in the decision making, decided to keep it as a reserve to be used in the future as needed.

The diamonds Lucy sold and the money was paid into the Trust so even after the cost of infrastructure, the Trust account remained steady.

Occasionally different government departments called but Lucy made sure all taxes were paid on time and so gradually over the next decade their enquiries waned. The island population grew and grew and when the Justice Department wanted to place a police officer on the island Lucy suggested that one of their own could be trained in Port Moresby and stationed here. They agreed. 'How ironic that one of Joseph's grandsons will become an island police officer,' Lucy mused.

One of the Chinese girls trained at the hospital in Port Moresby as a nurse and when her training was complete and she had fulfilled her practical experience, a clinic was set up at the main beach. After years without close medical aid it made Lucy giggle to see the population lined up for many 'perceived' ailments which had never seemed to bother them before.

For the next few years Lucy watched over her cherished island, often from the sanctity of her bedroom. Her violent past still haunted her and cold shivers washed over her when bad memories obsessed her. 'How did she allow herself to drift into such a lifestyle? How could she take another human being's life!' she agonised. Although suffering nightmares at night, during the day as she mingled with the island residents she justified her past, at least to herself.

Still there were times when she wondered if her life had been worth the horror and bloodshed and then memories of her misery and loneliness as a young housewife would confront her and she would say 'yes' to herself. 'It had all been worth it.'

Lucy Jones lay in her bed, the curtains floating lazily in the breeze off the lagoon. She could hear children's laughter below. That night she dreamed of her past and of her long journey from a simple upbringing in rural Tasmania to the life of a cold-blooded crime queen. It had been an often violent and bloody life. Visions of her daughter Sheridan, of her son Liam and her grandchildren, seemed to beckon her as she looked below into The Gulf. She struggled to hold on to the plane seat but an overwhelming strength pulled her below and she felt herself plummeting into the water. Looking to her right, as darkness seemed to surround her, Lyndon was there, smiling. She relaxed and allowed herself to fall.

The End

www.ingramcontent.com/pod-product-compliance
Lightning Source LLC
Chambersburg PA
CBHW062120170626
46813CB00002B/520